DEDICATION

For my daughter, Candice, and husband, Mike, who both, with unfailing grace, pretended it was perfectly normal to stay in a small room for days at a time, writing madly, with wildly disheveled hair and wearing the same shabby pajamas.

"But they shall dwell safely,
and none shall make them afraid."
(Ezekiel 34:28)

PROLOGUE

The sun was just breaking on the horizon and the sky was turning pink as the woman eased her car over to the side of the road. She put the gearstick in park and with the motor of her car throbbing quietly over the asphalt, took in the sleepy town nestled at the bottom of the hill. The sun ray's were growing warm enough to begin burning the fog away from the town, but from her position at the top of the hill, she could still see a thin blanket of mist hanging over the lush, green lawns that grew in the yards of the quaint village. The wave-tossed Atlantic Ocean surrounded the town on three sides, and herring gulls glided over the dark, blue water that glistened under the sun's rays. A small smile escaped her as she viewed the water and the gulls, and she turned around in her seat to say something to her nineteen-month-old daughter, Madeleine, who was strapped in the child's seat in the back, but merely smiled when she saw that her little girl was sound asleep.

She turned back around and looked out the passenger side window and scanned a wooden sign that stood off the road on a patch of grass about twenty feet ahead of her car that said, **Welcome to Leigh Falls, Maine, population, 5,252.**

Lord, please protect us, she whispered a prayer, before she pulled out onto the road and accelerated down the long hill that would lead them right into the town.

The main street, Ash Street, she had read, was quiet and almost deserted at this time of day. As she cruised slowly down the street, she cranked her window down and was immediately hit with the sharp tang of salt in the ocean breeze that blew inside her car. She felt groggy from the long drive, and took in a deep breath of the briny air to try to clear her head, and was surprised by the amount of warmth in the breeze, having expected much cooler temperatures in this part of the country.

One side of the street ran parallel with the water of the harbor and was lined with gift shops, boutiques, seafood restaurants, and cafes that pandered to the tourists. She peered curiously through the driver's side window to the other side of the street and saw a hardware store, a pharmacy, a combination beauty salon/barber shop, and a bakery with a sign over the front door that read '*The Icing On The Cake*'. As she passed by, the scent of fresh baked goods wafting out from the bakery reminded her that she hadn't eaten since supper time yesterday and that had only been a chicken salad sandwich.

She continued on down the street and saw a square, red-bricked building that was the library, another, square shaped, that was the town hall, and then another red-bricked building, but this one was a two-story with a sign over the door that said, **Leigh Falls Police Department**. Reading that sign made her heart give a violent lurch, and she pressed the gas pedal and accelerated past the police station to the end of the street where she spotted a Dunkin' Donuts coffee shop. She was dying for a coffee, and wanted to buy a bottle of orange juice for Madeleine, so she pulled into the lot, shut off the engine, and sat there for a moment trying to gather some courage before she went inside.

And then without warning, her mind slipped back to the day she had pulled a manila envelope from her mailbox. A seemingly innocuous envelope mixed in with the rest of her mail that at first glance looked like junk mail, and she had almost carelessly tossed it into the garbage. Yet even now, each time she recalled the moment she had pulled the threatening note and photograph of Madeleine and herself from the envelope, she relived the jolt of shock and horror that had pierced through her that day. She didn't recognize the handwriting on the note, but it didn't really matter. She knew there was only one person in the world that would want to harm them.

And so, to keep Madeleine safe, to keep them both alive, she made the decision to leave the city. It wasn't that hard a decision anyway. Not with her husband, Kent's, tragic death only a little more than one year past, no other living relatives that she knew of on either side of the family, and no job to hold her there. In addition, the church she and Kent had been attending was large, with over one thousand members, and although the people were friendly, she hadn't really made any close friends in the congregation that she felt she could turn to.

In truth, leaving Carlow was something that had entered her mind on more than one occasion since the day she had buried Kent. Living in their home, filled with its memories of her husband had been proving too much for her. Each and every night she dreamed of Kent. Dreams so vivid that in the morning when she would awaken, she would think he was alive and lying next to her in bed. The creep who had sent the photo and telephoned her had no idea that although he had succeeded in terrifying her; he had also helped her to do what she should have done months ago. Leave the city and start over somewhere else.

So that very night, decision made, she had raced through the house with her heart thundering in her chest and grabbed clothes, toys, and personal items, and crammed them all into suitcases. She tossed the suitcases into the trunk of her Malibu, added the stroller, and then ran back inside the house for her sleeping child, somehow managing to carry Madeleine out to the car and buckle her into the car seat without waking her. Before getting in herself, she had stood at the open car door, and looked at their house for the very last time. Once a home filled with love, warmth, and the sound of their laughter, now it stood cold, silent and dark, a house of anguish and despair. With tears streaming down her face, she turned her back to the house, climbed in behind the wheel, started the engine, accelerated away from the curb, and fled the city.

She had driven for hours that first night, a long night of passing though dark, quiet towns and cities, all of them growing darker and quieter as the hours passed. The next day they had stopped at a motel in a town called Rockwell, just outside New York. Not wanting to leave a paper trail, she had signed in under a false name and paid cash for the room, even though the motel's desk clerk had at first been very reluctant to accept it. She remembered how his features hadn't softened until Madeleine, who was asleep in her arms, awoke and smiled at him. After that, he had accepted the cash without further questions.

They had slept for the rest of that day and through the night, and the next morning had arisen before the sun came up. After stopping for breakfast at a roadside diner outside Rockwell, they had continued driving all that day, and although at times the tears still fell, she felt a little better with each passing mile.

They stopped once again for the night in another motel in a small town and she had talked the clerk into accepting cash for the room. The following day, sunny and bright, she was able to sing along with Madeleine, her mood somewhat lightened by the fact that they were getting closer to the state of Maine. That night when they had stopped at a motel, the female desk clerk had adamantly refused to accept cash, and she had been forced to use her credit card. She did so with a feeling of dread, at the same time hoping and praying that the distance would keep anyone from Georgia from tracking them. The next day, they had risen when it was still dark and had driven until at the crack of sunrise they had pulled over on the cliff above Leigh Falls.

The strange thing was how it had all worked out. Leigh Falls hadn't even been the town she had originally chosen when she had studied her map of Maine. She had actually decided on the neighboring resort town of Linden, which was larger, and had a bigger population that would allow them to blend in without too much notice. But that plan had gone right out the window when the engine of her car started to misfire, the **SERVICE ENGINE SOON** warning light came on, and to her dismay, stayed on.

She had to admit though, that when that light came on, she began to sense that through that unforeseen circumstance, God was leading them away from Linden and to the little seaside town of Leigh Falls. This feeling was additionally strengthened when she had learned, after reading a tourist guide booklet she had picked up at a gas station, that the town of Leigh Falls was also a hot spot for tourists and its population almost doubled in the summer months. That fact alone made Leigh Falls almost as good a choice as Linden, because she was sure they wouldn't be noticed there, and she didn't want to draw more unwanted attention than she already knew a woman and baby arriving alone in any small town should expect.

And as further evidence of God's care and provision for them, she had also found a place for them to stay. As a rule, the chances of finding a motel with a vacancy in the month of June in a tourist haven like Leigh Falls would be remote. But when she had stopped for gas at a station outside Leigh Falls, she had overheard the owner telling a customer that his brother, who owned a motel in Leigh Falls, had a sudden vacancy in one of his cottages.

Despite the early morning hour she had immediately called the motel from the pay phone at the station, and spoke to a very pleasant woman, who didn't seem to mind being awakened from sleep, and who had agreed to hold the cottage for them. As soon as they had eaten breakfast, they would drive over to the Blue Spruce Motel & Cottages on the Oceanside Road and finalize the rental. Thinking of that, she felt a renewed sense of strength and courage flow through her and she knew that she could do this. For her little girl, for her precious Madeleine, she could do this.

She flipped down the visor, glanced into the mirror and tried to fix her hair into something that looked halfway decent. She dabbed on a little lipstick and then noticed that her eyes were red-rimmed and bloodshot from the long drive and from the tears she had shed. She pushed the visor back up and bowed her head for a moment.

Lord, I know you are with us, she prayed silently, and then climbed out of the car on two very shaky legs and opened the back door. She gently woke her daughter, unbuckled the straps on the car seat, and lifted her up into her arms. She paused for a moment and took in a deep breath of the stimulating ocean air, and then prepared to enter the coffee shop like any other visitor to Leigh Falls, trying desperately not to appear as though she was a woman on the run. Even though that was exactly what she was.

CHAPTER 1

The eastern sky was turning from a dull gray to a golden red as the sun began to make its appearance at the edge of the horizon. I was standing out on my deck enjoying both the radiant sunrise and the ocean waves that were rolling up on the beach below my front lawn, ready to begin my day as I always did, rain or shine, with a four mile run. I was a dedicated runner, and my route was to run two miles along the edge of the surf to Cotter's Cove, my turnaround point, and then two back.

Most mornings, when the weather allowed, I would stop at a secluded spot at Cotter's Cove, and read my Bible and have a time of prayer. It has been my experience that being both a cop and a Christian is not an easy walk, and even though Leigh Falls is a small, relatively quiet town, it still has its share of the criminal element. I tried to faithfully have my devotions each morning before beginning my day as sheriff of Leigh Falls, for I have often found that staying close to God had been all that has kept me from overstepping the bounds of my office when dealing with some of these criminals.

An hour and a half later, I was back from my run, had my devotions, showered, shaved, dressed in my sheriff's uniform, and was driving in my cruiser along the Oceanside Road to the Dunkin' Donuts shop on Ash Street. The Oceanside Road, true to its name, ran parallel with the Atlantic Ocean, and gave a breath-taking view of the water. I pulled over to the shoulder of the road, got out, and stood silently beside the open door and watched the blue-green water surge in, smash against the large boulders of the sea wall, and then spray up in a white, frothy geyser. Even in the winter, when the pulse of the water seemed to change from a warm, tranquil blue to a frigid, stormy gray, this spectacular sight never ceased to make my heart quicken.

Ten minutes later I pulled into the parking lot of the coffee shop, and as was my habit, scanned the plates of the cars parked in the lot. Being a seaside resort town, Leigh Falls also had its share of criminals that arrived each summer, trying to blend in with the more law-abiding tourists. As sheriff, I felt a great responsibility for the safety and well being of every citizen and visitor in town, so I kept my eye out for any low-life's that drifted in and then swiftly helped them find their way back out of town.

I read the plates of the five cars in the lot. Two locals, owned by Marvin Warren, and Rollie Pugh, who were regulars at Dunkin' Donuts at this time of the morning. A '99 forest green, Toyota Camry with Massachusetts plates that I recognized as belonging to newlyweds who were staying at the Bayside Hotel, a '98 Dodge Stratus with New York plates that I knew belonged to a summer resident, and a car with Georgia plates that I didn't recognize. I pulled up beside the car, looked over and saw that it was a four door, black 2000 Chevy Malibu and there was a car seat in the back.

I shut off the engine, slipped off the seatbelt, and was about to reach for the door handle when out of the corner of my eye I caught movement at the door of the coffee shop. I looked over and saw a dark-haired, slender woman and a little girl emerge from the coffee shop. The woman was clutching a cardboard tray with coffee and juice on it in one hand, and with the other she was holding the hand of the toddler who was tottering along beside her.

They headed for the Malibu and when they passed the front of my cruiser the woman glanced sideways, our eyes met, her face blanched, and she flinched so badly that the tray flew out of her hands and crashed to the pavement. I peered out the driver's side window and saw that the lid had come off the cup, hot coffee was spreading out in a dark circle on the asphalt, and the bottle of juice had smashed to pieces. I quickly opened the door of the cruiser, jumped out and went over to help her.

"Good morning, ma'am," I said, and stooped down beside her and the toddler and began helping her pick up pieces of glass.

She mumbled something, but didn't turn her head to look at me and since her hair was hanging loose I couldn't see her face.

"I'm Sheriff Jake Cole. I'm sorry if I startled you."

I heard her take in a shaky breath and when she picked up a large shard of glass I could see that her hand was trembling badly. I looked at the little girl, who was staring sorrowfully at the shattered orange juice bottle. When she looked up at me I smiled at her and her lip puckered, then trembled, and she started to cry.

Great, I thought to myself.

"Ma'am, please allow me to buy you another coffee and a juice for your daughter," I said.

"Thank-you, but no, that won't be necessary," she said, and I heard a distinct quaver in her voice.

"Are you sure?" I said.

She shook her head and then stood up, lifted the little girl up into her arms, and walked briskly over to the Malibu, all without looking at me once.

Puzzled by her cool, yet nervous manner, I stood to my feet and silently watched her as she strapped the little girl in the back, and then opened the driver's side door and slid in behind the wheel. She fastened her seatbelt, slipped on a pair of sunglasses, backed her car up and drove to the end of the lot. I continued watching the idling car until finally her brake lights went off and she pulled out onto Ash Street and drove away.

I walked into the coffee shop, musing over how in my fifteen years as a cop here in Leigh Falls, hers was the strangest reaction I had ever seen considering that she appeared to be just an ordinary mom out with her child. I walked across the floor of the shop to the counter and stood in line behind Marvin Warren and Rollie Pugh.

Marvin was a tall, frail-looking, seventy-year-old retired librarian, with a long, thin face, a thick head of white hair, and bushy white eyebrows. He was wearing knee-length white shorts that were belted high up on his waist, a lime green golf shirt, brown socks, and brown dress shoes, on two, sparsely haired, milky-white legs that reminded me of a chicken.

Rollie Pugh, who owned and operated the only drug store in town, was the complete opposite. He was dressed in white slacks, a pale blue, short-sleeved dress shirt and black dress shoes. He was short, stout, red-faced, almost completely bald, and he had thick legs that looked nothing like a chicken's.

"Good morning, Jake," Marvin said, when he saw me there.

Rollie turned slightly, smiled and nodded at me at the same time as he passed the girl behind the counter a five-dollar bill.

"Good morning Marvin, Rollie," I said, and stepped up to the counter beside Marvin. He placed both his hands palm down on the glass countertop, and I could see brown liver spots and knobby blue veins covering the thin skin on the backs of his delicate hands.

"You're up out of the coop early too I see," Marvin said.

The coop, I thought, thinking of his legs, *that's a good one*, and had to suppress a smile.

Rollie pocketed his change, and then picked up his mug of hot coffee and a plate with a blueberry muffin on it and turned to face me.

"What'd you do to that poor woman out there, Jake?" he said, motioning with his head to the large plate glass window in the front of the shop that looked out on the parking lot.

"Not a thing."

"Seemed to me that you gave her an awful scare."

I shrugged. "I just looked at her."

He studied me silently for a few seconds.

"Well, that'd do it," he said very solemnly. "Wouldn't it, Marvin?"

Marvin picked up his mug of coffee and bagel from the counter, turned and eyed me for a moment, and then looked at Rollie and nodded sadly. Laughing together, the two men then walked over to a table.

I sighed and rubbed my face with one hand, feeling tired even though the day hadn't really started. I bought a coffee and then drove to the department and parked in the shade of the trees that lined the far edge of the parking lot of the Leigh Fall's police department building. I was walking to the front entrance when I spotted Freddie Leach sitting on a wooden bench along the edge of the sidewalk on Ash Street.

He was wearing soiled green pants, a plaid red and black flannel shirt, a pair of black work boots with the laces untied, and despite the heat, a heavy green winter parka. He had a brown liner from a hard hat on his head and the flaps hung down loosely over his ears. He was holding one hand out with the palm up, glaring hatefully at the tourists who were up this early, trying to intimidate them into giving him money.

Freddie was a sixty-two-year-old alcoholic who preferred to live on the street, despite the fact that his unmarried, older sister, Agnes, who had a home over on McAllen Avenue, kept a room there for him. Agnes was a fellow believer and a member of my church, and had been my Sunday school teacher when I was very young. I guess that was why no matter how many times I found Freddie intoxicated and passed out on a bench or on the ground inside a cardboard box in the park, I would take him over to Agnes' place instead of putting him in my drunk tank. He scoffed at me each time I witnessed to him about Christ, and he stormed angrily out of the house and back to the street whenever Agnes raised the subject of his salvation, and I knew it was just a matter of time before I would find him dead either of alcohol poisoning or of hypothermia.

"Good morning, Freddie," I said, my eyes searching the bench for a bottle.

"Mornin', Jake," he said, continuing to scowl at the tourists that were strolling down the sidewalk on their way to eat breakfast in one of the cafes or restaurants. I noticed that most of the tourists who walked past him gave the appearance of looking right through him.

"How's it going?"

"Okay, I guess."

"You're not panhandling are you, Fred?"

He grinned at me and held up a Styrofoam cup of coffee. His hazel eyes were rheumy and blood-shot, and the alcohol fumes that came off him were so strong I breathed through my mouth. He had short, gray hair, stood about five-ten, but was so emaciated from the years of alcoholism that he weighed not much more than a hundred and twenty-five pounds.

"I'm just sitting here drinking coffee," he said, his breath sour, waving the cup in the air, seemingly oblivious to the fact the hot coffee was shooting out of the small opening in the plastic lid and spilling onto his lap. "Gertie gave it to me," he said, smiling crookedly, his front teeth looking badly decayed. "She offered me breakfast too, but I can't eat nothin' yet."

I looked across the street to Gertie's diner and smiled to myself. Gertie, like so many others in town, had often given Freddie food, clothes or blankets over the years. In that way, I knew you just couldn't beat living in a small town.

Freddie suddenly growled and barked at a couple who had stepped out of a cafe, and were walking on the sidewalk toward us. The woman, who appeared to be in her early seventies, looked nervous when Freddie bared his teeth and growled once again at her.

"Freddie," I said sternly.

The man, who was also somewhere in his early seventies, held a folded newspaper under one arm, was dressed in beige shorts, a white cotton, short-sleeved shirt, and Doc Martin sandals with no socks. He had thick, wavy white hair, a ruddy face, and stood about six feet tall, and weighed two-hundred and a bit, but had the flat stomach of someone who was still in very good shape for his age. I glanced at his face and recognized the silent, no-nonsense expression of a former big-city cop. He halted in front of the bench and stared hard at Freddie, and then slid his eyes to me without speaking, but I knew what he was saying. Back where he was from, Freddie would have been locked up in his drunk tank.

"Good morning," I said to both of them, and then looked at him with an expression that said in a small town things are different.

"Morning, sheriff," he said, met my eyes and seemed to take my measure and then looked at Freddie again. He looked back at me with his steel-gray eyes, nodded curtly, and then put his arm around his wife's waist and they walked away.

Freddie growled and barked loudly after them.

"Okay, that's it, Freddie," I said, setting my coffee down on the bench before I reached for his upper arm. "Come on, stand up now."

"No, no, wait. Whoa, hold on a sec," he mumbled, and lost his balance as I stood him to his feet and I had to hang on to him with both hands to keep him from falling flat on his face on the sidewalk.

"I've got you," I said, and held him upright.

"Don't put me in a cell, okay," he pleaded, and his fetid breath, ripe with alcohol, filled the air.

"Let's go see if Agnes is home," I said.

He grinned and nodded, clearly not minding my hands around his arms or the idea of going to his sister's.

I let go of one of his arms to grab his coffee cup, which he was holding almost upside down, seemingly unaware that the coffee was now spilling out onto the sidewalk. I tossed it into a garbage can beside the bench, retrieved mine, and carried it in one hand while I walked him over to my cruiser.

"You know, you're okay for a cop, Jake," he said, as he tottered along unsteadily beside me.

Sure I am, I thought with much sadness. *That's why I'll take you to Agnes' place, she'll clean you up, feed you, let you sleep it off, and then you'll slip out on her and be back on the street by tomorrow morning, and we'll go through this again for what must be the two-thousandth time.*

CHAPTER 2

Thirty minutes later, I parked my cruiser in the police department's parking lot and went inside. I walked across a large room where three of my deputies and the dispatcher, Marney Jacobs, who also filled in as my secretary, all sat behind desks either talking on telephones or typing on computer keyboards.

"Night reports are on your desk, Jake," Marney barked, without lifting her fingers from the keyboard or taking her eyes from her computer screen.

"Thanks, Marney," I said, and tapped the shoulder of one of my deputies, Caleb Harrington, as I walked past his desk.

"Caleb, come into my office for a minute," I said, and then took the stairs two at a time up to my office on the second floor.

I sat down behind my desk, swiveled my chair around and looked out the window. The sun was shining brightly, and the early morning breeze was moving the branches of the birch and poplar trees outside the window so that they were scraping across the glass. My window looked down onto Ash Street, and gave a superb view of the water of the harbor and the ocean beyond and I constantly had to fight the urge to just sit there looking out at the seascape. After a minute, I turned to my desk, picked up the reports, propped my feet up on the edge of the desk and scanned them quickly. When I was finished I tossed the reports back onto my desk and turned my head to gaze silently out the window again.

When Deputy Harrington walked into my office he dropped down in the chair across from my desk, stretched out his legs, and then pushed up his glasses that were forever slipping down his nose. Caleb, with his thick rimless glasses, fair complexion, soft-spoken voice, brilliant mind, and very slight build, looked and sounded more like a college professor than a sheriff's deputy, but I knew he was as hard as nails.

"Good morning, Jake," he said softly.

"Morning, Caleb," I said, as I watched a power-boat pull away from the town wharf and roar over the water. "How's the family?" I asked, thinking of Caleb's young wife, Ashlyn, his son, Gabe and their eleven-month-old daughter, Haley.

"They're all good," Caleb said. "It's Gabe's third birthday on Friday, so Ashlyn's busy planning it and I think there must be fifty relatives coming over. Forty-nine of which are hers," he added with a long sigh.

I smiled and looked down to the street and the sidewalks that were filling up with townspeople and tourists. I watched a young couple argue as they stood on the sidewalk in front of a small gift shop. The man was pointing at a sign outside Cassie's Cafe that advertised a breakfast special for just $2.99, and the woman was pointing at the gift shop, her thin face set determinedly.

"What's so interesting out there?" Caleb said.

"I'm watching a hungry young man about to go shopping on an empty stomach," I said.

"Look at the reports yet?"

"Peeked at them."

We fell silent for a long time.

"Something on your mind?" he said finally.

"I was just thinking about this woman I saw at Dunkin' Donuts this morning. She came out of the shop carrying a tray with coffee and juice on it, and when she saw me sitting in my cruiser watching her, she jumped about three feet in the air and dropped the tray," I said, shaking my head.

"What," he said with a smile. "Really?"

I nodded.

"Probably overwhelmed by your incredible good looks."

"Sure."

"Tourist?"

"Most likely. She's from Georgia."

"Long drive," Caleb said.

"A very long drive for a woman alone with a young child," I mused, and pulled the piece of paper with her license plate number scribbled on it from my uniform shirt pocket, turned slightly in my chair and tossed it on my desk blotter.

"You took down her plate number?" Caleb said, shaking his head.

"Force of habit," I said with a shrug, and looked out the window again beyond Ash Street to the harbor and watched a lobster boat pull away from the town wharf and head out to sea. I recognized the boat as the *Madison-Ann*, owned by Jim Caplin. *He's late getting out this morning*, I thought, knowing that most of the lobstermen in town headed out long before the sun came up.

"Well, it's not all that unusual for a woman to drive alone with a child across country," Caleb said.

I dropped my feet to the floor and faced him.

"I know, but I can't seem to forget her reaction. What is it about me that would rattle her so much? I mean the woman dropped her tray. And when I tried to help her pick up the broken glass, her hands starting shaking and she wouldn't even look at me. I offered to buy her another coffee and juice and she practically ran away."

"Some people are really nervous around cops, Jake," he said mildly. "Doesn't make them criminals."

I nodded agreement at that.

"You don't exactly look like the stereotypical small town sheriff either. I think she saw you and found you so fetching she very nearly swooned," he said, and laughed softly.

I shook my head and gave him a half-smile.

"Look, don't take offense and forgive me for quoting an old tired saying, but I think you're making a mountain out of molehill," he said, and then heaved his slender frame up out of the chair and stood to his full five-foot, seven inch frame.

"It wouldn't be the first time," I said wryly.

He smiled and leaned over my desk and picked up the piece of paper that I had written the plate number down on.

"Didn't see you at church on Sunday," he said, as he scanned the plate number.

"I was there. I came in late and sat at the back."

"I must have missed you," he said, frowning a little. "I didn't see you downstairs after the service for the pot-luck dinner either."

"I slipped out."

"Party-Pooper," Caleb said, shaking his head sadly as he went out.

Wouldn't be the first time for that either, I thought.

Later that morning, I had just hung up the phone when Caleb walked into my office.

"Jake?"

"Yes."

"I went ahead and ran those Georgia plates for you."

"What'd you get?"

"Nothing much. Malibu's registered to a Kate LeRue, from Carlow, Georgia, and other than a speeding ticket from a couple of years ago, nothing else showed up."

"Okay. Thanks anyway."

He watched me with a silent smile.

"What?"

"Come on. Admit you made too much of this."

I shook my head.

He laughed and walked out, and for the next hour or more I buried myself in the never ending paperwork that made up the most aggravating part of my job as sheriff of Leigh Falls. At noon I left my office and stepped out into the glaring sunlight and walked across the street to *Gertie's Diner* for lunch. Ash Street and the sidewalks along it shimmered in the heat, yet, the tourists were out in full force, ranging in small herds along the sidewalks of town, apparently unaware of the torrid sun.

I opened the door to Gertie's and went inside. The diner was owned by a feisty, seventy-year-old, Canadian woman, who stood just under five feet, weighed about ninety pounds, dyed her hair blue, and was as testy as a porcupine. Not usually a good character trait when serving the public.

The diner had been a fixture in town for thirty years, since the day Gertie and her husband, Remi Carbonneau, had opened it after moving to Leigh Falls from a small fishing village in northern New Brunswick, Canada. In the entire thirty years, I could not recall the diner undergoing any renovations whatsoever. Not even so much as installing an air conditioner, which was badly needed during the hot summer months. The diner was cooled by one big, ancient fan that sat in a high side window and clattered and rattled noisily, and vibrated so bad that it felt like the building was shaking on its foundation. It did nothing to cool the diner down at all, and simply blew the oppressive heat and paper napkins right into your face if you were unfortunate enough to sit in its path.

Remi had died four years ago, and Gertie had continued to run the diner with only one other waitress to help her out in the busy summer months. She said she didn't need any more help than that, but I think she was just too stubborn to admit she really did. Gertie's specialty was seafood dishes, which she served up with more than a little pride, and although she did serve some of the usual fare you would expect in a diner, there wasn't a great deal of selection on the menu. And Gertie was not above grabbing a broom and chasing out any customer who was foolish enough to complain.

Inside the small railroad car shaped diner, there were five booths along the front window with red Naugahyde seats, the cracks taped with gray duct tape, and a row of eight stools at the counter with the same red Naugahyde, heavily duct-taped seats. I stepped up to the counter and sat on a stool beside Roger Wagner, the owner of the hardware store in town. He was a widower in his early sixties, a tall, lanky man, with chestnut brown eyes, thinning, steel-gray hair, and a narrow, prominent nose, and like me, he ate most of his meals at Gertie's. I chatted with him, getting advice on the best brand of stain to use on my deck, which I planned on painting sometime in the next couple of days.

"What do you want?" Gertie called out, anger evident in her face as she stood behind the counter, one hand on her bony hip and the other stabbing a stainless steel soup ladle in the air at me.

"Did I do something?"

"I guess you did."

"What?"

"Where'd you eat on Sunday, Mister?"

"What do you mean?"

"Don't act so stupid. You're the town sheriff for goodness sakes. You're scaring me."

"Oh, for crying out loud, Gertie," I groaned. "I only ate at Trina's because you're closed on Sunday's."

"You want food poisoning, fine, go right ahead then," she said, her dark blue eyes flashing in anger. She tapped her index finger against her forehead in an expression I understood full well.

Roger, chuckling quietly as he kept his head down over his bowl of steaming hot, clam chowder, reached over with one hand and patted me compassionately on the back.

"And you mind your own business," Gertie warned him.

"Gertie, I sincerely apologize," I said. "I won't ever eat there again."

"Good. What can I get you? Today's special is Clam Chowder."

"Clam Chowder," I repeated, making a face before scanning the menu once again. "It's almost ninety degrees outside. What kind of a fool would eat chowder on a day like this?" I said, and grinned at Roger whose entire face was covered with a sheen of perspiration.

He swallowed another spoonful of the hot chowder and scowled at me.

Gertie rapped my right hand hard with the soup ladle and I dropped the menu on the counter.

"Ow! Come on, Gertie," I said, wincing as I shook my hand. "It's too hot for chowder and canned soup is all I live on at home."

"Get married then!"

"Maybe nobody will have him, Gertie," Roger said.

Gertie slapped her skinny thigh and roared loudly at that.

"Why do I even come here," I said, blowing my breath out tiredly.

"Beats me," Gertie said, still cackling. "You want the chowder or not?"

"Sure, I'd love some," I said in defeat.

As Gertie marched triumphantly away, I swiveled around on the stool to look out the plate-glass window to the street and noticed a black Malibu with Georgia plates pull into the parking lot of Weston's Grocery Mart, which was directly across the street from Gertie's. I watched Kate LeRue walk into the store holding the hand of her little girl who was taking small, short steps beside her. I glanced over at the car again and noticed that her headlights were on.

"Gertie, hold my chowder for a couple of

minutes," I whooped out over my shoulder as I slipped off the stool.

"What!" she screamed.

"I'll be back in a couple of minutes," I said, heading for the door.

"If you go out that door, Jake Cole, don't you dare come back!" she roared, clutching the bowl of steaming chowder in her hands.

I stepped out into the blinding sunlight and jogged across the street to the grocery store. I walked through the sliding door and was instantly hit with a blast of ice-cold air conditioning that felt wonderful after being in Gertie's. Even though the store was filled with tourists it didn't take me long to find the woman. I could hear a child's voice bellowing out a song about an itsy-bitsy spider at the top of her lungs and I followed the sound to the dairy section. The little girl was belted into the child's seat of the cart, mouth wide open as she sang, and the woman was leaning over picking up a carton of eggs when I came up behind her.

"Good morning, ma'am," I said as pleasantly as I could because I was worried she might flinch again and drop the eggs on the floor.

She whirled around to face me, and when she did her entire body recoiled, but somehow she managed to hang onto the eggs. I found myself looking into deep blue-green eyes that held both intelligence and fear.

"Good morning ma'am," I repeated, but even more gently, and then said hello to her little girl who had stopped singing and was now staring wide-eyed up at me.

"You own the black Malibu with Georgia plates parked in the lot outside, don't you?"

"Yes, I do," she stammered, and I caught a clear tremor in her voice.

She leaned over to put the eggs in the cart, and then straightened up and placed her right hand on the little girl's shoulder. I noticed it was trembling badly. I wondered if it was something about my manner or if all cops made her this nervous. I caught her following my gaze to her left hand, and saw her quickly drop that hand from the side of the cart down by her side where I couldn't see it anymore, but kept the other placed firmly on the child.

"You left your headlights on," I said.

"What?" she said, and a tremor went through her.

"I was in the diner across the street and I noticed you left your headlights on."

"Oh," she said, and anxiously brushed back a strand of dark brown hair from her face, and then dropped her hand quickly to her side again. "I'll just pay for these groceries and go right out."

"Good idea. You don't want your battery to die on you," I said, feeling baffled by the genuine shakiness in her voice.

"Hi," the child called out to me.

"Well, hello there. How are you?" I said, and saw that the little girl had the same almond shaped, blue-green eyes, dark hair, and almost exotic looking facial features as her mother.

"That's mommy," she said, and pointed up at the

white-faced woman.

"And what's your name?" I asked, and then heard her say something else that didn't sound like any word in the entire English language that I knew.

I looked helplessly at the woman.

"She's telling you her name is Madeleine," the woman said, her voice still sounding unnaturally high and tremulous.

"Ah, Madeleine," I repeated thoughtfully, and then turned my eyes from the child back to the woman. "That's a pretty name."

She met my gaze for all of two seconds, swallowed hard and then averted her eyes to the floor.

"I'm Jake Cole," I said, introducing myself for the second time, but dropping my title this time. "We met earlier this morning."

"Kate LeRue, and yes, I remember," she said finally, reluctantly, her eyes still down.

"Are you up here visiting family, Mrs. LeRue?"

"No."

"Tourist then, I guess," I said.

She looked up, opened her mouth to speak but then closed it again. Her face was turning a light shade of red, and her fear of me seemed overtaken for a moment by a growing annoyance with my questions.

"Sorry," I said with an apologetic smile. "I noticed your Georgia plates and I was curious. Hazard of the job, I guess."

She slid her eyes from me to her child again and didn't say anything.

I watched her silently for a couple of seconds

before nodding. "Well, I shouldn't keep you any longer. Enjoy your stay in Leigh Falls, Mrs. LeRue. Bye-bye, Madeleine," I said with a little wave.

"Bye-bye," Madeleine said, and squeezed one hand open and shut in a funny little wave.

I walked out of the store and across the street to the diner again and sat sideways on a stool while I waited for Gertie to quit ignoring me and bring my lunch over. I saw the LeRue woman emerge from the store and push the cart over to her car. I continued watching as she opened the driver's door, reached in to shut off the headlights, and then opened the back door, lifted her child out of the cart and strapped her in the car seat. Then she loaded the groceries in the trunk, got behind the wheel, and drove away down the street. I swiveled my stool around, wondering why she was afraid of me and so reluctant to tell me what she was doing here.

CHAPTER 3

The sun was dropping behind the trees in the police department's parking lot when I left the office for the day. On the Oceanside Road, I followed behind a slow moving RV, only one of the vehicles driven by tourists doing ten miles an hour and congesting the road. I fought the temptation to hit my lights and siren for no other reason than to blow by them, but managed, just barely, to resist.

I passed Sadie's Cottages, Livingstone's Bed & Breakfast, The Coastal Inn, and then came up on the Blue Spruce Motel & Cottages. All displayed *No Vacancy* signs. I glanced in at the Blue Spruce and saw the LeRue woman's Malibu parked in the driveway of one of the cottages. I pulled over to the shoulder of the road and looked at the motel and five cottages. The motel itself faced the road, but the cottages sat further away, to the left of the main building and at the very end of a narrow paved lane.

They were small, cedar-shingled buildings nestled under the shade of a stand of thick pines and smaller birch and poplars on grassy land that faced the ocean and gave onto the motel's private beach. All of the cottages afforded some privacy from the motel office and from the road where I sat in my car, but I noticed that the one Kate LeRue was in provided the most. It was the last one in the row, and was set back amongst the pines, and all I could see from the road was a section of the back porch and rear end of her car poking out a little at the end of the short driveway.

As I looked at the cottage, I recalled something I had overheard Dennis Halton, the motel owner, telling the pastor at church on Sunday. A couple from Texas had suddenly canceled their reservation for a cottage because the man had suffered a massive heart attack and died. I realized Kate LeRue must have rented that very one, which surprised me because that meant she had arrived in town without a motel or cottage reservation. I took my foot off the brake, eased back onto the road and drove on.

Five minutes later I was on Meadow Lane, a narrow, dirt lane at the southern boundary of town that led straight down to my three-bedroom cedar and glass home. The lane ran for about one hundred yards, was lined with great old pines and oaks, and ended at my comfortable home, which was the only house on the lane and was hidden from the main road.

My house sat on an acre of mostly woodland, faced the ocean, and had a lush, green lawn in front that sloped gently down to my own, private, white sandy beach. It was surrounded on three sides by very thick pine and oak shade trees that kept the house in shadows and cool during the hot summer months. The many pine trees layered the ground around my house with a thick carpet of needles, and the breeze that came into the house always carried a mixture of the salty ocean and heady pine scent from the fallen needles.

All the walls and floors were wood, mainly oak, and I had put in two floor-to-ceiling windows in the living room that gave a heart-stopping view of the vast, wave-tossed ocean. I had built a floor-to-ceiling stone fireplace that took up another wall, and had put in bookshelves on the other two walls that were overflowing with books. Four summers ago, I built the wide, cedar deck on the front that ran the length of the house and faced the ocean. I owned a beautiful home and an impressive piece of land, yet, at times, I grew very lonely and my footsteps on the wood floors seemed to echo forlornly through the quiet house.

I walked into the kitchen and put a pot of coffee on to brew, and then stood with my arms folded across my chest and my back against the counter and thought some more about Kate LeRue. Why had she come to Leigh Falls alone with such a young child? And why did she act so fearful of me? I had seen a wedding ring on her finger and I wondered if she had fled an abusive marriage. As a police officer, I knew full well that that was one of the biggest reasons why women took off with their children. If that was true, and if she had crossed state lines with her husband's child without his consent, then she was a kidnapper. And that made her a fugitive from the law.

I grimaced at that, thinking that I had been a cop too long, and was becoming suspicious of everyone without good reason. I walked to the sliding patio doors in the living room that led onto my deck and stood breathing in the bracing ocean breeze that blew inside through the open screen door. When the coffee was ready I wandered back into the kitchen, made a sliced chicken sandwich, and carried it and a mug of coffee out to the deck and ate at my patio table while watching the sky turn a remarkable purplish-red as the sun slowly began dropping in the west. I sat out there listening to the sound of the ocean until it was dark, unable to let go of my thoughts of this woman from Carlow, Georgia.

CHAPTER 4

The cottage faced the ocean and was, like Kate LeRue had hoped, as clean as the motel office. It was cozy too, with a bright kitchen, tiny bathroom, living room, and a small bedroom with a double bed and a crib against one wall. In the livingroom there was a white and blue, oval shaped braided rug in front of the sofa, an armchair, a 19" television and a stereo system. One wall held shelves crammed full with books, there was a small woodstove set up on red bricks in the corner of the room, and an old, loud, air conditioner in one of the two windows.

They had eaten a late supper, and now Madeleine was down for the night. Kate wandered around inside the cottage for a while, and then walked to the front door and stood there looking out to the water that seemed to go on forever before her. The sun was dropping below the horizon, and the sky was filled with mauve and red streaks, and her breath caught in her throat at the magnificence of it. Maine was a beautiful state, she thought, and was glad to find that she didn't miss Georgia as much as she had feared.

She went into the living room, chose a book by Max Lucado from the shelf, and spent the next couple of hours quietly reading. Afterward, she put the book back on the shelf, glanced at her watch and saw that it was almost eleven o'clock and was surprised to find that she still wasn't all that sleepy. Probably overtired, she figured, and opened the screen door, walked out onto the deck and stood under the moonlit sky and breathed in the heated night air. The difference in the air outside hit her like a wet blanket. She noticed that the breeze coming off the water was more pleasant now that it was evening, and did offer some relief from the suffocating heat, but it still carried a good deal of humidity, and she was thankful that the cottage had an air conditioner.

Her mind went from the weather to the sheriff of Leigh Falls and she winced at the memory of dropping the tray of coffee and orange juice right in front of him outside the coffee shop. She tried to remember the name she had read on the gold nametag on his white uniform shirt. *Sheriff J. Cole*, she said to herself, frowning as she tried to recall what he had said his name was when he introduced himself later in the grocery store. *James, Jed, Jesse*? None of them struck a chord, and she frowned, thinking hard, and then she remembered.

Jake, she thought, and unconsciously bit her bottom lip as she also recalled his unbelievably penetrating gaze. His river-blue eyes were so serious, so unrelentingly intense that his gaze seemed to knife right through her. She was certain that his piercing stare had not missed the tremor that shook her when they spoke outside the coffee shop, and then again in the grocery store when it happened for the second time.

She had seen in his eyes that he was wondering about a woman arriving in town with a young child and no husband. She could have kicked herself, and not just for dropping the tray, but also for leaving her headlights on. That was a careless mistake that had drawn his unwanted attention. She had daytime driving lights and didn't understand why, in the brightness of the noontime sun, she had even turned on her headlights, or how she hadn't heard the car's warning system that always signaled when the headlights were mistakenly left on.

Stupid, stupid, stupid, she murmured in disgust, feeling sickened at the thought that he might be suspicious enough to do a background check on her. She recalled how when he had finally left, her legs had felt so suddenly weakened that she had to grab the push bar on the shopping cart with both hands to steady herself. She could see that he wasn't the stereotypical small town sheriff she had thought would be in office here in Leigh Falls, and she had a nagging suspicion he would come around asking questions again.

Her second mistake had been to use her credit card at one of the motels, twice for gas, and then again today to pay for the cottage, and she was appalled now at the realization that someone from Carlow might be able to trace her here. *So many things gone wrong already*, she thought despondently. She closed her eyes and listened to the relentless surf rushing up on the beach. She caught herself feeling a little unsure now about sensing God's hand in leading them here to Leigh Falls. Why, she wondered, would He lead them to a town with a sheriff who took his job so seriously that he made it his business to know who was in Leigh Falls, when any knowledge at all about them could have such deadly consequences.

She looked up at the sky and saw that clouds had moved in, and were crossing in front of the moon, obscuring its light, and the sudden inky darkness made everything eerie. Her mind suddenly strayed to another dark, shadowy night just like this one, and the deafening blast of the gunshot replayed in slow motion over and over again in her memory like an old horror movie. She pushed the memory out of her mind, but didn't feel any better for she knew it was a painful image that would live in her mind for the rest of her life.

She was suddenly chilled to the bone, and went quickly back inside the cottage, shut and locked the door, and then went into each room and made sure all the windows were locked tight. After that, she walked quietly into the bedroom, stood by the crib and placed on hand lightly on her sleeping daughter's back, and as a lone tear slipped down her face, she vowed that she wouldn't be caught, not by the sheriff, and not by that revolting man who was hunting them.

———————

Four hours later the sound of glass shattering jerked her from a troubled sleep. She turned over in her bed and faced the bedroom window and blinked a few times to try to adjust her eyes to the darkness. She listened carefully and before long heard muted laughter. She threw the blankets back, slipped out of bed, went to the bedroom window and slid it up a couple of inches and peered out through the curtains to the yard. She couldn't see anyone, but could hear voices and more glass breaking. *It's him. It's him!"* her brain cried in terror, *he had found them*. She slammed the window shut, locked it, and then stood by the window for a moment paralyzed with fear, her heart slamming against her ribcage.

She took a deep breath and then forced her legs to move. She padded out of the bedroom and across the kitchen floor to the window, reached up with two trembling fingers, opened the slats a crack and peered out. Clouds shrouded the moon and the yard was dark with shadows, so she reached under the mini-blind, opened the window just a half-inch, tilted her head toward the window and held her breath and listened intently. All she could hear was the buzz of night time insects coming from the woods around the cottage, and the soft slapping of the water as it eased up on the beach below. She darted across the room, yanked open the silverware drawer, pulled out a large knife and at the same time, heard someone calling her name.

"Mrs. LeRue. Please open the door."

She recognized Dennis Halton's voice and went to the front door, flipped on the outside deck light, pushed back the blind and saw the motel owner standing on the deck with a long, black flashlight held in one hand. She cracked open the door partway and peered out at the motel owner.

"Ma'am, I'm sorry to have to disturb you, but there was a problem down on the beach. I'm just checking on all the guests to make sure everyone is okay."

She held the door tightly with one hand and swiftly hid the other hand behind her back to keep the knife from view.

"Are you okay, Mrs. LeRue?" Dennis Halton said.

She nodded and opened the door another inch or so.

"Okay, well, good," he smiled. "I think the all the noise was probably just a bunch of kids drinking down on our beach. It's the nicest beach in town so they like to sneak in here at night and swim and party. I called the police just to be on the safe side though. They should be here any minute now."

Although her pulse had steadied when he said that kids had likely made the noise, her heart was thundering once again in her chest at the thought that the police were on the way. Her mind raced right to the sheriff and she desperately hoped it wouldn't be him that answered the call. She didn't think a town sheriff would even work the night shift, but she had to admit that the sheriff of Leigh Falls didn't exactly act like the average sheriff and it was entirely possible.

"Are you sure you're okay Mrs. LeRue? You're as white as a ghost."

She winced against the bright beam of light in her eyes from his flashlight and she wished he'd have the sense to put it down. With the outside light on, the deck was brightly lit and he didn't even need it.

"It's the flashlight, Dennis," Pam Halton gasped, as she came bounding breathlessly up the steps to the deck, dressed in a matching pink pajamas and housecoat, and tall, black, rubber boots on her feet that must have belonged to her husband. "You're shining it right in the poor woman's face."

"Oh, sorry," he said somewhat sheepishly and clicked the flashlight off.

Kate swallowed hard and began to close the door, desperate to escape the two of them, and also avoid having to speak with the police, in particular, the sheriff, if he arrived right now.

"Look, you go right back inside, Mrs. LeRue. We don't want to wake up your little girl," Pam Halton said, when she saw her starting to shut the door. "No need for you to lose any more sleep. Dennis and I will wait down on the road for the police."

She forced a smile and tried to appear cool and calm as she casually closed the door even though it took all of her willpower to refrain from slamming it shut. Only a second or two before the door closed all the way, she heard Dennis whisper to his wife.

"You won't believe this, Pam, but she came to the door with a great big knife in her hands."

CHAPTER 5

I woke up at six o'clock to the sound of seagulls screeching in the sky over the water, and the unmistakable bite of brine in the soft ocean breeze that puffed the curtains on my open bedroom window. Bright morning sunlight streamed in through the window and fell in a wide slant across my chest as I lay on the bed for a few minutes thinking of the day that was ahead of me.

I finally climbed out of bed and went outside to the deck and found the air heavy with humidity. *Rain's coming*, I thought, as I rolled the bottoms of my pajama pants up to the knees, and walked across the dew covered grass of my front yard in my bare feet to the small wooden steps that led down to the beach. I walked across the sand to the surf's edge and stood there with the warm sun against my face and the waves spilling up over my feet, finding something soothing in the constant, repetitive movement of the ocean. After a couple of minutes, I headed back into the house, changed into running shorts, a T-shirt, and Nikes, grabbed my pocket Bible and went for my run. Later, after a quick shower and shave, I changed into a fresh uniform and headed to work.

At seven-forty I was in my office, leaning back in my chair, sipping coffee and staring out the window at the water of the harbor.

"Earth to sheriff," Marney Jacobs said as she walked in through the open doorway with the night reports in her hand.

Her voice was raspy and sounded like the voice of a serious chain-smoker, but I knew that couldn't be farther from the truth. Marney was a bodybuilding fanatic, and worked out at a ladies only fitness center on Barrett Avenue five times a week. She lifted free weights, and worked out on Nautilus machines, and I knew she bench pressed more than I did, because before the ladies fitness center opened we used to work out at the same gym. She was also infamous for what she called her *stylin'* haircuts, which I thought was an opinion shared by no one else but her. Marney was twenty-nine, and had been engaged twice, but both times, without an explanation to anyone, she had broken off the engagement shortly before the wedding dates. But, broken engagements, huge muscles and strange hairstyles aside, Marney had worked as both the dispatcher and sheriff's secretary for the Leigh Falls Police Department for almost ten years and she was very good at her job. And although she was altogether bossy, and at times acted more like the sheriff than the secretary, she had a heart as big as the ocean and was the most unselfish person I had ever known.

"You going to read these sometime today?" she grunted.

I forced my eyes away from my window, took a drink from my coffee, sat forward and set my cup down on my desk blotter before taking the reports from her with my other hand. A noise complaint at the Seashore Campground, followed by an open liquor offense at the same site, a D.U.I., and one other that caught my full attention. I read it slowly because it had to do with the Blue Spruce Motel where the LeRue woman was staying.

"Dennis called in about a possible break-in at his motel?" I said.

"Yes. He heard voices and glass breaking," she said, and blew a stray strand of platinum blond hair out of her eyes. "Turned out to be a bunch of kids partying down on the beach. Happens every summer."

I nodded and read some more, and then saw that one of my deputies, Eric Malley, had answered the call. "Did Eric check the area thoroughly?" I asked, thinking of Eric, an overweight, bone-lazy deputy, whose coarse personality grated on my nerves.

"I imagine he did. But I say that only because Scott was on duty with him," she said, exchanging a knowing glance at me.

I nodded in agreement. Scott Moore was a young, painstakingly meticulous cop, and I often put Eric on patrol with him in the hope that some of Scott's thoroughness on the job would rub off on him.

"Good morning," Caleb said, nodding to the two of us as he entered the room. "Are you talking about the incident at the Blue Spruce last night?"

I nodded.

"I was talking to Eric downstairs on the shift change. He said he found a couple of broken beer bottles on the beach behind the motel. Likely just teenagers drinking down there again."

I nodded in agreement.

"He also mentioned that he spoke with that actress from California that's renting that huge summer home not too far down the beach from the motel, and she told him that she heard the noise and looked out her window and saw an old, noisy, black pickup truck leaving the area. She told Eric there were three young males in the cab," Caleb said, and then paused and said very quietly. "For a very beautiful woman she is remarkably unobtrusive."

"Remarkably unobtrusive. Eric's words or yours?" I said, suppressing a smile.

Caleb frowned. "Mine. Why?"

"No reason," I said.

Marney grinned at me.

"Well, I'll let you guys get on with it," Marney said. "I have work to do, not to mention that Eric and Bryce Gorley have planted themselves by my desk and are crying like a couple of newborns."

I looked at her and raised my eyebrows in a question.

Marney made a wry face. "They're complaining about being scheduled for night shift on the July fourth holiday. Say they want to take their kids to the fireworks."

"Do you believe them?" I asked.

"Bryce, maybe," she shrugged. "Eric? No way. He's just too lazy to work."

I nodded and then gazed out the window to the harbor. The blue-green water shimmered under the brilliant early morning sunlight. I had eight deputies and all of them worked three different shifts, day, midnight and graveyard, one week on each shift, and although I would juggle the roster on occasion, I didn't like to do it too much. And it seemed to me that Eric and Bryce were always asking to get off the night shift.

"I can't give them the night off," I said after a moment. "With the number of tourists in town I don't have enough deputies on patrol as it is. The weather's not the only thing breaking records this year. And it's not fair to the other men."

"That's what I told them," Marney said. "And I'll be more than delighted to tell them again. They're always whining about something. The two of them make me feel like I'm the secretary of a day care center."

Caleb chuckled softly.

"Tell away then," I said.

"Done," she grunted.

Remarkably unobtrusive, I said to myself, and shook my head slowly as I watched Caleb follow Marney out of the room. Although he looked and sounded so much like a schoolteacher, and was called, *The Professor*, by the other deputies, he was a cop through to the bone. And I also knew that despite his own, quiet, unassuming manner, he was the toughest deputy on the force.

At noon I went outside, and was walking across the street to Gertie's, when I saw a black, Ford half-ton with three teenage boys in the cab cruising noisily down the street. I walked out into the middle of the road and stood there until the truck came to a stop a couple of feet in front of me, and then stared at the thin-faced, auburn-haired, bristly chinned teenager wearing a ball hat who sat nervously behind the wheel. I recognized him as Clayton Dixon, the son of Leonard Dixon, a lobster fisherman in town.

"Pull over against the curb please, Leonard," I said, and when he did I walked over to the open driver's side window. "What'd we do, sheriff?" Clayton blurted out.

I stuck my head in through the window and inhaled deeply. "Were you guys down at the beach behind the Blue Spruce Motel late last night?"

"No way," Clayton Dixon said, shaking his head vehemently, but the other two boys, smaller and younger, both dropped their chins and stared at the floor of the cab.

"You're sure about that?"

Clayton mumbled something and then fell silent.

I watched them for a long moment.

"So where are you guys headed now?"

"To the wharf. We got a job helping Mr. Hachey repair his lobster traps," the boy sitting in the middle replied.

I studied the young teen that had answered; a rail-thin kid whose name was Riley Shaw. The boy next to him was his younger brother, Andy. I knew Riley lived with his mom, Andy, and two young sisters, and took pretty good care of them ever since his dad, Paul, had died at sea during a storm five years ago.

"Were you down behind the motel drinking, Riley?" I asked.

"He looked at the others and then looked back at me.

"Yeah," he admitted finally. "But we only had one beer each. I swear. That's the truth. School finished last week and we were just celebrating. I guess we got carried away and threw the empties against a rock."

They were silent as I considered what young Riley had said, and also the fact that I couldn't smell alcohol inside the cab of the truck or on his or Clayton's breath. I studied all their faces quietly. Young, pale, faces that held more fear than belligerence.

"Okay," I said. "This is what I want you to do. Before you go to the wharf, go back down behind the motel and clean up the broken glass from the beach before someone walks on it."

They all nodded quickly in unison.

"And it would be a good idea to remember two things," I said firmly, but not unkindly. "You're all under the legal drinking age, and the beach below the motel is owned by the Halton's and is private property. I don't want either to happen again."

They all nodded again, and then waited and watched me apprehensively.

"Okay then. Have a good day," I said, and waved them on.

"Thanks, sheriff," they all said in unison, big smiles of relief on their faces.

When I walked inside Gertie's, James Dawson, the lawyer, who was sitting on a stool beside Roger Wagner, hooted out at me.

"Stop another major crime wave, Jake?"

"You looked like Wyatt Earp out there, standing in the middle of the street like that," Roger added.

Hilarious, I thought, as the two men howled with laughter.

CHAPTER 6

L ater that afternoon, ominous, black clouds rolled in, and darkness fell over Leigh Falls. Loud thunderclaps shook the houses and buildings in town and lightning flickered through the window on the walls of my office. And then the rains came. Hard sheets of rain that beat down on the roof of the police department building and swept across town, pounding the dark water of the harbor. *Badly needed rain*, I thought, as I stared out at the wharf where boats that were tied up there bobbed up and down on the rough waves.

At five o'clock I gave up on the incessant paperwork in my basket, grabbed my jacket and went home, driving through rain so thick that at times I couldn't see the centerline. After a shower and a quick supper of canned tomato soup that I ate in the living room while I watched the evening news, I got back into my cruiser and headed across town to pick up my nephew, Jeb.

Jeb and his mom, Sandy lived in the house that my brother, Craig, and I had grown up in. It was a two-story, cedar and glass house that my dad had built with his own hands, and it sat at the end of a quiet street at the western edge of town. After our parents had died in a plane crash, Craig and I had continued to live there, and when Craig went off to university, I lived there alone, but purchased the piece of land on Meadow Lane and starting building my own cedar home. When Craig returned to Leigh Falls and married Sandy, I signed the family home over to them as a wedding present and moved into my almost completed home. But only three years after Jeb was born, Craig's half-ton pickup had careened across the highway on top of Drummond Cliff; plunged over the edge and sank beneath the churning ocean waves below.

Jeb, who would be eight at the end of July, considered himself the man of the house and took pretty good care of his mom. Sandy, on the other hand, seemed unable to cope with Craig's death, and at times, hardly seemed to notice that Jeb lived in the same house with her. For years a strong Christian, after Craig's death, Sandy had never again picked up her Bible or set foot in church again. It seemed to me that Jeb had taken on the role of parent, and Sandy, the role of child, and although for a long time I had been sympathetic, I was now quickly losing patience with Sandy.

I pulled into their gravel driveway and was about to get out and walk up to the door when I saw Jeb come flying out of the door.

"Hi, Uncle Jake," he said, and gave me a huge grin as he climbed into the front seat.

"Hey there, Jeb," I said with a smile.

"It's raining cats and dogs, isn't it?" he said, as he fastened his seat belt.

"It sure is," I said and pulled away from the curb, heading in the direction of Leigh Falls Baptist Church.

"Jake?"

"Yes?"

"Why do people say it's raining cats and dogs? It can't rain cats and dogs."

"It's just a saying."

He made a face. "It's dumb."

"Yeah, I guess."

"I guess so," he snorted.

"How's your mom?"

He shrugged and stared silently out the windshield.

"Wasn't sure if she would let you go to prayer meeting tonight with the rain coming down so hard."

"She doesn't care, Uncle Jake," he said quietly.

I took my eyes off the road for a couple of seconds to study his face. "That's not true, Jeb. She does care. She just doesn't always show it."

He shrugged again, his little face tight as he watched the windshield wipers sweep back and forth.

I took one hand off the wheel and reached over and ruffled his neatly cut, fine, sun-blond hair. Once a month when I went to the barber, Jeb came with me and had his hair cut in the same police regulation length as mine.

"How about after prayer meeting we get an ice cream sundae at Gertie's?"

He looked over and the tension on his face was replaced by a big grin.

"Okay!"

"Jake?"

"Yes?"

"Can I hit the siren?"

"Not yet. Mrs. Frost is driving right in front of us."

Jeb looked at me quizzically. "Isn't she deaf?"

"As a post."

He smiled hopefully.

I shook my head and smiled back. "We'd better wait anyway."

He fell silent for a few minutes as he impatiently watched Mrs. Frost's slate, blue, mint condition, 1988 Chrysler Dynasty crawl down the road.

"You know my friend, Cody Peters?"

"Sure."

"Well, he was walking with his mom along the side of the road and Mrs. Frost was coming behind them, and they had to jump into the ditch because her passenger door was open and it would have hit them. He said his mom screamed at Mrs. Frost, but she didn't hear her and just kept driving down the road with her door hanging wide open."

"Where'd this happen?"

"On the Whitney Road where they live."

I shook my head and blew out my breath hard.

"Why is she going so slow?" he sighed.

"She's just being careful."

He snorted at that and shot his eyes over to my speedometer and moaned in agony at the slow speed. "I bet she doesn't even know we're behind her or anything."

"Jeb."

He looked at me and suddenly grinned. "I heard you talking about her with Deputy Harrington at my baseball game last week, and you told him that she's a menace on the road and shouldn't even be driving any more."

I smiled. "You don't miss a thing."

He grinned proudly. "I know. Gertie told me that I take after you for that and I should be a policeman too when I grow up."

I laughed quietly.

After Mrs. Frost had finally turned left onto the street where she lived and the car's taillights disappeared from sight, he whipped his head around and fixed his eyes on me.

"Jake?"

"Yes?"

"Can I hit the siren now?"

"Sure."

"And the lights?"

"Sure."

At eight-thirty the rain had stopped and as we walked from the church to my cruiser I breathed in deeply of the balmy breeze which was stirring the leaves on the trees. Even after the rain, the breeze didn't smell all that clean or new, but carried the strong scent of the thick, green seaweed, dead fish, and the assorted seashells that cluttered the beach after the tide retreated.

Fifteen minutes later Jeb and I were perched on stools in Gertie's eating chocolate sundaes when Kate LeRue walked in carrying Madeleine in her arms. I moved the stool around a few inches and looked over at her. She was wearing black jeans, a dark blue short -sleeve blouse and a pair of brown leather sandals on her feet, and her shoulder-length, dark hair was tied back and shiny with health. She glanced over, and when our eyes met for a brief instant I saw her face go pale and she quickly cut her eyes away. She walked across the room to the last booth and waited for Leslie Simmonds, a college student who worked for Gertie during the summer months, to bring over a child's booster seat.

"Jake?"

"Mm?"

"Whatcha looking at?" Jeb asked, his eyes following mine.

"Nothing."

He snorted.

"What?"

"You're staring at that lady."

"I smiled and moved my eyes from the LeRue woman back to Jeb as he spooned up the last of his ice cream.

"It's rude to stare. You told me that."

"I know. Finish your sundae. It's getting late and your mom will be looking for you," I said.

"What are you still doing here?" Gertie growled as she walked around the counter and stood in front of him, holding a coconut cream pie in her hand.

"It's not late, Gertie. Besides, it's summer vacation," Jeb said.

"Don't you sass me. I'm ready to hit the coop and so are you," she growled, but it didn't bother Jeb at all and he just grinned at her for he knew that she loved him fiercely. "Here, I made this pie for you and your mom. Give it to her for me and tell her I said hello."

"Okay. Thanks, Gertie," Jeb beamed, for it was his favorite kind of pie.

"Where's mine?" I said hopefully, for it was my favorite too.

"Try Trina's Restaurant."

I closed my eyes and then opened them after a couple of seconds to find her watching me with a bemused smile.

"Yours is over there," she said, gesturing to the end of the counter where the pie sat next to the ancient cash register. "And you get home to bed right now," she said, giving Jeb a no-nonsense look.

"But, Gertie," Jeb said, swiveling his stool around to point his spoon at Kate LeRue's toddler. "That baby's still up and I'm almost eight."

"Mind your own business! You're getting as bad as your uncle," Gertie grumbled and then bent over and began searching the shelves below the counter.

I stood up and dug in my pants pocket for some money. "We're finished anyway, Gertie. I'll take him home now."

"Good," she said, but stayed down and rummaged around below the counter.

"Lose something?" I said to her.

She straightened up and jabbed her index finger down on the counter. "I'm sure I set my soup ladle down right here, but now it seems to have vanished."

"You probably just forgot where you put it, Gertie. It's awfully busy in here," I said, looking around at the customers in the booths.

"I know where I put it, Jake Cole!" she barked right back at me.

"You don't use it for soup anyway, Gertie. You just use it to hit Jake with," Jeb said, and then clutched his sides and started laughing so hard tears streamed down his eyes.

"Oh, you're bad," Gertie said, grinning as she came around the counter to where he sat roaring on the stool and gave him a bone-crushing hug.

"Maybe you should think about hiring another waitress," I said, after she had released him. "There's more tourists in town than any other year, and it seems like it might be too much for you and Leslie."

"I'll give it some thought," she said, but her tone said she wouldn't, and then she walked back to the oven, yanked on oven mitts, opened the door, and pulled out a long glass dish from which the aroma of seafood casserole rose in delicious waves.

As Jeb and I walked across the floor of the diner to the door, each with a coconut cream pie held carefully in our hands, I risked another glance at Kate LeRue. She was staring out the plate glass window to the street, but suddenly turned her head and caught me looking, so I quickly cut my eyes away from hers and studied the floor of the diner as I walked out.

"Jake?" Jeb said, as we walked across the sidewalk to where my cruiser was parked up against the curb.

"Yes, you can hit the siren on the way home."

He squinted his bright, blue eyes at me. "How'd you know I was going to ask you that?"

CHAPTER 7

I was jolted awake from a dream of Craig's accident around four-thirty in the morning. My body was drenched in perspiration and I tossed and turned for another hour on the sweat-soaked sheets, but couldn't go back to sleep. Despite that my bedroom window was open as far as it would go, and I had a small fan on the night table that was blowing right on me, it didn't make much difference. The humidity had returned and the air in the room was too stifling to sleep.

I lay there staring at the ceiling and thinking back to that hot, August day almost five years ago, when I had sped to the accident scene at the top of Drummond Cliff, only to learn that the victim was my brother. Stunned, shocked, none of those words can describe the emotion that swept through me when as I looked over the edge of the cliff and knew that it was Craig's half-ton truck that had dropped down more than two hundred feet and smashed into the ocean.

Scott Moore, the first deputy on the scene, told me that Craig had swerved across the road and gone over the bluff to avoid rear-ending a car driven by an elderly man from Florida, who had become confused and had stopped his car dead in the road at the top of the cliff. There was a minivan carrying a young family from New Hampshire coming toward Craig in the oncoming lane, and he had less than five seconds to decide whether to rear-end the stopped vehicle, swerve around it and hit the minivan head-on, or avoid doing either by driving over the edge of the cliff. Courageous and selfless to a fault, he veered straight across the highway and went over the bluff. In my dream I could hear Craig's engine hissing as it hit the water, and see his brave face filled with heartache for Sandy and Jeb, as his truck slipped beneath the cold, dark ocean waves.

I gave up on getting any more sleep and threw off the tangled sweaty sheet, climbed wearily out of bed, and wandered outside to the deck in my bare feet. The breeze was slightly cooler outside, that due in part to the perpetual morning fog that rose from the water and rolled inland, yet, the air carried a heavy warmth that promised another brutally hot day.

My mood as dark as the sky, I sat down on a chair at the patio table and listened to the waves coming in, cresting close to shore and then flattening out on the sandy beach below my back yard. I rarely dreamed of Craig, or of his accident, but I thought a lot about the elderly driver who had stopped his car in the road and caused the accident. And I thought even more about who he was, and how he had happened to arrive at the top of Drummond Cliff on that terrible day. And when I did allow my mind to dwell on all that, I was almost overwhelmed by a feeling of despair that I found hard to shake for hours after.

When the first pink hue appeared in the eastern sky, I went back inside. I pulled on dark blue running shorts, a gray T-shirt, and my blue and white Nike running shoes, made my way across my short grassy lawn to wooden steps and took them two at the time down to the sandy beach. I started out a slow jog along the edge of the surf where the sand was hard and packed down from the water, and then gradually increased my speed until I was running as hard and fast as I could. Sweat streamed down my face and back as I poured it on and pushed myself to the brink of exhaustion. After two punishing miles, I stopped at my turnaround point and walked up to the seawall. I dropped down, gasping harshly, on a large boulder that was in a curved section of the high wall and was secluded from the road above and from Cotter's Cove, the public beach about a half-mile further down the beach from where I sat.

I sucked in huge gulps of the early morning sea air as I tried to get my breath back. The sun was rising and was burning off the mist and fog, and its rays radiated off the water right into my eyes.

I slipped on my sunglasses, and when I was breathing somewhat more evenly, took out my pocket sized Bible and read for awhile. After a time of quiet prayer, I rose and jogged slowly back home, feeling slightly better, yet, at the same time, aware of a nagging sense of disquiet in my heart.

Just after one-o'clock that afternoon, the sun was a hot, red sphere in the sky, and sweat once again poured down my back as I stood on the road at the top of Drummond Cliff, behind a shiny black, Lincoln with Florida plates and wrote the driver a speeding ticket. Five minutes before, I had been parked on the side of the road when the Lincoln had passed me at a high rate of speed. Shaking my head in disbelief, I had pulled out onto the road, hit the siren and took off after the speeding car.

I was filling in his license plate number when I heard the sound of the car door opening.

"Please stay in your car, sir," I called out.

"Boy, it's a scorcher today, isn't it, officer?" he said.

I looked up, but didn't reply.

"I can't believe you people get this kind of heat out here along the coast," he said, and continued walking toward me.

"It's unusual," I said flatly, and began writing again. "Would you please wait in your car, sir."

"Officer, listen, there's no need for you to fine me. Come on, give me a break, will you? Back home, I serve on the city.."

"Get back in your car, sir," I cut him off, my patience waning.

The driver was a portly man in his early sixties, dressed in a loose fitting, oversized, white cotton shirt, plaid blue and green shorts, white sports socks and white Adidas running shoes that looked like they just came out of the box. His face was fleshy and red, and he was perspiring heavily despite the air conditioning he had just been enjoying in his car. He wore a false grin as he approached me, seemingly unconcerned that he had passed my cruiser while doing eighty in a fifty mile an hour zone.

"Listen, officer," he said.

I glanced at his name on the license, and then looked up and gave him a brief, warning look. "I'm not going to ask you again, Mr. Newman. Wait in your car."

He kept coming, not losing the insipid smile.

I sighed, removed my sunglasses and stared hard at him.

He stopped when he caught the expression on my face, but then leaned against the rear fender of his Lincoln, folded his arms over his chest and glared right back at me. Then he glanced at my badge and looked astonished.

"You're kind of young for a sheriff, aren't you?" he said.

I didn't reply.

He glanced back over his shoulder at the town of Leigh Falls spread out at the bottom of the long hill before turning his eyes back to me and fixing me with a withering glare.

"I can't believe that a town sheriff would be even out on patrol, let alone writing out speeding tickets. Surely you must have more important things to do."

I didn't say anything to that either. I was aware that this section of the road wasn't far from where Craig's truck had gone over, and as I glanced to my right and gazed out at the open water, my mind slipped back to the accident.

"Do you usually give tourists such a hard time, Sheriff Cole," he said, reading my nametag over the pocket of my white, uniform shirt.

"Only the ones who break the law," I replied, and pulled my thoughts back to the present. "The sign back there clearly says the speed limit is fifty miles an hour. You were doing eighty when you passed me sir, and I noticed that your driver's side headlight is damaged."

"Yeah, so what?"

"What happened to it?"

"I hit a deer in Massachusetts," he shrugged.

"Did you report your accident, Mr. Newman?"

"What accident!" he groaned, and slapped his pudgy pink hand down hard on the fender in irritation. "I just bumped into a deer. Only stunned him too, because I saw him run back into the woods. Ask my wife, she'll tell you the same thing."

I stared at him silently for a few moments while I considered his explanation.

Then to my disbelief, out stepped a thin, frail looking woman dressed in knee length, baggy pink shorts, a white sleeveless blouse, and too much blush in what I thought might be a weak attempt to appear healthy.

"Officer? Is there a problem?" she said, and her voice sounded as fragile as she looked as she stood shakily beside the car.

"He wants to know about that deer we hit, so why don't you tell the man," Newman snapped at her.

"Oh, that. Of course," she said and then smiled first at him and then at me, apparently so used to his rudeness that she never noticed it any longer. "Yes, officer, we hit a deer not long after we crossed the Massachusetts state line. Outside a small town called Anderson. The deer wasn't hurt seriously because by the time Harvey pulled over to the side of the road it had run back into the woods. We stopped in Anderson and Harvey reported it to a police officer. An Officer Harris, I think, wasn't it, honey?"

Newman shot her a harsh look. "Norris, and he was the Chief of Police of the town of Anderson," he hissed.

"Yes, pardon me. That was it, Norris. He took the report and looked at our car, and I have to say, he seemed dreadfully bored with the whole thing," she said, and pushed back a strand of blonde hair from her face. Her hair was very blonde, too blonde actually, and cut in a style that I thought was more suited for a teenager than a woman in her sixties. I figured 'honey' probably had a lot to do with that.

"Thank you, ma'am."

"You're very welcome, sheriff," she said with a pleasant smile.

"You can get back in the car now," I said.

"Certainly," she said, and did as I asked.

I walked around to the front of the car and examined the damaged headlight. There was a small speck of blood on the corner of the smashed headlamp, and a tiny tuft of coarse brown hair that did resemble deer hide stuck in the dried blood. I straightened up slowly and faced the man. Other than a broken headlight and a very slight dent, there wasn't enough damage to dispute the fact that he really did hit a deer. I began writing the ticket up, but made a mental note to give the police chief in Anderson a call just to be certain.

"Do you always treat your tourists like this, sheriff? Not real good for the economy I would think. After all, the money tourists spend must be very important to the survival of a small town like Leigh Falls," he snarled when he saw what I was doing.

Both money and tourists are a necessary evil, I was thinking.

"Where I'm from, the cops tend to give the tourists a little slack."

"Is that right, sir?"

"Maybe you're just not aware of how things work."

"I know how things work in Leigh Falls," I said.

He blew his breath out hard.

"Where are you staying, sir?"

He seemed to think I was relenting, and immediately dropped the sneer and flashed me an ingratiating smile.

"At the Coastal Inn. We've been there three days now."

"And how long will you be staying in Leigh Falls?"

"Oh, we're staying until the end of July. The wife's sister and brother-in-law are summer residents here and we're visiting them," he said, his smile slowly fading. "But why would that concern you?"

"Because I want you to follow me right now to a garage to have your headlight repaired."

"You can't be serious," he said incredulously, and his double chin seemed to quiver with his anger.

I waited for the traffic to pass before I spoke again. Two huge motor homes; and a station wagon pulling a hardtop tent-trailer headed down the hill toward town. More tourists, I sighed inwardly.

"Sir, you have been driving around Leigh Falls for three days with a broken headlight. You should have stopped at a garage immediately after you hit the deer to have it repaired. I have asked you three times to wait in you car and you have refused. I don't think I am being unduly harsh. If you don't follow me to a garage right now, the next place you will find yourself is in my lockup."

"Unbelievable," he said through gritted teeth and his face and neck flushed red with his anger.

"Enjoy your stay in Leigh Falls, Mr. Newman," I said, and handed him the tickets.

The guy looked like he was going to say something, but instead just shook his head, his eyes narrowing until they were just slits in his pudgy face. He snatched the tickets from my hand, stormed back to the driver's side door, yanked it open, climbed in, and then slammed the door shut behind him so hard the window rattled.

I walked back to my cruiser, climbed in, and then sat quietly for a long moment, seriously contemplating making a career change before it was too late. Then I put the car in gear, pulled back out onto the road and led the Newmans to Samuel's Garage. At the garage I asked the owner, Samuel Lynch, to inspect the damage to the front highlight area, but not to repair it until I gave him the okay. Sam had been a mechanic for almost forty years, and had seen every kind of damage done to a vehicle, and if the Newmans had hit a deer, he'd know it.

At five o'clock I left the office and walked down the sidewalk to the garage. The air was so humid it was hard to breathe, and the leaves on the trees that lined the sidewalk looked dry and were motionless. By the time I got to Sam's, sweat ran in rivulets down my back, soaking my uniform shirt at the small of my back. As I walked into the coolness of the cement walled garage through one of the two open bay doors, I saw the Newmans' Lincoln Continental parked in the far bay of the garage, and Kate LeRue's Malibu in the first bay with its hood up.

"Hey, Jake," Samuel said, wiping his greasy hands on a rag before tucking it into the pocket of his oil-stained orange coveralls as he stepped out from behind the Malibu's hood.

"Hi, Sam," I said, and walked behind the Malibu to the Lincoln in the next bay and closely examined the front bumper and broken headlight again. "Had a chance to look at the Lincoln yet? The police chief from Anderson called and confirmed the guy's story, but I wanted to see what you found anyway."

Sam lifted his Red Sox ball hat up and ran a hand across his steel gray, crew-cut hair, and then dropped the hat down again and smiled at me. "Well, what I found was very minor damage to the car and a small spot of blood and tiny piece of deer hide caught in between the busted headlight and grill. The guy hit a deer, and a small one too," he said with a shrug of his beefy shoulders.

I nodded and blew out my breath.

Sam looked at me with his dark brown eyes with a slight smile. "You don't like the guy much, do you?"

"No," I admitted with a small smile.

"Look, if it's any consolation, I wasn't real fond of him myself," he said, and lifted his ball hat up and down a couple of times. "Thought he was a real loudmouth and treated his wife like a piece of dirt every time she tried to speak. Wanted an estimate on the bill and argued over every cent. Looks like he's got a wagon full of money, but bickered with me over every penny. I gave him the cheapest price I could without losing money myself and it still wasn't low enough for him. Why is it the ones that got the money hate to part with it the most?"

I shook my head.

"Uh, Jake, I should tell you this. He was bad-mouthing you when he was in here. I told him to can it, and he did, but not before he said he was going to lay a complaint against you for harassment."

"Let him."

Sam smiled.

I pointed to Kate LeRue's car. "So, what's wrong with the Malibu?"

Sam lifted his baseball cap and scratched his head again. "Oh, nothing serious. The engine was misfiring. I checked it over and all I found was a faulty plug wire. I replaced it and she's running good now. Odd to have a faulty plug wire in a car this new, but you never know, I guess."

I nodded.

"I was on the phone with the owner just before you got here. Lady from Georgia. Although I think she's probably a Canadian because she told me she was on her way up to Canada to visit family before she had car trouble."

"Now why in the world didn't she just tell me that," I said, thinking aloud.

Sam frowned. "You know her?"

"No, not really. I spoke to her in Weston's a couple of days ago."

"Oh, I see," Sam said, and lifted his hat up and down again. "Well, she's a real nice lady, isn't she?"

"Seems to be," I said. "She didn't happen to mention anything about a husband?"

"No!" Sam hooted, his eyes going wide. "And I didn't bring up the subject either. None of my business, and there's enough nosy old coots in this town already if you ask me. We sure don't need another one."

I smiled at that.

A few minutes later I walked back to my office,

cleared some paperwork and then went home. I fixed two chicken salad sandwiches, watched some television, and then went to bed early. After I shut out the light, I lay there waiting to drift off to sleep and thought back to the events of the day and a shadow of guilt sliced through me. In my heart I knew I had been convinced that Harvey Newman had only hit a deer, but had given him a hard time over it just because I didn't like the guy. And I had to admit that if he had refused, or not bothered to take his car to Sam's, I would have like nothing better than to have thrown him in jail.

I flipped my pillow and lay on my back and allowed the sultry night breeze slipping in through the curtains to puff gently across my face. It wasn't that Newman didn't deserve the tickets, he did, and I had no regrets for that, it was just that I knew in my heart I had used my authority as sheriff to give him a hard time about the broken headlight just because I disliked him. I stared up at the ceiling and grimaced in the dark, disgusted with myself.

CHAPTER 8

Sunday morning the air was once again damp and the sky filled with haze when I picked up Jeb and we drove across town to Leigh Falls Baptist Church. It was too hot for a suit, and since I never wore one anyway, I opted for black dress pants, a short sleeve white shirt, and a cobalt blue tie that Jeb gave me for Christmas the year before, and yet my skin felt sticky under my shirt by the time I pulled into the parking lot.

We were late, so we hustled across the lot and in went in through the door. Jeb threw me a quick wave, turned right and went down the stairs to the basement for his Sunday school class, and I went upstairs and into a small room at the back of the church for my class. I sat down in an empty chair in between the town's mayor, Leighton Marshall, and James Dawson, who was a lawyer in town. Roger Wagner and Rollie Pugh were seated across from me talking quietly, and the class teacher, Morgan Dunn, was standing up at the head of the table, shuffling through some papers in his Bible as he prepared to begin the lesson.

"Good morning," I said to them all.

They all returned greetings and then Leighton Marshall turned sideways a couple of inches in his chair to face me.

"Jake, I think we need to have a talk," he said.

"Now?"

"No, later is fine. Meet me outside in the parking lot right after the service," he said.

At ten past twelve I made my way down the aisle and was astonished to see Kate LeRue sitting at the end of the last pew in the back. She was wearing a matching mauve colored skirt and jacket, a white silk blouse, and her glossy dark hair was pulled back behind her head and held by a gold beret. I was so surprised to see her I almost stopped dead in my tracks. I worked to keep the shock from my face as I approached her pew, intent on saying hello even though she had her head down and was reading a church bulletin.

"Good morning, Mrs. LeRue."

She looked up and seemed flustered by my presence, and I was sure right then that she had already seen me approaching and had only been pretending to read in the hope that I would pass by without speaking to her.

"Good morning," she said finally, her face tight with strain. She met my gaze only briefly before sliding her eyes back down to the bulletin in her hands.

I was going to say something else, but decided against it, partly because she was doing her best to ignore me, but mostly because I had spotted a wedding band on her finger. I continued down the aisle, nodding greetings at people, and stopped at the entrance only long enough to shake hands with Pastor Vance Rayner, and his wife, Anne, made the usual small talk, and then went outside.

I walked across the paved parking lot, blinking in the bright June sun. I pulled my sunglasses out of my shirt pocket and slipped them on to shield my eyes from the blinding sunlight. I studied Leighton as I strolled toward where he was standing at the edge of the lot under the shade of a wide, oak tree. He was a tall, slim, silver haired, very distinguished looking man who was somewhere in his mid-sixties. I knew he didn't buy clothes here in Leigh Falls, but drove to Bangor and bought them from a well-known very high-priced men's clothing store there. In short, he dressed and looked like he had money, and carried himself with such polish and dignity you would have thought he was the mayor of New York rather than the mayor of a small, coastal town in Maine.

Today he was dressed in an expensive looking sky-blue summer suit, a white dress shirt, a wide, silk, dark blue tie, and a pair of shiny black, dress shoes that probably cost more than my truck. He had been mayor now for ten years and although we had always gotten along, after Craig's accident, it seemed that we had hardly spoken other than to argue. We blamed our arguments on the fact that he liked to give the tourists preferential treatment and I didn't, but we both knew that really wasn't what lay beneath the surface of our conflicts.

"Leighton," I said as I came up beside him and faced the front of the church so I could keep and eye on Jeb.

"Jake," Leighton said, and took out a handkerchief from his suit coat pocket, wiped his brow and then folded it neatly and tucked it carefully back in the pocket. He ran his fingers through his thinning, silver hair, combing his bangs over, which was an unconscious habit of his, and then turned to face me.

"Terribly muggy weather, isn't it?"

"Yes, it is," I said, but at the same time I was thinking, here we go.

"Jake, a man by the name of Harvey Newman came in to my office Thursday afternoon."

"Oh?"

"He's from Morganport , Florida. Told me he's a city councilor up there."

I waited, trying to keep my face free of any expression.

"He also told me he thinks Leigh Falls is a fine town. Apparently he and his wife like it here so much they're giving some serious thought to buying a piece of waterfront property over on the Shoal Road."

"Good for them."

"Good for the town, Jake, good for the town," Leighton admonished me sharply.

"Ah."

Leighton just looked at me for a few seconds without speaking, his lips compressed into a hard, thin line.

"I'd better get Jeb home," I said and started to walk away.

"Hold on, Jake. I'm not finished yet," Leighton said, anger in his voice now.

I stopped, let out my breath and waited. I noticed Kate LeRue coming out of the front doors of the church holding Madeleine's hand as the toddler walked with very small steps beside her. I watched them cross the lot, and when they passed in front of where Leighton and I were standing, Kate turned her head and glanced over at me. I nodded at her, and she quickly turned her head and stared straight ahead.

"I can't believe you gave the man two tickets," Leighton said, sounding outraged. "And if that wasn't enough, you made him follow you to Sam's like he was some kind of common criminal?"

"Just doing my job."

"Doing your job? He told me that you came on like Wyatt Earp."

"What a compliment," I said. "And that's twice this week."

"This isn't funny, Jake. Not at all," Leighton said coldly.

I kept silent because my own anger was growing and I didn't trust myself to speak. I searched the parking lot for Jeb and saw him running around on the grass with a group of boys his own age. He saw me watching him and grinned and threw me a quick wave before he tore off around the corner of the church and disappeared from sight.

I glanced to the right in time to see Kate LeRue back her Malibu up, straighten out and then drive through the lot and pull out into the street. I was surprised to see her in church, and very surprised to see her in the same church I attended, but I was more than puzzled by the fact she was still in Leigh Falls since her car was now repaired.

"Jake, are you with me on this?"

I turned and met Leighton's eyes. "With you on what?"

He fixed me with a stony glare.

"Leighton, this city councilor from Florida was doing eighty in a fifty and driving at night for almost an entire week with a broken driver's side headlight."

"I think one ticket would have been more than enough, Jake," he said.

"I don't tell you how to do your job. Don't tell me how to do mine."

"And you don't run this town, I do," he retorted.

"Really? And all this time I thought we had a town council," I said, and nodded at Caleb, who was staring over at Leighton and me with a look of concern as he walked across the parking lot carrying his baby daughter, Haley, in his arms.

"Look, you've got to try to get this through your head," Leighton said, grasping my forearm with his long, slender fingers. "This town rolls up and dies in the winter and so does the town's economy. Like it or not, and I'm well aware of that fact that you don't, we need the tourists."

I looked at him until he let go of my arm.

"The only problem I have with the tourists is that their numbers keep rising while the number of deputies on the police force remains the same," I said, keeping my tone even. "It's getting harder every summer to keep a handle on things with only eight deputies."

"They're tourists, not criminals! And if you don't think you're up to the job, then maybe we need to find a sheriff who is."

I let my breath out through my nose and fixed my eyes on a line of pine trees across the road from the church.

"Besides, eight deputies and one sheriff in a town this small is a fairly sizable police department. A lot more than some of the towns with bigger populations around here have and you know it."

I opened my mouth to say something to that, but could feel my own temper rising dangerously so I decided against it.

"Just ease up on the tourists a little bit, Jake."

"If they break the law I'm not going to close my eyes about it."

"Oh, that's not what I'm asking you to do!"

"Are we finished, Leighton?" I said.

"Almost," he said, narrowing his eyes. "I didn't want to have to say this, however you leave me no choice. You better ease up, because if you don't and the town's economy suffers because of your actions, then the first place I'll cut costs is at the police department."

"Are you still speaking for the entire town council, Leighton?"

"Don't kid yourself, Jake. They'll see things my way, so don't push me," he said, his tone ominous. He held my eyes for a few seconds and then walked away.

I was quiet in my cruiser on the drive to Jeb's house and out of the corner of my eye I could see him studying me intently.

"I saw you and the mayor talking. You guys looked mad."

"Yeah, the mayor's a little upset with me."

"For what?"

"Well, we don't always see eye to eye on things, Jeb."

"Are you mad at him, too?"

"I guess I am," I admitted.

"Are you mad at that tourist too?"

"What tourist?"

"The one you made follow you to Mr. Lynch's garage."

I looked at him in surprise. "How did you know about that?"

"I was in Gertie's yesterday and there was this man was there talking real loud about how you gave him two tickets. He was saying bad stuff about you and everybody could hear, he even called you a man's name, and Gertie got really mad and kicked him out before he even finished eating."

"Really?"

He grinned and bobbed his head up and down happily.

I smiled at the thought of little Gertie throwing Harvey Newman out of her diner.

"Jake?"

"Yes?"

"Who's Wyatt Earp?"

I smiled.

CHAPTER 9

After they had arrived home from church and had eaten lunch, Kate put Madeleine down for a nap. The she walked into the kitchen, sat down, dumped the contents of her purse on the kitchen table and began counting the bills and the change. She had a grand total of four-hundred and seventy-seven dollars, and less than three-hundred in her checking account, and she had just about maxed out her credit card paying for the motel room on the trip here, one week's rental on the cottage, and the car repair bill. She had enough cash to rent the cottage for another week, and buy groceries for at least that long. Maybe a little longer if she was careful. But that was it.

After Madeleine's birth, Kent had talked about buying life insurance, but his one fault, which she had always overlooked for she loved him so deeply, was that he was a terrible procrastinator, and he had put off it off until it was too late. And to keep the monthly payments lower, he hadn't taken out life insurance on the car loan, therefore, after his death, she was left to make those payments. On top of that, they had been renting the house in Carlow while they saved what they could for a down payment on their own home. But then Kent became terminally ill, and Kate had used almost all of their savings to pay for his medical bills, and then his funeral expenses.

After his death, Kate had been as frugal as possible, and although she had never allowed Madeleine to go without, she had often skipped meals many times to save money. She hadn't really had much of an appetite anyway, not after watching her husband die a horribly painful death, and then, not long after his death, witnessing a brutal murder. The days and months following Kent's death seemed to pass in a charcoal blur, yet, somehow over the past year, she had managed to pay the rent and utility bills and make the car payments. But now the money was almost gone. She had considered selling the car and paying off the loan, but had decided against it, knowing that they would need it if they suddenly had to flee Leigh Falls.

She glanced sadly over her shoulder to the bedroom door where behind it her little girl slept in her crib, realizing that if she wanted to stay in Leigh Falls, she would have to find a job here. And very soon. She simply had no choice about it. And she did want to remain in Leigh Falls, because other than the town sheriff, who, it seemed, watched everyone in town vigilantly, the small town was perfect.

She thought of the sheriff and recalled how astonished she had been to see him in church. She had to admit that she really wasn't all that surprised to find out that he was a Christian, for despite his serious manner, she had noticed a gentleness and compassion about him that were evidence of a man who walked closely with His Lord. She had only been astonished by the fact that he attended the same church she had decided to start attending. And with only one Baptist church in this town, she'd be hard pressed to avoid seeing him on Sunday's.

She considered that for minute, and then decided to keep attending the church anyway. She figured she could easily avoid him if she made certain to arrive late and sit at the back, and after the service slip downstairs to the nursery to get Madeleine and go out through the lower level doors. And if he did insist on speaking to her like he had this morning, she would simply ignore him, even at the risk of seeming unpleasant and horribly rude.

She put her mind on Leigh Falls again and knew she wanted to stay here. It was ideal because she had found that no matter where she went, whether it was the drug store, library or grocery store, there were so many tourists about she felt almost invisible. Even at church this morning she had spotted people dressed in shorts, sandals and souvenir T-shirts sitting in the back pews and knew they were tourists, so she didn't think that other than to the sheriff she stood out too much.

Her mind drifted to the sheriff again, and she recalled the startled expression on his face when he saw her in church. She hadn't missed the way his penetrating eyes moved over her face, studying her when he greeted her. She had tried to appear calm and composed, but she wasn't sure how well she had pulled it off. No matter, Leigh Falls, she decided, would be their new home, at least for the summer. But first, if that was to happen, she had to find a job and a baby-sitter for Madeleine.

She leaned back in her chair and stared out the open kitchen window to the sandy-white beach while she thought for a few minutes. She remembered something she had overheard the older woman named Gertie, who owned that little diner in town telling the young waitress that she had changed her mind and was now considering hiring another waitress for the summer months. The diner was closed on Sunday's, so she decided that tomorrow morning she would put Madeleine in the stroller and walk to town and talk to the woman about hiring her.

Before her marriage and Madeleine's birth, she had been an elementary school teacher, but she had worked in a restaurant in the summers during her high school years, she was a quick learner and very determined and she was sure she would catch on fast. In addition, Gertie had been very kind to her and Madeleine when they ate at the diner, and she thought the woman just might give her a chance. *I bet Gertie would know of a responsible baby-sitter she could hire too*, she thought.

Thinking of that cheered her up and so she rose from her chair, went to the fridge, took out a pitcher of iced tea, grabbed a glass from the cupboard, her Bible, sunglasses and carried them outside to the patio table on the deck. She set everything down on the table and then walked to the railing, slipped on her sunglasses, and still had to shield her eyes with her hands as she gazed out to the blue-green water.

The salt and kelp filled breeze, and sound of the waves was continuous. The gulls screeched overhead in the near cloudless, blue sky, and the hot sun blazed unmercifully down on the swimmers. She glanced at the sunbathers who lay sprawled out on towels on the sand, and didn't know how they could stand to be barbecued by the sun like that.

The tide was on the way out and she could see some of the motel's guests, clad in bathing suits, or shorts and T-shirts, strolling far out on the ocean floor, stooping every now and then to pick up a seashell left behind. She walked the few steps back to the table, sat down in the shade of the wide umbrella and opened up her Bible to the Book of Ezekiel, Chapter Thirty-four, where she had left off reading during her quiet time yesterday.

Every few seconds though, she would lift her eyes from the page to glance over at the dirt lane and up to the Oceanside Road. Despite the measure of safety she felt here, she was never really at ease, for she knew she couldn't allow herself to let her guard down completely. And then she read verse twenty-eight, and the words spoke to her with such power, with such peace, that she looked up from the page and smiled, her heart filled with wonder at God's love and protection for His children.

"*And they shall no more be a prey to the heathen, neither shall the beast of the land devour them; but they shall dwell safely, and none shall make them afraid.*"

She stared at the ocean while the words echoed comfortingly over and over and over again in her mind.

CHAPTER 10

At the edge of the town of Linden, Maine, neighboring town to Leigh Falls, a tall man with a muscular build stood inside a phone booth in the parking lot of a truck stop, dropping quarter after quarter into the slot, his index finger sliding down the line of names in the book. He had pale blue eyes that glittered in the sunlight like ice crystals, eyes that revealed a cold, black, evil heart. He had a neat goatee, long, black hair with streaks of gray in it that he wore pulled back in a pony tail, and he stood well over six feet tall. He was wearing a black, pin-striped suit, white dress shirt, blood red tie, black snakeskin cowboy boots, and a lightweight, gray summer topcoat over the suit. He was dialing the numbers, in alphabetical order, of every motel within fifty miles of where he now stood.

He heard the scuffling of shoes on the asphalt and heavy exaggerated sighs, and turned around and saw a short, heavy-set woman in her early fifties, waiting outside the booth, her face pinched as she tapped her foot impatiently. He turned back around, ignored her, and kept dialing. When he got to the S's, he dropped another quarter in the slot, cleared his throat before speaking, and then hit pay dirt at a motel in the seaside, resort town of Leigh Falls.

"Excuse me, but I've been waiting almost ten minutes," he heard the woman blurt out, her voice like the harsh cawing of a crow that grated and chafed on his nerves.

He turned around again in the booth and gave her an icy glare that carried one warning, one lethal caution that promised violence, and a cruel violence that he would greatly enjoy inflicting on her. When she met his eyes, she understood at once and her small mouth fell open, and her fleshy red face went completely ashen. She spun around and walked away, her legs pumping so rapidly her entire body was waggling and the sight was enough to make him smile.

Still smiling his chilly smile, he began talking to the owner of the Blue Spruce Motel & Cottages, a woman who said *'praise the lord'* repeatedly, and who sounded so jolly, he hated her at once. As they spoke, the man could hear suspicion creep into her voice, and she grew cautious and wouldn't answer his questions, or admit whether the woman and child he was asking about were staying at the motel. But, it didn't really matter. He had been at this long enough to know by the motel's owner's voice that they were there. He had found them, and found them very easily, for the woman he was hunting had made it all so easy for him by using her credit card to pay for gas twice, a motel room and now the cottage. She had left a paper trail so wide he would have had to have been a blind amateur to miss it, and the trail had ended abruptly at the Blue Spruce Motel & Cottages in the little town of Leigh Falls, Maine.

He hung up the phone and walked across the wide parking lot of the busy truckstop to his rental car. He was tired from the long drive so he decided to try to find a motel room somewhere in Linden, get a good night's sleep, and then head into Leigh Falls in the morning. He had a satchel in the trunk with a change of clothes, white cotton shorts, baggy T-shirt with a large flowered shirt to wear over it, wide-brimmed hat, sandals, and a Nikon 35-millimeter camera. *The consummate tourist*, he thought, and almost laughed aloud at the mental image of himself dressed in his costume, driving into the seaside town and cruising by the Blue Spruce Motel.

He climbed into his car, fit the key in the ignition and drove out of the parking lot with a thin, hard smile on his face. He felt a familiar tingling rush up his spine, and he mused that it was probably not unlike what any hunter experienced when he had cornered his prey.

CHAPTER 11

Monday morning the sky filled with dark clouds, the humidity had worsened, and the air carried the smell of the drizzling rain coming down. I was driving my cruiser, with Caleb in the passenger seat, slowly patrolling the streets in and around Leigh Falls. It was foggy, far too humid, and the morning seemed gray, and endlessly boring. We stopped just two cars in the space of three hours, one driven by a tourist from Wisconsin, for speeding, and the other, a local teen, for driving without proper tags. And just to prove Leighton Marshall wrong, I ticketed both tourist and townie equally.

At ten-thirty, Marney radioed me about a possible drowning at Cotter's Cove. Caleb hit the siren and lights and we raced across town, followed an ambulance down the lane to the cove and parked beside Eric Malley's cruiser in the dirt parking lot.

We sprinted across the beach behind Eric and Scott Moore, who were running about five yards ahead of us and looked to have just arrived too. We headed toward a group of people standing together talking at the water's edge. There was one man lying flat on his flat on his back on the sand, and two lifeguards standing side by side watching two paramedics who were kneeling down beside the man and were performing CPR. I could see that the man on the ground looked in very bad shape. He was a portly man with thick, gray-white chest hair, and was wearing a pair of baggy, bright red nylon swimming trucks that came down almost to his knees.

I stopped as I came up alongside the lifeguards, looked down at the victim, and my heart turned to stone. Although his fleshy face was a pasty gray-ish-white, his thick lips a deep blue, and his wet hair was plastered against his skull, I recognized him at once as Harvey Newman. His eyes, the same ones that had held scorn for me that day on Drummond Cliff were open and rolled back in his head, staring lifelessly up at the sky. I pulled my eyes away and searched the group of onlookers for Newman's wife but didn't see her anywhere on the beach.

I looked back down at Newman again and knew he was dead. I was filled with a sudden despondency because I knew I would have to find his wife and tell her that her husband was dead, and it was the one part of my job that I in no small sense dreaded. I was also feeling a deep sense of failure for the way I had spoken to him that day when I pulled him over for speeding on Drummond Cliff. My annoyance with Newman, had, if he didn't already know Jesus as His Savior, very likely cost me an opportunity to be any kind of a Christian witness at all to him.

I watched the paramedics continue to perform CPR, and uttered a silent prayer that they would be able to bring Newman back to life. When I was finished, I touched the arm of the lifeguard who was on my left, a well-built young guy whose name was Trent Holmes. I had gotten to know Trent well over the past couple of summers that he had been coming to Leigh Falls to work as a lifeguard to earn money for university, and I thought he was a fine, young man.

"What happened, Trent?" I asked, and motioned to Caleb, who was standing on my right, to break up the crowd and to close the beach for the day.

Caleb nodded that he understood and I turned my gaze back to the young lifeguard.

Trent ran his hand across the top of his buzz cut sandy bristles and looked distraught.

"Oh man, I still can't believe it. The guy tried to swim over to Sangster's Island. He must have been nuts to think he would make it."

I shook my head and blew my breath out as I looked over the blue-green, wave-tossed water to Sangster's Island. Not many people were strong enough swimmers to make it the mile or so across the choppy water. The current out past the yellow safety ropes of the swimming area was treacherous, and there were signs posted all over the beach area warning swimmers not to go out past the ropes. The only people I knew who had ever attempted it had been two members of Leigh Falls High School's swim team. And I knew that even though they had been young men, strong and healthy, they had only just made it.

Eric Malley, who had been talking to a group of swimmers, joined us then and I noticed that his white uniform shirt was stretched so tightly across his bulging stomach that the buttons looked close to popping off, and his shirt tails were hanging out in places. His brown hair was shaggy and went down past his shirt collar despite the police regulations that said it was to be worn above the collar. I felt irritation crawl up my back when I also took in the large yellow sweat rings staining his shirt under his arms, and the sticky looking stain on his tie.

"Hey, what happened here, Trent?" Eric blurted, his gray eyes filled with a strange excitement.

Trent seemed taken aback by Eric's boorish manner and looked from Eric to me.

I nodded at him to go ahead and tell his story.

"I was up in the chair and saw the guy swim out past the boundary rope and I yelled at him to come back," Trent explained with a voice quavering. "I know he heard me because there wasn't that many people on the beach or in the water on account of the rain. Anyway, I used the bullhorn and warned him a couple more times, but he just turned and kind of sneered at me and kept going. He ran into trouble not long after."

"Did you go out after him?" Eric asked in what sounded like an accusing tone.

"Eric, go give Caleb a hand," I said before Trent answered him.

"Why?" Eric said, and shrugged his meaty shoulders.

I ignored Eric's insubordination for the moment because I was watching Trent carefully. Although it was raining, and the sky was a hot gray haze, and the air sweltering and very muggy, Trent had begun shivering and I fearful he was going into shock.

"You okay, Trent?" I said.

He took in a gulp of air, shivered hard once, and then nodded.

"Go ahead, finish your story," I said gently, still keeping a close eye on him.

He drew in another deep breath and then continued.

"I went in after him on the board right away, but by the time I reached him he had already slipped beneath the surface. It was a miracle I even found him because it's so dark out there and the bottom is mostly thick sawgrass. Somehow I got a grasp on his hand as he was sinking into the grass, but when I hauled him to the surface, he was already unconscious."

"Guy wasn't a listener, I guess, hey Trent?" Eric snorted in a half-laugh as he gazed down at Newman's body. "He isn't anymore, that's for sure."

Trent stared at Eric in open-mouthed shock.

"Eric," I said tightly.

"What?" he said, wearing a callous grin on his face.

"Go over and give Caleb and Scott a hand moving the people off the beach. Now," I said sternly.

"Why? He's got most of the lookie-loos off the beach already. He doesn't need my help," he retorted, swiping the sweat and rain from his forehead with the palm of a meaty hand.

I took in a breath and then let it out slowly and quietly and stared hard at him.

He stared back and opened his mouth to say something else.

I shook my head once, firmly.

He shut his mouth and held my gaze, but after a short time, dropped his eyes, shrugged and grinned again.

"And lose the smile," I said.

"Okay, okay. Relax, will you? I'm going."

I watched him shaking his head in amusement as he walked away, and felt my face burn and I had a hard time controlling my anger. I wanted to fire him right on the spot. And I would have if it weren't for his pregnant wife, Louella, their unborn child, and his four other young children who were all under the age of ten. I forced my eyes from him and glanced down at the paramedics who were strapping Newman onto a stretcher while still performing CPR. When they picked up the stretcher and were hustling past me, I spoke quietly in the guy's ear that was closest to me.

"Is he going to make it?"

The guy shook his head. "Nah, he was dead before we even got here."

"Where's his towel?" I asked Trent, as I looked around the beach. Most of the other sunbathers seemed distressed by the drowning, and were picking up their belongings and leaving the area without much prodding from my deputies.

"Right over there," Trent said, pointing to a large orange beach towel about twenty feet away from where we stood. I could see a small pile of clothes and a pair of cheap yellow and white plastic flip-flops on the towel.

"Was he with anyone?"

Trent shook his head. "No. I saw him walking from the parking lot down to the beach. He came alone."

I nodded. There was only one towel there, but I had to check anyway.

I trudged across the sand in my regulation shoes, sweat streaming down my back, and squatted down by the lone beach towel. I picked up a pair of white cotton pants from the pile of clothing, and searched the pockets until I found a set of car keys for the Lincoln. I figured his wallet must be locked in the car.

When I stood to my feet again, I saw that Trent had walked over to the lifeguard chair and was leaning against one of the long posts of the high wooden structure with his hands over his face, shivering with what I knew from personal experience was the utter shock of seeing someone die right in front of you.

I walked over beside him, reached up and pulled a sun-warmed towel from the seat of the lifeguard chair, draped it around his shoulders and gave his arm a gentle squeeze.

"You okay?"

He nodded, but wouldn't look at me.

"Hey, this isn't your fault, Trent," I said. "He was an adult and he made the decision to go out past the rope."

Trent wiped tears from his face with the back of his hand and then shook his head. "In my head I know that, but, I'm a trained life-guard. I was supposed to save him. Man, all these years I've been a lifeguard and that's the first person I've ever seen drown. I thought I would be able to handle it, but it's a lot harder than I could have imagined."

"It is," I said quietly.

"I just wish I could have saved him."

"You did everything you could, Trent," I said again, and motioned to Caleb who was walking toward us to go get a blanket from the trunk of my cruiser.

A couple of minutes later Caleb joined us and wrapped the blanket over the towel that was already around Trent's shoulders, at the same time giving him a compassionate, yet, reassuring smile.

Trent seemed to gather some composure after that and his shivering eased and his voice grew stronger and I was sure he was out of danger of slipping into shock. I walked over to speak to Scott and put him in charge of clearing the beach with Eric, not so sure I wasn't really putting him in charge of keeping an eye on Eric, and then I got Caleb and we drove to the hospital.

We waited in the lobby of the emergency ward, and after only ten minutes, the doctor came out and told us Harvey Newman had been pronounced dead on arrival. Although, there wasn't much doubt that he had drowned, the body would be sent to Linden for an autopsy to determine the exact cause of death. The doctor told us that he thought there was a good possibility that Newman might have suffered a heart attack before he drowned, but he couldn't be sure until he got the results of the autopsy.

I called the Newmans' room at the Coastal Inn but there was no answer. Then I called the front desk at the Inn and learned that Mrs. Newman was out, but was expected back shortly. That done, we left the hospital and walked out to our cruiser in the parking lot. The clouds were gone, the rain had stopped and the sun was burning down even more unmercifully now. We climbed in the cruiser, rolled down the windows and sat there quietly. After a short time, Caleb and I then bowed our heads and closed our eyes, and prayed that God would grant us the wisdom, strength and guidance we needed before we drove over to the Inn to inform Mrs. Newman that her husband was dead.

CHAPTER 12

A little before noon on Monday, the man with the glacial blue eyes quickly and efficiently pushed his cart up and down the aisles of the small hardware store, picking out the camping gear he needed. He rolled the cart over to another aisle, saw that it contained shelves filled with boxes of nails, screws and brackets of every size and shape, so he proceeded to the next aisle. Although he already had in his cart a good, but relatively inexpensive, two-man dome tent and a sleeping bag, he didn't have hardly any choice in selecting any of them. The store had a lot of hardware items, and little in the way of camping gear, and that did nothing to improve his mood that was already very foul.

The reason for his bad mood was that he hadn't been able to find a motel room last night in Linden, and had been forced to sleep in his car. And at six-foot, seven inches, and two hundred and seventy-five pounds that was no small feat. Then, to add to his consternation, he had arrived in Leigh Falls this morning only to find the same thing. After hours of searching, all he had been able to find was a camping site in a campground at the southern end of town. He simply had no other choice. It was either sleep in his car or pitch a tent. He hadn't camped since the one time when he was ten or eleven-years-old, but he distinctly remembered hating every single minute of it. He was a born and bred city-boy and didn't like the outdoors at all, let alone roughing it in a tent. But, in the end, the more he thought about it, the more he realized that camping might just work to his advantage, for he would blend in with the tourists even better than he would have if he was staying in a motel.

He glanced over at the cash register and noticed the sales clerk watching him closely. He figured the guy probably found it strange for a tourist to arrive in town without any camping gear whatsoever, but the guy's intense stare didn't really bother him. When he had at first noticed the lack of camping gear in the store, he had considered driving back to Linden to shop at a large sporting goods store in the Linden Mall where he wouldn't attract attention, but, in the end had decided against it. If the sales clerk began asking him any questions he had a plausible explanation ready.

After searching through most of the store he finally found an aisle stocked with batteries and a wall of flashlights, and after searching through them, picked out a set of two, a hand held large *6v* battery that could be used in the tent as a lamp, and a smaller one he intended on using when he was out walking late at night. Which he most definitely planned on doing, he knew, and the thought of it caused a cruel smile to play at the corner of his mouth.

He pushed the cart over to the far wall of the store and found one lone, dust covered plastic package that held a double size, green air mattress, and he tossed that in the cart on top of the sleeping bag. He didn't bother looking for cooking utensils because he wasn't about to cook his meals outdoors. In the city he ate only at the finest restaurants and he wasn't about to change that just because he was forced to camp.

His smile a hard, thin line on his face, he rolled the cart into the next aisle and picked out a pair of big, purple framed, goofy looking sunglasses. He saw the sales clerk staring at him even more curiously, but it didn't concern him. He figured he'd pass as a tourist, dressed as he was in his hat, sandals, extra large yellow T-shirt, and knee-length, white cotton shorts. He had a Nikon, 35-millimeter camera slung over his shoulder and he smiled unconsciously at the picture of himself. He tossed the sunglasses into the cart and hurriedly finished gathering what he figured he would need for his stay in Leigh Falls, and then pushed the cart up to the cash register and began dumping the camping equipment on the counter.

"That's certainly a lot of camping gear. I hope you found everything you needed," the clerk said, his tone and smile friendly.

The huge man nodded once without looking at the clerk.

"I'm Roger Wagner. I own this store," the man said, and held out his hand.

The large man with the ice-blue eyes cleared his throat, ignored the outstretched hand and nodded once more.

"Good, good," the owner said, sounding slightly flustered as he dropped his hand. "I don't carry a lot of the larger camping equipment like tents and such, because most of the tourists who are camping have already have their own gear. If they don't, they tend to buy it at the sports store in Linden."

The man with the cold eyes cleared his throat again before speaking.

"I guess I should have explained. A rainstorm wiped out all my gear."

The storeowner's eyes moved over his face and he frowned, but didn't speak.

"Something wrong?" the tall man said thickly, sounding like his throat was clogged.

"No, not really. I just never thought that a rainstorm would wipe out a camper's entire gear. Must have been a real bad storm. Where'd you say this happened?" the owner said.

"I didn't," the man said coldly.

The owner seemed taken aback, but managed a brief smile after a moment.

"So which campground are you going to be setting up at?"

The man reached into the cart for the sleeping

bag, set it on the counter and stared silently at the owner.

"I only asked because I'm assuming it's either the Seashore or Pine-Air. There's a thunderstorm heading our way and I noticed you don't have a rain fly or a ground tarp in your cart. If you're setting up here in town you're going to need them. And if you don't already have an air pump, you're going to need one to inflate your air mattress."

The big man turned slightly and his eyes swept around the store. "You know, I was in such a hurry, I completely forgot. Which aisle would I find those items?"

The storeowner smiled pleasantly. "Hang on. I'll run and get them for you."

Sixty seconds later, he returned with an orange rain fly, a dark blue ground tarp and a small air pump.

"These okay?" he asked as he laid them on the counter.

"They're fine," the big man grunted.

The storeowner nodded, and began ringing in the items. "I wish had more equipment for you to choose from, but this is more of a mom and pop hardware store," he said, and shrugged apologetically.

"Really? Don't see mom around," the man snorted derisively, his cold eyes moving deliberately around the store.

The owner's smiled vanished. "My wife passed away seven years ago."

The man smiled a cruel smile at that.

The storeowner's face muscles tightened. "You know, that really is very strange that you lost all your camping gear to a rainstorm. I've never heard of that happening before. Not ever."

The man with the glacial blue eyes remained silent as he lifted items out of the cart and onto the counter. He was thinking he might have made a mistake about purchasing his gear here instead of in Linden, and that made him very angry. He didn't like making mistakes. Not at all.

"I mean, you might get your tent blown down by the wind and your gear might take a soaking, but that's usually about the extent of it," the storeowner went on.

The man reached into the cart again for the last item, and when he had straightened up completely, he drilled the owner with a cold, deadly glare.

The owner, a thin, older man, blanched, dropped his eyes, and kept them fixed on the camping gear and avoided any eye contact or conversation after that.

CHAPTER 13

At two-o'clock, I dropped a very quiet Caleb off at his house on the Dryden Road and then I drove back into town. He didn't usually go home for lunch, but I knew that with the drowning today, he wanted to be with his family for a little while and I didn't blame him a bit. If I had a family to go to, I would have done the same thing. As it was, Jeb and Sandy were the only family I had in town, and Jeb was at baseball practice right now, and Sandy was not inclined towards visitors, especially me, who reminded her so much of Craig, that at times she could barely look at me without bursting into tears.

So, I drove back into town and pulled the cruiser up close to the curb in front of Gertie's and went inside. To my utter surprise, I saw Kate LeRue standing at a booth with a pen and pad in hand, ferociously chewing her bottom lip as she concentrated on taking an order from a group of noisy tourists crammed into a booth.

I hopped up onto the only empty stool in the diner, which was the one between Rollie Pugh and Dr. George Hanssen, a family physician who had opened a practice in town just two years ago. In that short time, the doctor had acquired so many patients, chiefly female; he could no longer accept any new ones. The reason for this was that he was a young, well-built, blonde haired, blue-eyed, very handsome man, thus, his female patients called him either, *Dr. Handsome or Gorgeous George.* He was aware of that fact, and seemed to find it both flattering and amusing. As I chatted with him, Gertie, who shamelessly flirted with him, walked over with a big smile plastered on her face.

"Can I get you anything else, Doctor Hanssen?" Gertie asked sweetly.

"No thank you, Gertie," he said.

Besides the flagrant flirting, Gertie had also been known to frequently fake life-threatening illness or injury, in a blatant attempt to get him to accept her as one of his patients. Gertie 's doctor, who had been her doctor for almost thirty years now, was an older man named Dr. Ralph Izzard. He was cranky, demanding, and touchier than she was; thus, she had long ago dubbed him, *Izzard the Lizard* or simply, *Dr. Lizard.*

"Hey, Dr. Handsome," Gertie said with a wide smile. "Are you taking any new patients yet?"

He smiled and shook his head. "No, Gertie. Sorry. Full house."

Gertie leaned over, rested her elbows on the counter and looked mournfully into his eyes.

"I don't feel well," she said, wincing with pain.

"Is that right?" he said with a wide grin.

"Hey, I'm serious. I'm really suffering," she said very solemnly.

His smile faded and he frowned.

"Really, Gertie?"

"Yeah," she said, sounding suddenly short of breath. "Dr. Lizard's tried so hard, but he just can't seem to help me. Maybe you can?"

Dr. Hanssen looked concerned. "Well, what are your symptoms, Gertie?"

"I have terrible chest pain, my left arm is numb, I'm sweating all over, and I'm having trouble breathing."

"Gertie," I groaned and shook my head slowly.

Gertie turned her head and glared at me. "Mind your own business."

"If you're not going to drop dead of a heart attack within the next few minutes, could I get some lunch?" I said.

"Guess I'm feeling a little better now," she said, and flashed Dr. Hanssen an innocent smile before straightening up from the counter and facing me.

Dr. Hanssen sighed loud enough for every one in the diner to hear.

"You want her to take your order?" Gertie said to me.

"Who?" I said.

Gertie snorted. "The new girl, Kate."

"I thought you didn't need any help," I said.

She shrugged her thin shoulders. "I like Kate."

"When did you hire her?" I asked quietly.

"She came in first thing this morning asking about a job. She needed a baby-sitter for her little girl first though, so I gave her Miranda Renard's name and number. She hired Miranda and then came right back and started at noon."

"Oh," I said, my eyes following Kate when she walked behind the counter and went over to the coffeepot.

"Kate," Gertie called out.

"Gertie, wait, don't," I said.

"Kate!" she called again, raising her voice over the noise in the diner.

"Gertie, wait," I said.

She looked at me and winked. "Take Jake's order, okay?" she yelled out loudly. I closed my eyes and blew out my breath. When I opened them Kate LeRue was standing in front of me, pen and pad at the ready, looking nervous and uncomfortable.

"What would you like?" she said, and her voice carried a slight quake when she spoke.

Gertie heard and patted her compassionately on the arm. "Oh, Kate. Don't be afraid of Jake. He's not really as grumpy as he looks."

Dr. Hanssen looked at me. "Well, I don't know about that, Gertie," he said gravely.

"That's what they call a cop's face," Rollie informed him.

"Oh, is that what it is?" Dr. Hanssen said, and then he and Rollie laughed together.

The doctor was still chuckling as he wiped his mouth with a napkin, tossed it on his plate, and then slid off his stool, patted me on the shoulder and went out the door.

I sighed aloud, not really in the mood for jokes.

Kate LeRue was still waiting to take my order, and when I looked at her, all color drained from her face and her hands that were clutching the pen and order pad began visibly trembling. She fastened her eyes on the pad and wouldn't meet my gaze again.

"I'll have a sliced chicken sandwich on whole wheat, with lettuce and mayonnaise. And a glass of iced tea," I said quietly, feeling subdued not only by Newman's death, and how devastated his wife had been when we gave her the tragic news, but also by the way Kate LeRue reacted to my presence, which no doubt had something to do with the uniform I wore. I was getting kind of sick and tired of everything about this job.

"What! A sandwich! The special's Cream of Mussel Soup. Give him a bowl of that too," Gertie yelled from the other end of the counter, shaking her head.

"No soup, Gertie," I said, raising my voice in annoyance. "You know I don't like mussels."

"Then he'll have *two* chicken sandwiches, Kate," Gertie roared right back at me.

Kate looked at Gertie, than to me, and then back to Gertie with an expression of shock and confusion, unfamiliar with Gertie's bossiness when dealing with me, the town sheriff.

"Fine," I said, too weary to argue with Gertie.

Kate nodded, scribbled the order on the pad, and strode away, all without actually speaking to me again or meeting my eyes.

Gertie watched her walk away and then came over, shaking her head as she studied me.

"What?" I said crankily.

"It's her first day. She's a nice girl, and a real good worker. Would it hurt you to smile?"

"I don't feel like smiling right now, Gertie. A tourist drowned this morning at the cove, and I just came from telling his wife. She took the news really hard," I said in a low tone.

Gertie's wrinkled face broke. "Oh, I'm sorry, Jake. Roger was in earlier and he said something about that to me, but I was too busy to pay attention. Besides, I thought he was just teasing me about throwing that guy out. So, it's true? It was the same man?"

I nodded and rubbed my face hard with both hands.

"I feel bad about that now. You know, I chased him out with a broom," she said, shaking her head ruefully.

Despite my own remorse for how I had dealt with Harvey Newman, I had to bite back a smile at that.

She stayed patting my hand until Kate called her over to the stove. Not long after Gertie brought my lunch over, and returned later to pat my hand again while she refilled my glass of iced tea, but the LeRue woman stayed as far away from me as possible, and when I did catch her looking at me, it was with an expression of fear and apprehension. I found that irritating on top of everything else that had happened that day, so as soon as I was finished, I threw a bill on the counter, grabbed my hat, and headed out the door in a dark mood.

Two hours later black storm clouds had appeared from the north, the sky turned black, thunder rolled in and the trees began to sway fiercely in the strong wind. I stood at my office window looking out at the street, and felt like my mood matched the weather pretty good. I watched as a tour guide hustled a group of seniors out of a gift shop and into their tour bus, but before she could manage to get them all in, the clouds opened up and torrents of rain came down. A few minutes later I watched through my rain blurred window as the bus pulled away from the curb and disappeared down Ash Street.

My office grew as dark as night as the storm clouds moved over the town, lightning lit up the sky and flickered in on the walls, and earsplitting thunderclaps followed a few seconds later. I walked back over to my desk, sat down, flicked on my desk lamp, glanced at the overflowing in-basket and blew out my breath in exasperation. No matter how steadily I worked, the thing never really emptied. I folded my arms behind my head and leaned back in my swivel chair, put my feet up on the desk and let my thoughts drift to Kate LeRue. *It was frustrating having a woman scared to death of you*, I was thinking, when Marney came through the open doorway with an armload of paperwork.

"Somebody shoot me," I said in disgust as she slid the load into my basket.

"Quit daydreaming all the time and you won't have such a pile," she scolded me.

I looked back out through the window in time to see a bolt of lightning light up the sky, and then thunder followed it, the boom sounding like the crack of a rifle shot.

Marney walked to the window and looked up at the black sky.

"Do you believe this?" she said, shaking her head.

I didn't say anything.

"One minute it's hazy and humid, the next it's sunny, and then we get a storm like this," she said. I don't think the weather knows what it wants to do."

I nodded silently.

"Be nice if the storm gets rids of the humidity though. I can't remember muggy weather like this in June ever before," she said, and had to raise her voice over the rumbling thunder. When I remained silent she turned around and studied me carefully for a minute.

"I wish you'd let me get a word in once in a while," she said.

I gave her a half-smile.

"What's wrong with you?" she asked.

I only shrugged for an answer.

She raised her eyebrows. "Is this about the drowning at Cotter's Cove this morning?"

"That's part of it," I said.

She nodded. "It is tragic. Although I'd like to know why a sixty-year old man who was overweight and in poor physical condition, would try to swim all the way over to Sangster's Island."

"Who knows."

"I heard his wife passed out when you broke the news."

I nodded.

Marney shook her head sadly. "Poor woman. Is someone staying with her right now?"

"Her sister and brother-in-law. They own a summer home on the Shoal Road. She's staying there with them until the autopsy's completed and the body's released. Then they'll drive her back home to Florida."

"Let me guess. You're feeling bad about the tickets you gave him."

"Not the tickets, but I regret making him follow me to Sam's."

"Hey, guess what, you're human."

"I'm also a Christian, Marney," I said.

She nodded slowly.

We were quiet again.

After a time, Marney cleared her throat loudly. "So what's the other part?"

"What?"

"You said that's part of it. What's the other part?"

I looked at her and gave a little shrug.

"Is it the fact that we have more than two-thousand tourists in town already, and it's not yet July."

"No."

She nodded once, slowly, but eyed me thoughtfully.

"You're not going to leave my office until you get an answer, are you?" I said.

She folded her arms across her chest. "You got it."

I dropped my hands from behind my head and laid them on my stomach.

"Okay. It's this woman that's in town. She's from Georgia. She's working over at Gertie's now, and I don't know what it is, but any time I go near her, her face turns deathly white and she starts shaking. It's starting to drive me crazy."

Marney frowned only for a second before she smiled. "Oh, wait a minute. I know who you mean. Slender, dark-haired woman in her early thirties?"

I nodded.

"Kate LeRue," she said, nodding thoughtfully.

"How do you know her."

"Gertie introduced us when I was over there at lunch time."

"Oh."

Marney watched me now with a look of amusement on her face.

"What?" I grunted.

"I can see why that would bother you. She is an exceptionally attractive woman."

"Oh, Marney, it's not that," I groaned, and shook my head. "And believe me, you wouldn't say that if you had seen her reaction the first time she saw me."

"Why? What happened?"

"She was coming out of Dunkin' Donuts carrying a tray of coffee and juice, and when she saw me watching her, she jumped about a foot in the air and dropped the tray on the ground."

Marney threw her head back and laughed.

"What's so funny about that?"

"Well, you are pretty grim looking at times."

I sighed.

"And that's the only reason she has caught your attention."

"Yes, that's the only reason," I said firmly. "And not that it matters, but the woman does wear a wedding ring."

"So you noticed her ring," she said, with a knowing smile.

"I'm a cop. I'm paid to notice things," I said dryly.

"Well, for your information a lot of widows wear their wedding rings. Some for years after their husbands have passed on."

"She's a widow?" I said in surprise.

Marney nodded.

"How do you know that?"

"I heard it from a very reliable source."

"Gertie," I snorted.

"I can't say," she said, grinning as she lifted her right hand up in the air, palm out and two fingers held up and pressed together. "I'm sworn to secrecy."

"It was Gertie," I said, and rolled my eyes.

"Do you want some advice?"

"No."

"Too bad. You're getting it anyway."

"Before you do, my I remind you that although you have been engaged twice, you're still single."

"Yeah, but I'm young and I have plenty of time. On top of that, one of my fiancés was lazy, and the other was as dull as an unsharpened skate blade. I'm still counting my blessings to have escaped the two of them. You, on the other hand, have never even been engaged."

"I came close once."

She shook her head. "That was years and years ago, and close doesn't count. What's more, you're getting up there."

I closed my eyes and shook my head slowly.

"Look at me."

I opened my eyes and looked at her.

"Good. Okay. The next time you see her, do like this," she said, and then smiled a broad smile that revealed almost all her even, white teeth.

"Funny," I said.

"Try it," she ordered.

I exhaled loudly and then smiled.

"Never mind," she said, and walked out of the room.

CHAPTER 14

When I drove home at suppertime, the storm had passed and thin gray clouds scudded by in the even grayer sky. A light mist fell gently on my windshield, and a much cooler breeze that smelled clean and fresh blew inside the car through the open windows. When I pulled up into my driveway I saw Jeb sitting on the steps of the front porch, and spotted his red mountain bike leaning against the sidewall of my garage.

"Hey there, Jeb," I said as I came up the steps and looked at him. His blond wet hair was plastered down on his head and his clothes were and running shoes were drenched.

"Hi, Uncle Jake," he said in a low voice and kept his eyes on his Nikes.

"Come inside. You're soaking wet," I said, and stepped to the door, unlocked it and held it open for him.

He stood to his feet and went inside without looking at me.

"Why don't you go change into some dry clothes," I said gently.

Since Jeb stayed at my place so much he had his own bedroom at the end of the hall right across from mine, and he kept extra clothes and personal items there. Three years ago, we had painted the room together, hung model airplanes from the ceiling, and he had decorated the walls with baseball and basketball posters of all his favorite players.

I followed him inside, kicked off my shoes, went into my bedroom and changed out of my uniform, and then went into the kitchen and was rooting hopelessly through the fridge for something to make us for supper when he came into the kitchen and sat in a chair at the kitchen table.

"Something happen at home, Jeb?" I asked, turning around from the fridge to face him.

He shrugged; set a pair of dry blue socks down on the table, crossed one leg over the knee on his other, and started picking off the wet white lint was stuck to his bare foot.

"Does your mother know you're here?"

"No," he said, his face set in a hard expression. "She's been in her bedroom all day and won't come out. She was in there when I told her I was going to ball practice this afternoon, and she was still in there when I got home."

I walked over to him and put my hand on his shoulder. "She cares, Jeb. She's still sad about your dad and she's not handling it very well.

I'll call her in a minute and let her know you're here, okay?"

"She won't answer. I told her I was coming here and she didn't say anything."

"I'll leave a message then," I said evenly, hiding the fact that I was very angry with his mother.

He kept his head down but stopped picking at his foot and was quiet for a minute.

"Jake?"

"What?"

"How come she's so sad, but I can't even remember my dad?" he asked, looking into my eyes with a dejected expression.

"You were only three-years-old when he died, Jeb. Of course you can't remember him. Listen, don't feel bad about that, okay?" I said, squeezing his shoulder gently.

He nodded but I could still see that he was troubled by it.

"How about some supper? You must be hungry."

"Yeah, I'm starving. I ate a bag of corn chips I found in the cupboard, and three dill pickles, but that's all I had," he said, and dropped his foot and starting picking at a blister on his thumb and I could see that his hand had a slight tremble.

Corn chips and pickles, I groaned inwardly.

"Well, I'm sure glad you're here, Jeb. It isn't any fun eating alone every night," I said, and gave his shoulder a soft squeeze.

He continued working on his thumb, but I caught a smile starting at the corner of his mouth.

I knelt down and faced him. "Promise me something though."

"What?"

"If it's storming like that again and you need to come here, I want you to phone me at my office or here at the house, and I'll drive over and get you. It was dangerous to bike over here during a thunder and lightening storm. Promise me you won't ever do that again."

"I promise."

"Good," I said, and smiled at him.

I stood up and went over to the fridge again. I was standing there staring at the meager, unappetizing contents on the shelves when the phone on the kitchen counter rang out.

"Hello," I said into the receiver, watching Jeb at the same time.

"Didn't catch you eating supper did I, Jake?" Pamela Halton said cheerfully.

"Not much hope of that," I murmured, as I moved a bottle of blueberry jam aside to see what was behind it. A jar of mayonnaise and another of mustard. "What can I do for you, Pam?"

"I wanted to talk to you about one of our guests. Her name is Kate LeRue."

That got my attention and I straightened up and shut the fridge door.

"What is it?" I said.

"Well, a couple of things that have happened that concern me, Jake. I thought I should talk to you about it and see what you think."

I smiled and nodded at Jeb, who had gestured to

me that he was going to watch television in the living room.

"Go ahead, Pam."

"I got a strange phone call on Sunday night. Some guy called the office wanting to know if there was a woman with a small child staying in one of the motel rooms. The description he gave sounded like Mrs. LeRue and her daughter. He said he was a relative and was worried about them, but there was something about this guy that creeped me right out."

"What do you mean?" I said.

"His voice, his manner. I don't know exactly, but it put my guard right up."

"Did he have a southern accent?"

"Yes, he did."

"Not Canadian then," I said, thinking aloud.

"What?"

"Oh, sorry. It's just that Sam told me that Mrs. LeRue was on her way up to Canada to visit family. If this guy had a southern accent than he must be from her husband's side of the family. Could be her father-in-law or a brother-in-law."

Pam snorted into the phone. "I doubt it. He pronounced Madeleine's name all wrong. He called her Madelyn, you know, in the English way. And why wouldn't he just say who he was? When I pressed him about it, he got evasive and hung up on me."

"Did he mention where he was calling from?"

"No, I asked him that too, and he wouldn't tell me. I have caller ID though, and it showed that he was calling from a pay phone."

"You didn't tell him she was staying there did you?"

"What! Of course not, Jake!" she exclaimed.

"Sorry, I had to ask."

"Well, I wouldn't give out that kind of information. But, listen, I'm serious. There was something about this guy that sent chills up my spine. He has the creepiest voice I ever heard. Sounds clogged with phlegm, and he clears his throat constantly. It's kind of gross. Made me want to keep clearing my own throat. I don't know what's going on, but maybe Kate had good reason to leave Georgia. This guy sounds nasty. There's something else too. Do you remember the night Dennis called the department because he thought we had a break-in?"

"Yes."

"Well, he went around checking on all the guests that night, and when he knocked at Mrs. LeRue's cottage she came to the door holding a big, butcher knife in her hands. She was shaking badly, and her face was sheet-white. I've never seen anyone look so terrified in my life."

"Really," I murmured.

"I didn't think it was that big a deal at the time, but now with this guy calling about her, I have to wonder."

"Did she pay for the cottage with cash or a credit card?"

"Both," Pam replied. "She paid for the first week with cash and the second with a credit card."

"It's a bit unusual to pay with cash, isn't it?"

"Yes," Pam said. "And as a rule, we don't accept cash at all, but in her case I let it go. I thought her credit card might be maxed out after paying for her car repairs and I didn't want to embarrass her."

"I see. Well, that would explain why she took a job at Gertie's. She probably needs to make some money before she can continue on up to Canada."

"I don't know about that, Jake," Pam said. "She was in the office not more than fifteen minutes ago asking me if I knew of any apartments for rent in town."

"What?"

"I know. I found that strange too," Pam said.

After I said goodbye to Pam and hung up the phone, I dialed Jeb's house and let it ring for five minutes straight and then hung up, dialed again, and let it ring until finally, Sandy picked it up.

"Hello," she said, and her voice was heavy with sleep.

"Sandy," I said, keeping the anger I felt from my tone. "Jeb is over here with me."

"He is?" she said, her voice dull. "I must have fallen asleep. What time is it?"

"It's after five o'clock. How long have you been sleeping?"

"I'm not sure. I lost track of the time," she said quietly.

"Listen, Sandy," I began.

"I know what you're going to say, Jake, so please just don't," she interrupted me. "I'm sorry. Look, tell Jeb I'm sorry for me, will you? And bring him home tomorrow morning. Things will be better. I swear, Jake."

"Things had better be, Sandy," I whispered harshly, keeping one eye toward the living room. "He biked all the way over here in a thunderstorm, and he's had nothing to eat today but corn chips and pickles," I said, and had a hard time keeping my voice calm. "Look, Sandy, this has been going on too long. You've got to get some help."

"Bring him home in the morning, Jake. I'll be up and better. I promise," she said, and hung up before I could reply.

Feeling more frustrated with Sandy than I could ever remember, I walked into the living room and got Jeb, and we jumped in the cruiser and headed to Gertie's for supper. We rode to town in silence with the windows of the car down, letting the cool, ocean breeze blow in on us. My mind skipped from Sandy to Kate LeRue and to the man who had called the Blue Spruce Motel looking for her. *Who is Kate LeRue and what is she really doing here in Leigh Falls? I wondered. If she was supposed to be on her way up to Canada to visit relatives, why was she now looking for an apartment in town?*

Kate LeRue's actions were a mystery, and Sandy's a source of frustration, and not knowing what else to do or where else to turn, I silently prayed while I drove.

"Lord Jesus, I don't know what to do about Sandy and I need your guidance so I can help her.

And, Lord, I am certain that Kate LeRue needs my help, but she is afraid of me and I'm not sure how to let her know she can trust me."

A couple of minutes later I felt much better and had made two decisions. The first was that I would go see Pastor Rayner tomorrow morning and talk to him about Sandy, and the second was that I would drop into Gertie's one morning this week when the diner was quiet, and try to strike up a conversation with Kate LeRue.

Jeb never looked at me at all during the drive, but stared straight out through the windshield with a frown on his face and his forehead creased with small lines. I recognized the look because it was the same expression Craig and I usually had when we were concentrating hard on something, and I knew I would only have to glance in the rearview mirror to see the same frown now on my own face. When I had parked in front of the diner, and shut off the engine, Jeb finally looked over at me.

"Jake?

"Yes?"

"Was my dad just like you?"

"Do you mean did he look like me?"

'No," he shook his head. "I know you look like him, except that he had blond hair and you have dark hair. I mean, was he just like you?"

I thought of my brother, Craig, and recalled how our smiles, tone of voice and laughter had been so similar. And although I was quiet and serious look-ing, which I blamed mostly on my job, and Craig had been very outgoing and much quicker to smile and laugh, we had shared almost identical strong, yet, gentle-hearted temperaments.

"Yes," I nodded. "We were a great deal alike, Jeb."

"I knew it, Jake, I knew it," he said, beaming happily.

CHAPTER 15

Wednesday morning I drove to town and parked in the police department's lot, and then walked across the street and went into Gertie's. I slid on a stool and looked around the room. It was just after eight-thirty, and the early morning breakfast rush had died down and two booths and five stools were empty. Gertie was frying eggs at the grill and Kate LeRue was taking an order from a customer at the end of the row of stools.

"What are you doing here?" Gertie said with a frown, wiping her hands on her dark blue apron as she approached me.

"Buying a coffee."

"Since when?"

"What do you mean?"

"Don't you usually buy your morning coffee at *Dumpy Donuts*?"

"I thought I'd try yours today," I said, and gave what I hoped looked like a casual shrug.

"I thought you didn't like my coffee."

"I heard it has improved considerably since Mrs. LeRue started making it," I said.

"Don't be a wise guy," she warned.

From the corner of my eye I attempted a discreet glance at Kate LeRue, who had just walked around the counter and was heading for the coffeepot. She was wearing navy blue dress slacks, a plum colored blouse, matching gold earrings and necklace, and she had her hair pulled back and held with a gold clasp. She wasn't overdressed, and the apron she wore around her waist was stained, yet, there was such elegance and grace about her she seemed out of place working in a diner.

I forgot how sharp Gertie was, and got caught staring at Kate.

"Kate!" she called out, a playful smile appearing and wrinkling her face.

"Gertie," I said, and moaned under my breath.

"What?" she said, opening her dark blue eyes wide in a feigned innocence.

I determined right then to stop looking at Kate LeRue so much.

Kate walked around the counter, stood behind the counter next to the cash register and looked over at us.

"Surprisingly, it seems Jake would like a cup of my coffee," Gertie told her. "Since this is quite a momentous occasion, I thought you might like to do the honors."

I shook my head almost imperceptibly.

Kate looked a bit bewildered, but nodded and stepped over to the coffeepot. "Is that for here or to go?" she asked, glancing at me from over her shoulder.

"Oh, for here I think," Gertie put in before I could answer, chuckling as she went back to the grill.

Kate turned around, held the coffeepot in one hand for a moment, looked at Gertie, who had her back to her now, and then looked at me with a questioning expression.

"For here," I said.

She nodded, and set a coffee cup on a saucer in front of me and filled it.

"Thank you," I said.

"Can I get you anything else?" she asked.

"No thanks," I said.

She nodded again and walked away.

I took a gulp and decided it was pretty good. I sipped it slowly after that, and in spite of my primary intention, which was to strike up a conversation with Kate, for some reason, I remained silent. And despite my earlier resolve to stop staring at her, it seemed my eyes were drawn to her unbiddenly. A while later, when I had finished my coffee, I motioned to Kate to come over.

"I'll like another cup of coffee, but make this one to go please," I said, and noticed that when she poured the coffee and cream into a Styrofoam cup, gave it a stir, and snapped the lid on top, her hands weren't trembling very much at all.

"Thanks," I said, and feeling greatly encouraged by the fact she seemed slightly more at ease around me, I gave her a brief smile.

She seemed startled by my smile, but gave me a small, tentative smile back.

"Have a nice day," I said, and smiled again.

"You too," she said, and smiled wider and more easily this time.

I dropped a bill on the counter and slipped off the stool. I headed for the door, ignoring Gertie who was standing in front of the grill, facing me with her hands on her skinny hips and grinning like a fool.

"Was the coffee good, Jake?" she hollered out.

"Yes it was."

"I'll bet," she said, shaking her head and laughing as she turned back to the grill.

I walked back to the department, went into my office, sat down behind my desk and set the coffee down on my desk blotter and stared at it without taking a drink. I didn't even want it and wasn't sure why I had even bought it, but the one thing I was sure about was that I hadn't learned anything new about Kate LeRue. I turned my head and gazed out the window, feeling thunderstruck, because for the first time in almost twenty years as a cop, an attractive woman had left me at a complete loss for words.

CHAPTER 16

Saturday morning at a little past nine I pulled up into Jeb's driveway, cut the engine to my personal vehicle, a '97 metallic blue, Jeep TJ Sport 4 x4, which I hardly ever drove because Jeb complained it didn't have lights and a siren. I climbed out and walked up the sidewalk to the front door and raised my hand, but Jeb yanked it wide open before I could knock.

"Hi, Uncle Jake, I'm almost ready," he said, and stepped back, and squatted down and began tying the laces of his cleats.

"Where's your mom, Jeb?" I asked, peering down the short, cluttered hallway of the small bungalow.

"In the kitchen," he said, and lifted one hand from his cleat to thumb over his shoulder. "Guess what. I ate six pieces of bacon."

"What! How are you going to run around the bases now?"

He grinned up at me. "Easy."

I smiled at him. "Hey, I need to talk to your mom for a minute. Go wait in the car and I'll be along shortly, okay?"

He nodded; bent his head over his cleats again, and in all of ten seconds had them laced, grabbed his glove from the floor, stood up, and was out the door.

"Sandy," I called out, stepping over shoes as I made my way down the hallway.

"In here, Jake," she said.

I stepped into the kitchen and saw her standing at the sink washing dishes, dressed in peach colored cotton pajamas, a silk peach housecoat and white mule slippers.

"How are you, Sandy?" I said, my eyes taking in the oak table and the counters. I was pleasantly surprised to find that the kitchen wasn't too chaotic, and I could smell the leftover scent of bacon, eggs and toast in the air.

She turned around, wiping her hands off on a towel and faced me with a weak smile. "I'm okay," she said, throwing the towel on the counter and then blowing a strand of strawberry blond hair out of her eyes.

I noticed that the dark circles that were normally around her eyes had faded some.

"For how long, Sandy?" I said gently.

She smiled, although it was still a weak smile. "Ease up, Jake, please. I'm trying. I really am."

"I know you are, but I can't forget that he biked over to my house in a thunderstorm while you slept. He could have been really hurt."

"I know," she said, and covered her mouth with her hand, her eyes filling up. "I'm sorry. I had no idea he had even left the house."

"I went to see Pastor Rayner," I said quietly.

She crossed her arms over her chest and looked at me. "I know. He called me."

I raised my eyebrows.

"He and his wife are going to come over tonight at seven o'clock," she said softly, and then smiled.

I looked at her in surprise.

"I want to take better care of Jeb. I know you may not believe that, but I want that more than anything. I've lost Craig, and I can't lose Jeb too," she said, and her voice cracked with emotion.

I watched her quietly, keeping my face free of how concerned I really was, for she had made appointments with Pastor Rayner before and had never kept them.

"I know, Sandy," I said after a moment. "And I'm here for you. You know that."

She nodded. "Thanks, Jake. And who knows, maybe I'll get out to Jeb's next game," she said with a small smile.

"That'd be nice, Sandy. He'd like that a lot," I said and then glanced at my watch and saw it was getting late. "Well, I'd better get him over to the game. When do you want him home?"

"Can you take him for the rest of the day, and I was going to ask you if he could stay over at your place tonight," she said quietly. "Pastor Rayner and Anne will be here at seven and I'd rather talk to them alone."

Sure, no problem," I said. "We'll grab some lunch after the game, and then get to work staining my deck for the rest of the day. We've been putting off doing it long enough."

She smiled and looked relieved.

An hour later, I was sitting on a bleacher in McDougall Park, sweating in the hot sun and screaming for Jeb as he ran around the bases and slid into third. When he stood to his feet he looked over with a wide grin and waved at me. When I waved back at him I looked past him to the outfield, and beyond the wire fence that separated the ball field from the rest of the park and caught sight of Kate LeRue pushing a stroller toward the swings. I watched as she stopped next to a swing, bent over and lifted Madeleine out of the stroller, and then slid her into the seat and begin pushing the swing gently back and forth.

I turned back to the game and watched Jeb cross home plate. When a time-out was called by the other team, I slipped off the bleacher and walked along the fence at the edge of the ball field, cut across the green grass of the park in the direction of the swings and a couple of minutes later approached Kate LeRue. She was standing with her back to me, laughing softly with her little girl as she gently moved the swing. She was wearing black shorts, a white sleeveless blouse, brown leather sandals, and her hair was loose around her shoulders. Madeleine was dressed in a pink and white short set, and on the shirt was the word, '*Precious*', in pink letters. She was laughing so hard tears were streaming down her chubby cheeks, and I smiled, thinking the shirt certainly said it all.

"Good morning, Mrs. LeRue," I said.

She turned and put one hand over her eyes to shield them from the sun, squinted at me, and kept the other hand on the back of the swing as she slowly pushed it.

"Hello," she said uncertainly and tilted her head to study me.

"Jake Cole," I said, and then saw her flustered expression and added. "Sheriff Jake Cole."

"Oh, I know who you are," she said, and I heard a slight tremor in her voice. She stopped pushing the swing, held onto the seat tightly, and took a breath and seemed to gather herself enough to give me a brief, but somewhat strained smile. "You just look so different it threw me for a second. I've never seen you wearing anything else but your uniform."

"Oh, right," I said, glancing at my clothes. I was wearing blue jeans, a dark blue T-shirt, tan leather hiking sandals with no socks, a Boston Red Sox ball hat and aviator style sunglasses. About the only clothes I ever wore when I was out of uniform.

She continued pushing the swing, but she was looking at me somewhat cautiously.

"Beautiful day, isn't it," I said.

"Yes, it is."

"At least the humidity's a bit more bearable," I said.

She nodded.

"Although being from Georgia, you must be used to it."

She simply nodded once again, but this time looked beyond my shoulder and kept his eyes pinned on a spot somewhere over there.

"Gertie gave you the day off, I guess," I said, changing the subject since she clearly didn't want to talk about Georgia.

"Well, I only work three days a week," she explained. I don't want to be away from Madeleine any more than that."

"I don't blame you," I said, and smiled and waved at her little girl who was smiling at me.

"Hi, Madeleine."

"Hi," Madeleine called out, and let go of the chain with one hand to wave at me with her funny little wave.

Although still clearly nervous, Kate LeRue gave a small smile when she saw us waving at each other. When she looked at me again, I thought how much her clear, blue-green eyes reminded me of the color of the ocean water when it surged up over the white sand and pebbles on the beach below my house. In fact, I found her to be a remarkably attractive woman. This shocked me more than a little, and I turned my gaze away to the tennis courts on the other side of the park and we fell silent again.

The air was filled with the creaking of Madeleine's swing, the symphony of the birds in the trees around us and the laughter of the children of the children on the swings and teeter-totters at the playground.

"Looks like we go to the same church," I said after a spell.

"Yes. It seems like a nice, friendly church," she said, and seemed to relax slightly, and I wondered if it was because we were talking about church, or because I was out of uniform.

"It is," I said, and then heard the voices of the fans on the bleachers start up.

"Sounds like the game is underway again. I should get back over there," I said, thumbing over my shoulder to the ball field, but for some reason I didn't move.

"Is your son playing?" she said.

"No, I'm not married. It's my nephew, Jeb."

"Is he that little guy with blond hair and a big smile?"

"Yes, that's him."

"Oh, so that's who he is. I've seen him with you in Gertie's, and you two look so much alike I just assumed he was your son. I've seen him with you in your cruiser too, or I should say, heard him with you," she added with a smile, and I noticed that she had a warm, genuine smile.

I gave a quiet laugh at that. "He loves turning on the lights and siren, and I don't seem to have the heart to say no to him. His dad, my younger brother, Craig, died about five years ago, and since then I've kind of looked out for him."

"I'm sorry about your brother. It's good Jeb has you to," she said, and her voice trailed off as a shadow of sadness crossed her face. After the shadow passed she looked away and seemed lost in thought for a moment.

"Well, I'd better get back to the cottage. It's time for Madeleine's nap," she said finally.

"I'd better get going too. It was nice talking to you, Mrs. LeRue. Have a nice day," I said.

"You too, Sheriff Cole."

"Oh, call me Jake. No one around here calls me sheriff except the tourists."

"Okay, ah, Jake. And call me Kate, if you like," she said, still sounding a bit unsure of me.

I smiled and then looked at Madeleine and gave her a smile and a wave. "Bye-bye."

"Later, alligator," she said, giggling as she waved back at me.

"It's her new phrase," Kate said with a smile. "She thinks it's hilarious."

"After a while, crocodile," I said, joining in her game.

"Later, alligator," Madeleine repeated, and burst into a long fit of giggling like only a toddler could.

I was chuckling softly as I turned to leave. I took a couple of steps and right at that moment it hit me. A man had phoned the motel looking for this woman and her daughter, a man Pam described as creepy, she was supposed to be on her way to Canada, yet, she was still here and looking for a place to live, and all I could think about was what a nice smile she had and how much I liked it when she smiled at me. My cop's common sense finally took over and gained control of my mind, and I knew that no matter how alluring, no matter how incredibly charming I found this woman, I needed to talk to her. I took a breath and then whirled back around.

"Kate," I called softly.

She turned to face me and had to shield her eyes from the sun again.

"Yes?"

"I guess you're planning on staying in Leigh Falls for a little while?"

She dropped her hand, quickly turned sideways, stepped up to the swing and raised the safety bar up with one hand, and attempted to lift Madeleine from her seat with the other.

"Here, let me help you," I said softly, and walked over to the other side of the swing. I held the bar high above Madeleine's head and Kate let it go at once so that she could lift her up and out with both hands, and when she did, she faced me, although warily now.

"Thank you," she said.

I stood there and watched her, waiting for her answer.

"I hope to stay for the summer. After that, I'm not sure," she said finally, quietly, and shifted Madeleine more comfortably in her arms.

"I see. So, you're not going up to Canada to visit your family after all?" I asked, hoping the question sounded casual.

It didn't. Her entire body stiffened and she wouldn't look at me.

"Small town. News travels fast," I said.

She nodded curtly. "Maybe in a few months," she said, her manner much cooler now.

"Kate, I need to ask you this. Is there any reason someone might be looking for you?"

I could see my words gave her a jolt. She recovered, but her face paled considerably and she seemed fearful again.

"Why would you ask me that?" she said, and a discernible tremor was back in her voice.

"I have good reason," I said more gently.

"More small town gossip?" she said incredulously.

I shrugged apologetically.

"Well, don't believe everything you hear, Jake," she said, and then whipped around and turned her back to me, slid Madeleine in the stroller, and began fiddling with the straps to belt her in.

I watched her for a couple of seconds, unsure of what to say next, though it didn't really matter because she kept her back to me. When she was finished, she straightened up, unlocked the brakes and pushed the stroller away without speaking another word or looking at me again. I felt an unexpected catch in my throat and almost called out to her. But, as I strode across the grass toward the ball field the cop in me took over again and I was thinking that she hadn't answered my question.

CHAPTER 17

After the ball game, Jeb and I bought four sliced chicken sandwiches, two pieces of deep apple pie, and two half-quarts of chocolate milk from Gertie and then drove over to his house. After he changed out of his ball uniform into his bathing shorts and a T-shirt, we drove over to a scenic picnic area that was located beside the Blue River.

The river, which was the northernmost boundary for the town, ran through a densely forested area, and was narrow and not very deep, and flowed languidly for a few miles before cascading over an eight-foot ridge, which was called Leigh Falls, and gave the town its name. The falls were pretty subdued as far as falls go, and the water didn't exactly roil and roar down over the gorge, but kind of gently tumbled down and emerged again as a tranquil, clear green pool below the falls.

Most of the tourists, and nearly all of the town's residents, avoided swimming in the river or at the falls, opting instead for the sandy, white beaches and salty ocean water that surrounded the town. Not Jeb though. He loved it here and always preferred swimming in the tree-shaded, deep, quiet pool of water. I, on the other hand, loved the ocean, had paid a lot of money for my own private beach, and preferred swimming there, but because Jeb loved the falls, and was so fair he burned badly no matter how much sun screen I poured on him, I brought him here without complaint.

After Jeb took a long swim, we sat on a wooden picnic table under a stand of pine trees next to the river and ate our lunch, washing it all down with the half-quarts of chocolate milk. As we ate, the river flowed gently past us, the soft, steady roar of the water cascaded down the falls, two crows argued in a tall pine tree, while gray and blue jays rebuked them loudly before flying away. Jeb looked up into the trees and watched the birds for a few minutes before he looked over at me.

I finished chewing my mouthful of apple pie, swallowed and then noticed him studying me intently.

"What?" I said.

He shrugged, his cheeks bulging with the food in his mouth. He looked like a little, blond-haired chipmunk.

"You got some good hits today," I said.

"That's cause Pete Reynolds told me that I hit like a girl. He made me so mad I swung really hard.

I guess I showed him."

"I guess you did."

He bobbed his head vigorously up and down, grinning so broadly that I could see the mashed up pie crust in his mouth, but then his smile faded slowly away.

"What's wrong, Uncle Jake?"

"Nothing. Why?"

You didn't swim with me today."

"I guess I've got something on my mind."

"Are you thinking about that lady?"

"What lady?"

He snorted. "The one you always stare at."

"I don't always stare at her."

"Then how do you know who I mean?"

I shook my head at him.

"I saw you talking to her in the park today too."

"You really don't miss a thing," I said.

He grinned broadly.

You know, we should be staining my deck right about now," I said, but returned his grin with one of my own.

"We can do it next weekend," he said hopefully.

"We can do it in about an hour," I said, after glancing at my watch.

He sighed.

I heard voices coming from the trees and knew that there were people walking on the dirt path that wound through the woods behind us. The narrow trail, which was the only entrance and exit to the falls, began at the parking lot located just off the highway, and threaded through the dense trees for about two hundred feet before coming out onto the open grassy picnic area.

I turned my head and saw a trim, elderly man with short, gray hair, carrying a wicker picnic basket, and a thin woman with bushy snow-white hair, who had a dog on a leash, step out from the tree-lined trail and head over to a picnic table beside the falls. I recognized them as Joe and Amelia Fisher, summer residents from Michigan. They both looked over and waved, and Jeb and I waved back at the same time.

"They have a Golden Retriever," Jeb said miserably.

"I see that."

"Lucky," Jeb whispered, his eyes following them to a picnic table that was positioned very near the falls.

I smiled sympathetically at him for I knew he loved dogs, especially Retrievers, and wanted one badly.

"Jake?"

I groaned inwardly, thinking, *here we go again.* "What?"

"Do you think I could get a dog?"

"We talked about this before, Jeb. It's not up to me. Your mom has to okay it first."

Jeb frowned and his forehead filled with thin creases. "She never will."

"Maybe she will someday soon."

"Couldn't you talk to her about it for me?"

"Jeb, I have at least two-hundred times already. You know that."

"Could you try again?"

"Jeb," I said, and turned my head when I heard more footsteps on the pathway.

"Please, Uncle Jake."

A giant of a man with a goatee and long black hair tied back in a ponytail stepped out from the dirt path onto the grass, and stood motionless for a minute as he viewed the river and picnic area before him. He was wearing baggy white shorts, a white T-shirt, sandals, purple sunglasses, and he was holding a wide-brimmed hat in his hand.

My body stiffened and my eyes narrowed as I studied him. He was dressed like a tourist, he was looking at the river and the falls like any visitor to the area would, and yet, there was something about him that struck me as peculiar. I kept my eyes riveted on him as he wandered over to the quiet pool of water below the falls, squatted down, and dipped one hand into the water.

"Will you try one more time?" Jeb pleaded.

The tall man stood up again and sauntered along the bank of the river, and then hiked across the grassy picnic area, passing the Fishers who were eating lunch at their table. He gave them a short, cool glance, looked around and saw me watching him, and gave me the same icy glance before continuing on to the woods where he strolled along the edge of the forest, stopping every couple of feet to look in at the dense trees.

"What's he doing," I said under my breath.

"Oh forget it. You're not even listening to me," Jeb said.

"What?" I said, as I observed the guy glance surreptitiously at the Fishers once more, and then me again, before he pushed the thick evergreen branches out of the way, entered the woods at one spot and disappeared from sight.

"Just forget it," Jeb said in a low voice.

I quickly turned my head to face him. "Hey, I'm sorry. I'll talk to your mom again about letting you have a dog. I promise."

"Really?" he said.

"Yes."

"Thanks, Uncle Jake," he beamed.

I tousled his hair, and then turned my head and slid my eyes back to the spot where the guy had gone into the woods.

"What are you looking at?" Jeb said, craning his neck to see around me.

"Nothing," I said, but kept my eyes pinned on this guy as he emerged from the trees and once again wandered around the picnic area. After a few minutes, he turned around and walked in the direction of the dirt path. He spotted me at the table watching him, and gave me a chilly glare before striding quickly down the path.

"Jeb, I want you to sit right here and don't move until I get back."

"Where are you going?"

"I'll just be five minutes. Wait here."

"Could I go pat the Fisher's dog?"

"No. Promise me you won't move from this table."

"What's wrong?"

"Jeb!"

"Okay, I promise."

I jumped to my feet, jogged over to the entrance to the pathway, and then stopped and glanced back over my shoulder to Jeb. He was sitting at the table eating his second piece of pie and watching me, his forehead full of frown lines. I turned and sprinted down the path at a good pace, but didn't meet up with the guy. I came out of the woods into the dirt parking lot and stood with my hands on my hips, breathing hard, while I scanned the lot. There were only two vehicles in the lot, my Jeep, and a Ford Focus that I knew belonged to the Fishers, and the highway was deserted. The guy had vanished. I could hear the sound of a car's engine fading in the distance further down the highway and knew it had to be him. I turned around and ran back down the trail to the picnic area, sat down next to Jeb at the table and tried to catch my breath.

Jeb looked at me, his expression serious.

"Did you find that man?"

I shook my head.

"Can I go for another swim?"

"In a couple of minutes. Let your food settle a bit first."

We were quiet for a time. The sun shone down warmly on us through the canopy of trees overhead and the river breeze was cool and soft against out skin. The leaves of the trees above the table seemed to almost tremble in the breeze, and the steady drone of insects that came from somewhere in the dense bush behind us was lulling.

"It's a great day, isn't it Uncle Jake?" Jeb said.

I took it all in and knew he was right, but for me, there was something about the man who had been here that had cast a cold shadow over what should have been a very, fine, early summer day. And I intended to find out who this guy was.

Two hours later, Jeb and I were dressed in old clothes and were busy staining my deck. The sun was breaking through the branches of the trees and beating down on our heads, and I could feel trickles of sweat running down my back under my T-shirt. There was a slight breeze coming off the water, cooling us only a bit, and carrying the strong scent of the ocean. We were about half-finished when I heard a car pull up into my driveway. A door opened and slammed, and then Leighton Marshall came around the side of the house and stood on the ground facing the deck.

"Looks real good," he said.

"Yeah," I said, burying a sigh. I stood to my feet and examined the section of decking that we had stained so far.

"Hello, Mr. Marshall," Jeb said.

"Hello, Jeb. You're doing a great job there."

Jeb grinned, wiped his fingers across his sweaty forehead and squinted in the sunlight. "Jake says I have a flair for painting."

"I think you do too," Leighton said kindly.

"Want to take a break, Jeb?" I said. "There's lemonade in the fridge."

"Okay. You want some too?" Jeb said.

"Sure. Leighton?" I said.

"I'd love a glass," he said.

Jeb set his brush down on the edge of the lid of the paint can, kicked off his sneakers, and then went in through the open patio doors to the kitchen.

"You have real nice piece of property here, Jake," he said, his eyes taking in my cedar and glass home with the wide oak and pine shade trees all around, and the vast blue-green ocean that lay before it.

I nodded.

"You were fortunate to buy this when Mrs. Bunting put the land up for sale. I had my eye on it for awhile, but you beat me to it," he said. "It must be worth a lot of money right now. Ocean front property's going fast and high these days."

I smiled and kept my face free of what I was thinking, for I knew Leighton, who had already owned a good amount of property in town, including a beautiful oceanfront acreage with a large, three-story, colonial style home on it, had done everything he could to try to buy this land before I had.

"You did a great job of building this house," he said. "You seem to be a man of many fortes."

"Not really. My father was a carpenter. He had a love for cedar homes and built most of the ones you see around Leigh Falls. Anything I do know, I learned from him."

"Ah, that's right. I forgot that," Leighton said with a smile, and ran a hand through his thin, silver hair. He combed his bangs over a couple of times and seemed to be trying to think about how he was going to say what he had driven out here to say. He straightened his tie, unbuttoned and then rebuttoned his suit jacket and then quietly cleared his throat. He was dressed for the office in a dark blue silk shirt, a white silk tie, and an expensive looking white suit, despite the heat and the fact that it was a Saturday.

"Terrible thing about Harvey Newman, isn't it?" Leighton said finally.

"Yes, it is," I said, careful to keep my tone pleasant.

Leighton nodded grimly.

"Look, I don't want to sound callous, but it is Saturday, Leighton. My day off. Do we have to do this right now?"

"Well, I'm sorry about that, but I went over to your office on Wednesday and Friday afternoon, and you were out both times. At least that's what Marney claimed. I tried to take a look in your office, but I couldn't get past her to see in. It's unnerving to see such a pretty young woman with that much muscle. What's wrong with her anyway?"

"Not a thing. She's a professional body-builder, and from what I hear, she's very good at it. She's won quite a few out-of-state competitions."

He shook his head in disgust. "Well, if you ask me, it's completely unnatural. And you mark my words, Jake. There isn't a man in the entire state of Maine that will marry a girl who has more muscle than he does. Good-looking or not."

I bit back a chuckle at the ludicrousness of that.

Jeb stepped out of the house with the jug of lemonade in one hand, and three glasses stacked together in the other, paused, looked suspiciously at Leighton and then back to me. I went over to him, took the jug and one of the glasses from him, poured a glass for Leighton and passed it to him, poured another for Jeb and gave that to him, and then poured mine. I handed the jug back to Jeb and tried to ease him in through the door to the kitchen.

"Are you guys going to fight again?" he whispered, glancing over his shoulder at Leighton.

"No, we're just going to talk. Listen, you're getting pretty red anyway, so why don't you go inside and stay out of the sun for awhile."

Jeb bit his bottom lip, a worried expression on his face. He had a cedar-colored streak across one cheek from the wood stain.

"Why don't you play some games on my computer," I said, and gently squeezed his shoulder.

He trudged slowly to the door, but before he stepped inside he peered over his shoulder one more time at Leighton and then at me. I gave him a small, reassuring smile and a nod, and he opened the door and went in, but very reluctantly.

When I turned around and looked at Leighton, he was looking straight at us, one hand holding the glass of lemonade, the other cupped under his chin with the thumb and fingers splayed out around his mouth.

"He's the spitting image of Craig, isn't he?" Leighton said.

"Maybe you don't want to bring Craig into the conversation," I said crisply, and sat down on the deck steps. I took a long drink of the cold lemonade, and then looked up and faced him where he stood on the lawn. I gestured to the step beside me with a tilt of my head.

Leighton studied the step carefully for any signs of spilled wood stain that might ruin his fancy suit, and when he was satisfied that it was safe, he brushed the step first with one hand, and then sat down beside me, although he still seemed awfully worried about it.

"Thing is, Jake, a drowning can scare people away if they think our beaches aren't well supervised," he began, and then brushed something, a minuscule piece of lint or dirt, I figured, from his pant leg.

"Our beaches are extremely well supervised," I said. "Newman swam out past the boundary ropes despite Trent's repeated warnings."

"Trent?"

"Trent Holmes. And before you say anything, he's a good, brave kid. He did all he could."

Leighton's face looked strained. "That's not how people will see it."

"I don't really care how people see it."

"Yes, well, that's always been pretty obvious."

"Look, Leighton, maybe I'm wrong, but you seem to be more concerned about tourists and the money they spend here, than you do about a man's death."

Leighton's neck grew as red as his tie. "That's not true," he said hotly.

I shrugged and we fell silent, the ocean air around us thick with tension as we watched the frothy surf rush in on the beach below my back lawn.

"Tell me something, Jake. When we talked that Sunday at church, were you aware that Gertie had run Harvey Newman out of her diner the day before?"

"No, I didn't know then. I heard about it later."

"We can't afford to have Gertie treat our tourists like that. I want you to talk to her for me."

I looked at him with a pained expression. "Leighton, give me a break."

"Give you a break! Listen, between you, Gertie, and Freddie the wonder drunk, it's a miracle that we have any tourists here at all."

"This conversation's over," I said, feeling burning heat crawling up the back of my neck.

"I want you to talk to Gertie."

"I don't think so," I said, and shook my head once, firmly. "If you've got something to say to Gertie, you go tell her yourself."

"So she can chase me down the sidewalk with a broom too. I don't think so. That woman's a mental patient. I only asked you because you two are so close. Although I have to say, Jake, I've always found that more than a little disturbing."

"I think it's time for you to leave," I said, and stood to my feet.

He stood to his feet too and faced me, clasping

his glass of lemonade so tightly his knuckles were white. "Fine. But you might want to warn that old woman that there is more than one way to close down a diner."

I gave him a cold, silent stare.

"I'm serious," he said, but dropped his eyes from mine. "It would just take one complaint about unsanitary conditions in that dump, and the department of health will shut her down."

"You know Leighton, it's getting harder to tell you're a Christian more and more everyday," I said, unable to hide the disgust I felt for him from my voice.

"You should talk," he shot back angrily, and slammed his full glass of lemonade down so hard on the deck the liquid slopped over the sides and ran down the glass. "At least my failures occur only because I am concerned about the welfare of Leigh Falls."

"What's that supposed to mean?"

"Oh, come on, Jake. You can blame our verbal battles on the tourists, but we both know the real reason is that you have never forgiven me for what happened to Craig."

I stiffened at his words. "Maybe I have good reason," I said.

"Not as a professing Christian you don't," he said harshly.

I opened my mouth and was about to respond, but knew there was some truth in what he said so I closed it again. Nonetheless, I was thinking at the same time that it didn't excuse him of his own responsibility for what he had just threatened to do to Gertie.

He watched me for a moment, and then just nodded tersely once again, as if he had made his point, and then stormed across my lawn and disappeared around the side of the house. I heard him yank open his car door, slam it shut, and then back up rapidly out of my driveway and speed away, his expensive Buick bouncing recklessly down the narrow dirt lane. I grabbed my paintbrush and began staining the deck again, my strokes quick and angry.

CHAPTER 18

Monday morning a shaft of early morning sunlight streamed in through the gap in my curtains straight into my eyes and woke me up. It had rained overnight, the humidity had eased slightly, and the cooler breeze coming from off the water through my open window was invigorating after the steamy temperatures of the previous couple of weeks. I felt my mood, which had been somber since my talk with Leighton on Saturday, change with the promise of more pleasant summer day.

Jeb had gone home Sunday afternoon, and as I climbed out of bed, I thought the house seemed so empty and silent without him there. I smiled to myself, thinking that I even missed his endless questions. I crossed the floor to the bedroom window, looked out, and decided to take advantage of the cooler temperature and go for a longer run than my usual four miles.

I pulled on running shorts, a dark blue tank top, my running shoes, and grabbed my pocket Bible and went for a hard run down the beach. After three miles, I sat down on the sand with the warm sun against my face and had my devotions while the incoming tide rushed up on the beach, and when I was finished the frothy ocean water was nearly touching my Nikes.

I thought about what I had just read. I tried to read through the Bible every year, and was now in the Book of Matthew, and had just finished reading Chapter 18, where Jesus spoke to Peter about our need to forgive our brethren. As I sat there I sensed a familiar prick in my heart, but as I had been doing for some time now, I filled my mind with arguments for why I couldn't, and shouldn't, and when that didn't ease the sense of disquiet I felt, I simply ignored it.

An hour later, I stood in line at Dunkin' Donuts behind Rollie Pugh, and chatted for a few minutes with him while one of the two girls working behind the counter poured my coffee. I heard another customer shuffling his feet behind me, but it wasn't until I had picked up my coffee and turned around to leave, that our eyes met, and a bad feeling about the guy pierced through my body like a rod of hot steel. Not only was he the same guy I had seen at the falls on Saturday, but he had the coldest eyes I had ever seen on a human being before. His eyes were such a glacial pale blue that he appeared to be completely devoid of any human emotion other than sheer and violent evil.

"Good morning, sir," I said, and shifted so that I could study him more carefully.

"Good morning," he said, and cleared his throat. He spoke with a distinct nasal tone.

"Going to be a nice one," I said, his voice triggering my mental alarms.

He nodded just slightly, cleared his throat again quietly, and averted his eyes from my gaze.

"Up here on vacation?" I said, holding him there because I wanted to hear his voice again.

"That's right," he replied. "Little vacation."

He was a huge man, standing well over six feet, and weighing over two-fifty. He had a massive neck, a thick chest, and enormous hands that looked like they could crush the neck of a rhino without much effort. He was wearing the same outfit I had seen him in on Saturday at the falls. Baggy, white cotton shorts, an extra-large T-shirt, brown hiking sandals on his feet, a wide-brimmed hat on his head, and he had a Nikon 35-millimeter camera hanging around his neck. But despite the costume, this guy was no tourist. I was certain of that.

"I'm Jake Cole, sheriff of Leigh Falls," I said, holding out my hand.

He hesitated for a second, and then shook my hand somewhat reluctantly, but didn't offer his own name.

"Enjoy your stay in Leigh Falls, sir," I said. With or without his help, I'd find out who he was and I'd know before noon today.

He gave me a brief nod before stepping up to the counter to give the girl his order. He may have looked as solid as a redwood tree, but I noticed he had the springy walk of a boxer. *Maybe he fought as a heavyweight at one time*, I thought as I walked slowly out of the store, my cop alarms screaming in my head.

Once in my office, I roared out for Caleb through the open door and when he walked in he had an odd expression on his face.

"What?" I said gruffly.

"Get up on the wrong side of the bed this morning?"

"Sorry."

Caleb nodded and continuing studying me. He seemed to want to say more.

"Something on your mind, Caleb?"

He took a breath before continuing. "The tension between you and Leighton in Sunday school yesterday was pretty thick. What's going on with you guys?"

"Caleb, I don't want to talk about that right now."

"Are you sure? Ashlyn says I'm a pretty good listener. For a man anyway," he said, and laughed quietly.

I smiled at that and saw that his concern was genuine.

"I'm sure. But thanks, and I'll keep that in mind," I said, softening my tone.

"Okay. But you won't mind if until then I pray about it."

"Not at all. I'd appreciate that."

He nodded.

"Have a seat," I said, and stabbed my finger to the chair across from my desk.

"What's up?" he said, his eyes widening at my tone as he sat down.

"There's a guy in town we need to check out, and fast. I've got a bad feeling about him. He's dressed up like a tourist, but he's no tourist," I said.

"What's he look like?"

"He's a giant. He's about six-six or six-seven, and weighs about two-seventy, two-eighty. And it's all muscle. Not an ounce of fat on him that I could see. He's got a goatee, and long black hair that he wears in a pony tail. I think he has severe allergies or some kind of adenoid trouble because he's real nasal sounding when he talks, and he clears his throat every thirty seconds."

"Where'd you see him?"

"At Dunkin' Donuts this morning. But, you know something. I actually saw him at the falls on Saturday, and there was something about him then that set off my alarms. I followed him out to the parking lot to try to talk to him, but I missed him. For a big guy he moves like a flyweight. Anyway, I went back there with Jeb on Sunday right after church, hoping I might spot there again, but I never saw him. Funny thing is I planned on looking around town for him today, and then I ended up bumping into him at Dunkin' Donuts."

"Did you see what he's driving?"

"A 2002 black, Grand Am with Georgia plates. It's a rental from Avis."

Caleb arched one eyebrow. "Georgia?"

I nodded at him.

Caleb fell silent and stared at me, looked about to say something and then changed his mind and watched me some more. Finally he smiled a little and then spoke.

"Don't tell me you think this has something to do with your swooner from Georgia?"

"As a matter of fact I do."

He looked skeptical. "I saw her at church on Sunday. What's her name? LeRue?"

"Yes. Kate LeRue."

"I heard she's working at Gertie's now. So what's her story anyway?"

"I don't know yet. But something's going on and I think it involves Mrs. LeRue and this guy. I didn't get a chance to tell you that Pam called me the other night at home. She said some guy, who gave her the creeps, phoned the motel asking about a woman matching Mrs. LeRue's description, and she mentioned that he had a real nasal sounding voice and cleared his throat all the time. Sounds like the same guy I bumped into."

Caleb shrugged one shoulder. "Could be he's her husband, and he just came up to join her here."

I shook my head. "Then why would she take a job waitressing at Gertie's? Besides, she told Gertie she's a widow."

"Maybe she's lying about that."

I shook my head. "I don't think so, Caleb."

"People lie all the time, Jake. Especially to cops."

"I know. But I've talked to her, and I've noticed

that she'll say nothing at all rather than lie."

He nodded quietly.

"And there's more to this. Pam said this guy that called the motel pronounced the little girl's name wrong, and she hasn't seen any visitors at Mrs. LeRue's cottage since she's been there. I know this guy's been in town since at least Saturday, so why hasn't he gone over to see her by now?"

"Maybe he's not the same one that called Pam. Could be just a coincidence that he sounds like the guy," Caleb said.

I rubbed my face with one hand. "No, I've got a gut feeling that he's the same one."

"Okay," Caleb nodded, having been a cop long enough to trust gut feelings.

"He looks like he's been in the system before," I said.

"He's likely got a sheet then," Caleb said. "Shouldn't be too hard to put a name to him."

I nodded and handed Caleb the piece of paper I had written the plate number down on. "I've got the rental number on there too. Call the head office for Avis in Georgia, and find out who he is, and then run his name through the computer. I'm sure something will show up on him."

I sat behind my desk, drumming my fingers on the armrest of my chair and staring out the window to the water of the harbor until Caleb returned. He walked in five minutes later carrying a sheet of paper that he read aloud from.

"Avis Rental Company says the Grand Am was

rented by a Wesley Gary Roberts, in the city of Carlow, Georgia. He paid with an American Express card. He gave his date of birth as September 8, 1969, and his address as 189 Floral Avenue, Apartment 5, Carlow, Georgia."

"Carlow! I knew it," I said, and stood to my feet. "That's the same city Mrs. LeRue's from."

"Hold on a minute, Jake," Caleb said, holding a hand up, palm out. "There's no sheet on him at all. I ran his name through twice and nothing came up. He's clean. Not even a speeding ticket on his driving record."

"What! Can't be. Something's not right," I said. "This guy's dirty, Caleb."

"Could be just a fluke they're both from Carlow."

"No, it's more than that," I said, shaking my head in disgust as I walked to the window. I stood staring out with my hands on my hips, thinking hard. After a moment I turned and faced him again. "If he doesn't have a sheet that might just mean he's using a phony ID, or maybe even he's never been convicted of any crime, although I find that hard to believe. I still think this has something to do with the LeRue woman. I'm certain of it."

Caleb chewed on his bottom lip for a minute while he thought.

"Okay," he said finally. "Why don't we run through a couple of different scenarios and see what we can come up with?"

"Good idea. You go first."

Caleb held his index finger against his chin;

looking and sounding like a schoolteacher. "She claims to be a widow, and you believe her, so that rules out the husband theory, and since he not only pronounced the child's name wrong, but hasn't gone over to see her yet, that probably rules him out as any kind of a relative or friend. So, I'm thinking that he could be a boyfriend or ex-boyfriend. Maybe she broke up with him, and he's the type who won't take no for an answer."

"You'd think a boyfriend would know how to pronounce her little girl's name," I said doubtfully.

"Maybe they didn't date that long," Caleb said. "What's your hypothesis then?"

"I'm thinking stalker. She's a widow, living alone in a big city with a young child. If he was stalking her in Carlow, maybe she decided she had enough and had no one to turn to in the city, so she packed up and fled to escape him, but he tracked her here. That would explain his phone call to the motel."

Caleb tapped his finger against his chin. "That's definitely plausible. But there could be a third possibility."

"I know where you're going," I said, nodding slowly. "You're thinking maybe he tracked her here for another reason. She might have something that belongs to him."

"Perhaps it doesn't belong to him at all, but he wants it nonetheless," Caleb added.

I blew out my breath heavily. "What I can't understand is that if any one of those theories is the right one, then why is she so afraid of cops?"

Caleb slid a finger up under his glasses and

rubbed one eye at the same time as he spoke. "And what I don't quite comprehend is, if this guy's been in town for a few days already, and the reason he's here does involve Mrs. LeRue, why hasn't he gone over to the cottage yet? What's he waiting for?"

"I don't have all the answers yet, Caleb. But I do know these two things. Mrs. LeRue acts likes she's running from something or someone, and he looks dirty."

Caleb smiled. "We can't pick up him up just because we don't like the look of him."

"No, but we can find out where he's staying and go talk to him. No law against having a quiet chat with the man."

"What about Mrs. LeRue? Are we going to give to have a quiet chat with her too?"

"Depends on what Mr. Roberts has to say. Maybe we'll find out that we're way off base on this and we won't even need to speak with her," I said, but my heart's heaviness betrayed what my cop's intuition told me.

CHAPTER 19

Five minutes later I sat behind the wheel and Caleb was in the passenger seat of the cruiser and we were driving down the Oceanside Road. I accelerated past Sadie's Cottages, Livingstone's Bed & Breakfast, and the Coastal Inn without even glancing in, but eased my foot off the gas and drove slowly past the Blue Spruce Motel and looked in at the cottages. I saw that Kate LeRue's driveway was empty and assumed she was working at Gertie's today. I pressed the gas down and headed straight for the Seashore and Pine-Air Campgrounds that were further down the highway.

Just before the campground I saw a blue and white, town patrol car parked off the road with the front end facing the ocean. The driver was slouched in his seat with his head reclining back on the head-rest and looked to be sound asleep. Anger rose in my throat and I turned in off the highway, drove over the grassy patch of land, and eased the cruiser up alongside the patrol car. I leaned around Caleb to look out the passenger side window. Eric's eyes were closed, his mouth was wide open, the patrol car's engine was idling, and the windows were all rolled up and the air conditioner was blasting inside.

"I don't believe that guy. He's sleeping," Caleb said, sounding appalled.

I hit the siren twice and watched Deputy Malley jump awake in his seat. His head whipped around and when he saw us his mouth dropped open. Eric rolled his driver's side window down and poked his head out. He flashed me a big smile and when he did his small gray eyes became little more than slits in his beefy, red face. His chin was bristly and I could see green sleep crust in the corners of his eyes.

"I want to see you in my office at the end of your shift today, Eric," I said sharply.

"Oh come on, Jake. Give me a break will you?" he pleaded. "I've been up all night."

I took a breath to contain my anger.

"Look, I'm serious, Sheriff," he said, reverting to my title when he saw the anger in my eyes. "I was up half the night at the hospital with Lou-Lou. We thought she was having the baby. I only got about two hours sleep before I came on shift. I was practically falling asleep behind the wheel, so I thought it'd be best if I pulled over for just a couple of minutes and caught a couple of winks. I guess I was so tired I conked right out and slept longer than I meant to."

I considered what he had said for a moment. "Did Louella have the baby?"

"No, it turned out to be false labor pains, but Doc Hanssen says she could have it any time now."

I looked at him quietly for a long time before speaking.

"Okay, I'll give you a pass this time, Eric," I said finally. "But don't ever let me catch you sleeping on duty again. And make sure you shave and get a haircut before your shift tomorrow. Understood?"

"No problem, Jake," he said with a grin, bobbing his pumpkin shaped head up and down a couple of times before putting the gearshift in reverse and backing out onto the highway.

"You believe him?" Caleb asked.

"Louella is pretty far along. I'll give him the benefit of the doubt this time," I said quietly, watching Eric's patrol car move languidly down the road.

Caleb looked at me.

"You think I'm too soft on him," I said.

He shrugged slightly.

"Louella and the kids already have a pretty rough life with him, Caleb," I said mildly. "I have to admit that my patience is wearing very thin, but I'd hate to do anything that would make things even worse for them."

Caleb's features softened and he nodded.

I backed up, straightened the cruiser, and followed Eric's cruiser until we came to the Seashore Campground & RV Park. There, I pulled off the highway and steered through the white, wooden gates, drove past the RV section, which was really just a large, grassy field in the front of the park, and headed down the dusty dirt road to the back section which was the wooded tenting area. Caleb, who had lived in Leigh Falls his entire life, and knew what the odds were of anyone getting into a motel or one of the B& B's in town at this time of the year, didn't so much as bat an eye when he saw where we were going.

Caleb and I both preferred the fresh air to air conditioning, so the cruiser's front windows were down and the car's exhaust kicked up dust that blew inside with the first blast of hot, early summer air. The campground was located right across the road from the ocean, yet, the breeze that blew in off the water was still only a few degrees cooler than in town.

"It won't be July for another week, and it's as dry as a bone already," Caleb said, choking on the dust that was as granular as talcum powder.

"Yeah, I know. We've had hardly any rain this spring," I said.

Caleb coughed again and then rolled his window about three-quarters of the way up. He pulled off his clip-on sunglasses, breathed on them, and cleaned them on his uniform shirt, and then fastened them on again. He went right back to searching the lots, which were surrounded on three sides by thick evergreens which provided privacy for the campers, but made it hard for us to see into the lots until we were almost directly in front of the short, narrow lane that was the entrance to each site.

"Looks like the back end of a black Grand Am sticking out of the lot up right up ahead," he said.

"I see it," I said, peering through the windshield to the back of a black car parked in the lane. I slowed to a crawl as we came up on the car.

"Pennsylvania plates," Caleb said.

I pressed the accelerator and steered around the dusty, tree-lined road as it came around in a circle and led back to the front of the campground. Almost all of the sites were filled, and had tents of all shapes and sizes pitched at the back of the lots. Most also had checkered red and white table cloths draped over their picnic tables, and clotheslines fashioned from ropes strung from tree to tree, a myriad of dish-towels, bathing towels, and beach towels hanging from the lines. But there only a few people about and not too many cars parked in the lots. And no more black Grand Ams.

"Office is closed," I said to Caleb as we stopped at the camper's registration building next to the front gates, and I read from a sign the owner, Emily Lauron, had taped to the door. "Sign in the window says she'll be back in a half-hour. Let's go try the Pine-Air. If we don't find him there, we'll head back here later."

A couple of minutes later, I pulled the cruiser over across the road from the registration office at the Pine-Air and we went up the small set of steps. A blast of ice-cold air from a noisy air conditioner set up in the one window of the small, white shingled building buffeted us when walked inside. We stood just inside the door and waited for the owner, Wally Powers, to finish serving two little boys wearing bathing shorts and hiking sandals, who were at the counter counting out change for two Popsicle's. The office also served as a canteen and tourist information center and there were racks of potato chips and chocolate bars, a cooler of pop, a small freezer containing ice cream bars and Popsicle's, and a wooden stand against one wall filled with brochures advertising whale-watching tours and sea kayaking excursions.

"Hello Jake. Caleb. What can I do for you guys?" Wally asked as soon as the boys went out.

"Need some information, Wally. Do you have a guy tenting here by the name of Wesley Roberts? Arrived in town probably sometime in the past two or three days."

Wally's ruddy, weather-beaten face burrowed with deep lines while he thought. He was a short, wiry man with chocolate brown eyes, a high forehead, stooped back, and wavy salt and pepper hair. His face was craggy and deeply lined from his years fishing at sea. Seven years ago he had hurt his back, and had given up lobstering and opened the Pine-Air Campground on his land. Although that had been seven years ago, Wally still dressed in the same clothes that he wore when out at sea. A pair of faded blue jeans, and either a wool sweater or a flannel work shirt over a ratty, gray T-shirt. *At least he stopped wearing his knee-high black rubber boots*, I thought, when he stepped back from the counter and I saw white Nikes with blues stripes on his feet.

"He's not staying here, Jake. I'm all full up. My regulars reserve their usual sites every year by the first week of May. I do keep about twenty unreserved sites at the back, but they're all taken and no one's moved in or out in the past week. Tourists are here in droves already this season."

I nodded while I thought.

"There's a campground on the bay about twenty miles beyond Linden," Caleb suggested.

I turned to look at him and shook my head. "I think he's staying in town."

Wally was hanging on every word. "He's likely at the Seashore then," he put in. "I know Emily has more unreserved tenting sites than I do, and she did mention that she had a couple left the last time we talked. If he's not there, then he's pitched his tent in someone's back yard or he's sleeping in his car," he said with a smile.

"Okay, thanks, Wally," I said. "We were just at the Seashore, but the office was closed. Should be open shortly."

"What'd he do? Besides being a tourist, I mean?" Wally said, and laughed hard.

"You reputation precedes you," Caleb said, and chuckled softly as he followed me out the door.

"So it seems," I said dryly, as we stepped out into a wall of heat that had earlier seemed tolerable, but now felt unbearable after the frigid air conditioned office.

It turned out that we didn't have to go into the office at the Seashore Campground to speak with

Emily Lauron, the owner, because just as we neared the entrance, a black Grand Am with Georgia plates was going through the front gate. I quickly turned right and pulled in behind it, and we followed the car through a cloud of dust it kicked up all the way to the back section of the campground. When the car pulled into the last lot at the end of the road, I pulled over onto the side of the road across from it, cut the engine and Caleb and I climbed out.

As we crossed the dirt road and approached the campsite I scrutinized the lot carefully. There was a blue and red, four-man dome tent set up and a bare wooden picnic table that sat close to a fire pit. That was it. There was no other camping equipment around at all. Evidently, he didn't cook his food at the campsite, and I found that kind of odd since most campers either barbecued or cooked their meals on small propane stoves.

Wesley Roberts was already out of his car, saw us, stopped, leaned against his car, crossed his arms over his thick chest, and stared with undisguised hostility at us as we neared him.

"He doesn't look happy to see us," Caleb said, under his breath.

"I see that."

"Good day, sir," I called out, my eyes not leaving his face. "I'm Sheriff,"

"Cole. I remember," he said, cutting me off. He cleared his throat, crossed one muscular leg over the other and stared at me coolly.

"That's right," I said, stopping in front of him. "This is Deputy Caleb Harrington."

He ignored Caleb and remained silent, his expression and posture belligerent.

"Enjoying your stay in Leigh Falls, sir?" I asked, keeping my tone casual.

"So what are you two, the welcome wagon?" he snorted, his icy-pale blue eyes bold as they met and held my stare.

My alarm bells were all screaming and I studied him with care. He wasn't only hostile and aggressive he clearly wasn't disturbed at all by our unexpected presence. This was a man used to having cops talking to him. He was dressed in the same white shorts and T-shirt, but the sunglasses, hat and camera were gone. I noticed he wore a gold Rolex on his wrist, and one gold ring on his left pinkie finger with the initial, 'W', on it, but no wedding band. I figured his real clothes, city clothes, were in the tent or in the trunk of his car. I moved over a couple of inches, and glanced casually into the front seat of his car. A band of sunlight that broke through the treetops shone into the car by the side window and fell onto a map of Leigh Falls spread out on the front seat.

"You might say that. We do like to meet all the new tourists. You know, public relations and all," Caleb said, and stepped past him, and looked around the campsite, his eyes taking in everything.

"With the amount of tourists here, it must be a full time job," he said, sounding amused.

"It does keep us busy," I said.

Caleb stepped to within inches of the side window in the tent.

Roberts turned his head sideways and saw what Caleb was doing. "I'd advise you to stop poking around, deputy," he said, his tone venomous.

"So what exactly is your business here in Leigh Falls, Mr. Roberts?" I said.

He snapped his head back around in surprise at my knowledge of his name, but then seemed to compose himself, and folded his arms across his chest and regarded me with a hard, silent, stare.

"You didn't answer my question," I said.

"I've forgotten what it was you asked me."

"Probably the heat. It can make a person kind of drowsy," I said. "Although I would think you'd be used to that, coming from Georgia I mean."

He remained silent.

"I asked what you are doing here in Leigh Falls."

"And I would think that's kind of obvious," he said with a sarcastic grin, moving one thick arm to gesture to the tent. "But then, like you said, the heat can make a person kind of drowsy."

I nodded, and studied him with a cold, hard gaze of my own. Just that tiny movement and his biceps in one arm bulged. Caleb and I were both lean, yet, muscular, but his biceps were more than twice the size of ours, and his neck and chest were so thick, I was certain it would take all of our strength to snap cuffs on the guy if it came to that. And I had no doubt that one day soon it would.

"Curiously, you don't strike me as the camping type," I said.

"My thoughts exactly," Caleb said, as he came up alongside me.

"Is that right?" Wesley Roberts said, and cleared his throat, only to sound the same when he spoke again. "Well, I could care less what you two think."

We fell silent, and the squeals of sea gulls and the shouts and laughter of young children playing in the park's playground sounded around us. I took a deep breath and could smell the ocean, dank and briny, but as I watched him, all I could think about was that his pale, blue eyes glinted coldly in the sunlight like thin ice on a pond on a bright, winter's day.

"How long will you be staying in Leigh Falls, Mr. Roberts?" I asked finally, my voice hard.

"I'm not really sure," he said, and yawned, revealing a mouthful of square, even white teeth that had obviously had quite a bit of expensive dental work.

"Do you know a woman by the name of Kate LeRue?" I said.

He tried hard not show it, but I caught something flicker across his face. Whatever it was it disappeared fast, but I knew I had seen a reaction to her name.

"You know, it's been a real treat, but this little tête-à-tête is over. I'm going to take a nap now," he said with a sneering grin, and then turned his back to us, walked over to his tent and languidly slid the zipper up.

"We'll be talking to you again soon, Mr. Roberts," I said, my voice sharp, my facial expression full of anger.

"I can hardly wait," he said, turning his head to look over his shoulder at us while moving his eyes up and down in a dance of vast amusement.

Caleb looked like he wanted to grab Roberts and throw him up against a tree, so I touched his arm lightly and then we walked back to the cruiser without speaking. I started the engine, glanced over at the site and saw that Roberts hadn't gone into his tent after all, but had walked to the end of the short driveway and was standing behind his car watching us.

"Your gut feeling was certainly right about this guy. He is not here to go out on a whale-watching tour," Caleb said.

"No, he's definitely not here for that, Caleb."

"I don't understand why he guy doesn't have a sheet," Caleb said. "He looks and sounds like he's been in jail before."

"When we get back to the department try running his name through the computer again. Maybe we overlooked something," I said.

"I will."

"Did you see his reaction when I asked him if he knew Kate LeRue? He tried to hide it, but I caught something flit across his face. He knows her."

Caleb nodded in agreement.

We cruised slowly past Roberts, who hadn't moved and was standing there glaring icily at us.

"His eyes," Caleb said quietly. "They're so chillingly evil."

I nodded, my mouth a rigid line in my face.

CHAPTER 20

W e strode hurriedly through the doors into the department, and Caleb headed for the computer. I made my way past the front desk and up the stairs to my office, and then shouted back over my shoulder two seconds before I stepped through the doorway.

"Marney!"

I walked around my desk and dropped down heavily into my chair, and then used my feet to push my chair around so I could stare out the window to the water of the harbor while I thought.

Marney walked in a minute later.

"I am not deaf," she growled irritably.

I swiveled my chair back around and looked at her and my mouth fell open. I shut it at once, and quickly averted my eyes to the oak coat rack in the corner of the room.

"Don't like my new hairstyle, do you?"

"Sure I do."

"Oh, just be honest, Jake," she said, giving me a pained look.

I studied her hair with its fiery red spikes that started at the hairline above her forehead and went all the way across the center of her head. Each spike looked like an individual flaming torch, and the hair on each side of her head above her ear had been buzz cut so short that I could see her white skull gleaming in the bright sunlight that streamed in on her head through the window.

"Well," I said, unable to think of anything else.

"If you're wondering, I took a half day's vacation this morning for my appointment."

"I wasn't even thinking about that, Marney. Believe me."

"Well, you've got such a strained look on your face, I wasn't sure."

I shook my head and tried to look more natural. The only way I could was to move my eyes to the right of her, and keep them focused on my gun belt, which I had draped over the coat rack when I came in the office.

"What's so fascinating about the coat rack?" she demanded.

"Nothing. I was just thinking it's been a while since I cleaned my gun."

"Sure you were."

I shrugged and kept my face free of any expression.

"So, what's all the hullabaloo about?"

"Sorry about that. Would you get the police chief, or sheriff of the city of Carlow, Georgia, whatever they have down there, on the phone for me. Please," I added.

She turned and walked away, muttering something about my lack of fashion sense under her breath, and almost collided with Caleb who was coming through the door at the same time, but who had skidded to a sudden stop when he saw her, and was gaping at her hair with wide open eyes.

"Oh, Marney," he said in what sounded like quiet despair.

"Something wrong, Harrington?" she demanded, glaring at him with a murderous expression.

"Uh, no," he mumbled, and then walked over to my desk, but kept glancing back over his shoulders as she walked away.

"What'd she do to her hair? Is it supposed to look like that?" he said in a low voice, when he was sure she was out of hearing range.

"Don't ask me. I've had the same hairstyle now for over twenty years. She thinks I'm fashion impaired."

"That might not be such a bad thing," he said. "Her hair looks terrible."

I almost agreed but caught myself when Marney stuck her head of fiery spikes through the doorway into the room a couple of inches, jabbed the pen she was holding at the phone on my desk, glared at the both of us again and then pulled her head back out and disappeared.

I picked up the phone. "Hello."

"This is Sheriff Ned Casey," said a deep voice with a soft, Georgian accent. "You wanted to speak with me, Sheriff Cole, is it?"

"Good morning, Sheriff Casey. Yes, I'm Jake Cole, sheriff here in Leigh Falls."

"What can I do for you, sheriff?"

"I wonder if you could give me some information on a guy from Carlow who is here in town."

"I'll try. What's his name?"

"Wesley Gary Roberts."

There was silence over the line for a moment.

"Does the name ring a bell at all?"

"Nothing's jumping right out at me," he said, with a slow, soft drawl. "But that doesn't necessarily mean anything either. I should tell you that I've only been sheriff here for the past six months."

"I see," I said, feeling a bit disappointed.

"Why don't you go ahead and give me the story on this guy anyway."

I recounted the entire story, starting with Kate LeRue arriving in town with her young daughter and ending with Wesley Roberts

"Did you run his name through the computer?" he asked. "He sounds like he'd be in there."

"Yes, we did," I said. "Nothing showed up at all. But this guy's a predator."

"Well," he said. "If he's up there on account of this woman, it could be a domestic situation. Maybe she took off with his kid. Those things can be nasty sometimes."

"She's a widow. But we are considering that he could be her boyfriend or an ex-boyfriend.

Although my gut instinct tells me it's something else. He's just doesn't seem her type."

"Well, it's been my experience that some real nice woman get hooked up with some pretty bad characters."

"You're right. But, in fifteen years as a cop, I've learned to trust my feelings about people."

"I know what you mean. I've had to go on nothing more my own gut feelings many times myself. I'm sorry to have to tell you though; the name doesn't jog anything in my memory. But like I said, I'm new here and just starting to become acquainted with some of Carlow's less than fine and upstanding citizens."

"I understand."

"You have his picture there?" he asked.

"Yes. DMV faxed us a copy of his driver's license with his photo."

"Fax me his picture and I'll pass it around to my men. All of them have been here longer than I have. If he's dirty, one of them should recognize him."

"I hope so."

"Me too. I don't envy you though. He sounds like a very, big boy."

"He's a giant. Tall, and close to three hundred pounds of pure muscle. Looks like he lifts weights daily."

"You know, I think I've got about ten guys that look just like him in my jail right now. And they're all likely pumping iron in the weight room as we speak," he said dryly.

I chuckled softly.

"Give me a couple of hours, a day or two at the most, and I'll see what I can dig up on your body-builder."

"Thanks. I appreciate your help, Sheriff Casey."

"No problem," he said. "And call me Ned."

"Okay, Ned. And it's Jake."

"Don't use the weights myself, Jake. Do you?"

"Once or twice a week at the most. I guess I'm more of a runner."

"I guess I'm more of a belly-builder," he said, and I could hear him laughing right up until he hung up the phone.

CHAPTER 21

I hung around the office the rest of the afternoon waiting for Sheriff Casey to call back with some information on Roberts. When he didn't, I left the office at four o'clock and walked across Ash Street to Gertie's. I had missed lunch and decided to eat an early supper even though I was too edgy to be hungry, and the reason I was going there had everything to do with Kate LeRue and nothing to do with eating.

As I entered the diner, I headed for my usual seat, the empty stool beside Roger Wagner, and from the corner of my eye saw Kate standing at the last booth across the room, taking an order from a middle-aged couple. I twisted my stool around an inch or two so I could keep an eye on Kate, and saw Leona Walton, a teller at one of the two banks in town, who was sitting in a booth with two other bank employees, wave at me from the only booth in the row that didn't hold tourists. I waved back and then slid my eyes quickly back to Kate, and she suddenly looked over and our eyes locked. After a couple of seconds she dropped her eyes and looked away.

"Hi, Jake," Roger said, and I eased my stool back around again.

"Hey Roger, how are you?"

"Can't complain," he said. He pointed his spoon at his bowl of oyster stew. "Special's pretty good tonight."

I grimaced.

"Where have you been?" Gertie whooped out as she walked over, drying her hands on her apron. "You don't eat lunch anymore?"

"Just busy, Gertie. Looks like you're pretty busy too."

"Ah, tourists," she grumbled, casting a deadly look toward the booths. "They come in here asking for breakfast at three o'clock in the afternoon. Must be nice to be able to sleep the whole day away."

I smiled slightly, and turned my gaze from the crowded booths to Kate, my eyes following her as she walked across the floor of the diner and came around the counter, picked up two orders and left again. But not before she glanced over in my direction and our eyes met again.

"I'll call Kate," Gertie said, and turned sideways.

"Wait a second, Gertie," I blurted.

Gertie turned back around, raised her thin eyebrows and looked at me.

I lowered my voice. "Why do you get Kate to take my order every time I come in here now?" I said.

"Because you want me to," she said very quietly.

"I never said that."

"You didn't have to."

I didn't say anything to that, and could feel my neck and face getting hot.

"But today, I'll do it," she said, giving me a kind smile. "What do you want?"

"I'll have bacon, eggs, hash browns and toast."

Roger threw his head back and laughed loudly.

Gertie's eyes narrowed and she glared at me.

"Oh, and Gertie, I like my eggs easy over," I added, with a grin.

"Kate!" she screamed as loud as she could. "Jake would like you to take his order."

Gertie grinned right back at me and then walked away.

Kate came over a couple of seconds later and stood quietly in front of me, pen and pad at the ready. She was wearing a pale green silk blouse that brought out her eyes, and black dress pants with the regulation apron tied around her waist, her cheeks were flushed red from the heat in the diner, and her gleaming hair was pulled back and held with a silver clasp.

"Hi, Kate," I said guardedly, because after our conversation in the park on Saturday, I wasn't sure if she would even speak to me again.

Hi," she said, and her tone and manner were a little cool.

I paused, and then looked at her and lowered my voice.

"I'm sorry if I upset you the other day," I said gently.

She didn't say anything to that but her expression softened.

"How are you?" I said.

"I'm fine. Hot, but fine," she said, and brushed back a loose strand of hair that had fallen across her forehead.

I felt a good deal of comfort because even if she still sounded a bit wary, at least she was talking to me.

"This place could use some air conditioning," I said.

"Yeah, and who's going to pay for it, Mister! You?" Gertie hollered out from the grill.

I smiled and shook my head. "She has eyes like a hawk and ears like a bat," I said.

"What!" Gertie shrieked, her eyes narrowing dangerously as she marched over and stood facing me from her side of the counter, wielding a soup ladle in her hand. "Did you just call me an old bat?"

I threw my head back and laughed hard and heard Kate burst out laughing at the same time.

"No, Gertie," I said, still laughing. "I said you have ears like a bat."

"He did," Kate put in when she had stopped laughing and saw Gertie glaring dubiously at me.

"Hmm, just remember who is cooking your food," Gertie grunted, before walking over to the cash register where a customer stood waiting.

"What can I get you?" Kate asked, and I could see she was fighting back laughter.

I smiled, and then she did too, and our eyes locked and not for the first time, I heard myself take in a quick breath of air.

"I'll have a sliced turkey sandwich on whole wheat, with mayonnaise and lettuce," I said, turning my eyes up to the clock on the wall so I could conceal my emotions from her.

"What!!!! A sandwich!" Gertie screamed as she walked past. "I eat more than that, and I don't have to catch criminals."

I closed my eyes for a second. "My mistake. Whatever was I thinking? I'll have the special."

Kate laughed quietly to herself as she wrote down my order. When she finished writing, she looked up from her pad and our eyes met once again, and I felt my heartbeat quicken.

When Kate walked away to get my stew, Roger, who had been watching all this, smiled at me.

"What?" I grunted at him.

"Nothing," he said.

I tried to be more discreet after that, but I seemed entirely incapable of not looking at Kate, and told myself it was only because I was deeply concerned abut the threat Wesley Roberts might very well pose to her and Madeleine.

When Roger finished his stew he wiped his face with a napkin, tossed it in his bowl, and then cleared his throat a little. "Jake, I need to talk to you about something," he said, his expression grave.

I looked over at him and nodded because my mouth was full.

"Did you ever meet someone that raised the hair on your neck?"

I swallowed first and then spoke. "Yes, more than once in this job."

He rubbed his face tiredly. "Yes, I guess you would. Well, it happened to me the other day. This guy came into the store and boy, did he ever give me the creeps. Sent shivers right up my back. He was that strange, you know?"

I nodded for him to go on.

"There was something else that bothered me about him too. He told me he came here for a camping vacation; yet, he didn't bring so much as a tent or a sleeping bag. I mean who drives all the way up here from Georgia for a camping vacation without any gear whatsoever?"

"How do you know he's from Georgia?"

"I watched him load the gear in his car from my front window, and I saw his license plate," he explained.

I nodded and let out my breath slowly. I had a pretty good idea who the guy was already.

"Sure," Roger went on. "I sell some camping equipment, like flashlights, naphtha gas and batteries. But that's about it. The tourists arrive already well-equipped, and the locals drive over to the big, sporting goods store in Linden to buy their gear because it's cheaper and they have a large selection. I'm more of a nuts and bolts hardware dealer. Oh, of course you know that. Sorry, this guy's got me so rattled, I'm not thinking straight."

"What did he buy?" I said.

"Tent, ground sheet, rain fly, air mattress, sleeping bag, flashlight, propane lamp, the whole kit and caboodle. Everything except cooking supplies. I've had that tent and sleeping bag in the store for years and I never thought I'd sell them. He cleaned me out of what little camping gear I did have in stock."

I frowned. "Did you ask him about it?"

Roger raised his eyebrows and nodded. "He told me he lost all his camping gear in a rainstorm, but he wouldn't say where it happened."

"Do you believe him?"

Roger snorted. "No, I don't. I'm no cop, but you wouldn't lose all your gear in a rainstorm. You might get your tent blown down, and everything would get a good soaking, but that's about it."

"Describe him," I said, my pulse racing now.

"He's a big man, really big. Looks like one of those professional wrestlers on television. He has a goatee, long black hair and he was wearing it in a ponytail. And he sounds all phlegmy when he talks. He must have allergies or something because he clears his throat all the time, but it doesn't seem to do much for his problem. It was his eyes that shook me though," Roger said, dropping his voice down lower when Kate walked by.

I followed her with my eyes and my felt my throat lock up.

"I'm almost ashamed to tell say this, but the man scared me to death," Roger went on, looking down at his plate. "He has ice-eyes. Evil, like he has no feelings at all inside.'"

I nodded understandingly, and reached over and squeezed his shoulder.

Roger rubbed his face roughly with one hand and then tilted his head sideways a little and caught the expression on my face. "You know who I'm talking about, don't you?"

"I do," I said quietly.

Roger looked relieved. "Good, I'm awful glad to hear that, because there's something else. Even though I found it strange, I probably wouldn't even have mentioned the camping gear thing to you at all if it weren't for this," he said, and reached into his pants pocket, pulled out a slip of paper and handed it to me. "He dropped this in the store when he pulled some change out of his pocket."

The writing was large and loopy, and when I read it my heart turned to ice in my chest. The name, address and telephone number of the Blue Spruce Motel & Cottages was written on it, as well as Kate and Madeleine LeRue's names.

We fell silent and I shoved the paper into my shirt pocket just as Kate came over and refilled my coffee cup. She smiled at me, and then at Roger. He smiled at her, shook his head, and covered his cup with the palm of his hand, so she walked down the counter to refill another customer's cup.

After Roger left, I lingered, drinking two more cups of coffee as I waited for Kate to finish for the day. When I saw her untie her apron and take it off, say goodbye to Gertie, and come out of the back carrying her purse and then head for the door, I slipped off my stool and followed her out.

"Kate," I called out, as she walked swiftly down the crowded sidewalk.

She stopped and turned around on the sidewalk, tourists pushing past and around her as she faced me, squinting against the brightness of the sunlight after being inside the diner all day.

"What is it, Jake?" she said.

"I wonder if we could talk for a minute?" I said.

The sun was right behind her, breaking through the alleyway in between the diner and the gift shop next door and hitting me right in my eyes. I reached into my shirt pocket for my sunglasses, and slipped them on as I approached her.

"I'm sorry, but this is not a good time. I promised Miranda I'd be back at the cottage no later than five-thirty," she said.

"Why don't I drive you home and we can talk on the way."

She shook her head and motioned behind her with one hand, and I could see that it was shaking once again. "My car's parked around the back of the diner. This will have to wait. I really am in a hurry today."

"This is important, Kate."

"Well, I don't mean to seem rude, Jake, but I really can't talk right now," she said, and then whirled around, and quickly ducked into a paved alleyway next to Gertie's diner and disappeared from sight.

I strode rapidly behind her, followed her down the alley, and caught up with her just as she reached the driver's side door of her car. She kept her back to me and searched through her purse for her car keys.

"Kate, hold on a minute, please," I said.

She shook her head adamantly as she dug through her purse.

"Kate," I said, and put my hand around her upper right arm and held her gently.

"Please let go of my arm," she said, and I heard a distinct tremor in her voice.

"Sorry," I said, dropping her arm at once.

She found her keys and slid one in the lock, opened the door, and climbed in. I reached over and caught the door before she could slam it shut behind her. I held the door open and watched her trying to fit the key into the ignition, but her hands were trembling so much she ended up dropping the keys on the floor. She bent down and groped around on the floor in front of the driver's seat and found them, tried twice more, and then finally started the engine. She pulled the stickshift into reverse, but her foot was still on the brake. She turned her head to look at me.

"Let go of the door, Jake."

"Just answer one question first, and then I'll shut it."

She didn't say anything, so I quickly spoke before she took off.

"Do you know a man named Wesley Roberts?"

"No, I do not know anyone by that name," she said.

"He's a real big guy. He stands over six and a half feet tall, and weighs close to three hundred pounds. He's got a goatee, and long, black hair he wears in a ponytail. You sure you don't know him?"

"I've already answered your question, so please shut the door."

"Wesley Roberts is from Carlow, Georgia, too."

She shook her head in disbelief, and fell back against the car seat, seemingly staggered by my words.

"So you do know him," I said.

Two bright red spots appeared on her cheeks and anger flashed suddenly in her eyes.

"No, I don't know him," she hissed. "But what I do know is that I never told you or anyone else that I'm from Carlow. How do you know that's where I'm from? Have you been checking up on me?"

I didn't reply to that right away because in truth I felt a little embarrassed.

"Shut the door now," she said, and reached over and tried to pull it shut.

"He had this in his pocket," I said, and clutched the door tightly with one hand, pulled the slip of paper that Roger had given me from my shirt pocket with the other, and held it in front of her face so she could read it.

She read the note, squeezed her eyes shut for a couple of seconds and then opened them again.

"So what?" she said.

"Why would this guy have a piece of paper with your name on it?"

"I don't know. I don't care. And I do not know him," she said, her mouth set rigid now with a determination that gave evidence that the name meant nothing to her.

I kept my hand firmly on the door, blew my breath out, and looked back over my shoulder to the high sea barrier of large, gray boulders that lined the end of the parking lot behind the diner and tried to think. The air down here smelled of a mixture of diesel, kelp and the barnacles that clung to the pylons and rocks in the small harbor, but I hardly noticed for my thoughts were only of how I could reach her.

I turned back to look at her. "You're afraid and you're on the run, Kate," I said.

"To be perfectly candid, Jake, the only man I'm afraid of is you."

I was acutely taken aback by that, and let go of the door and backed away from the car a couple of steps.

When I did, she immediately took her foot off the brake, stomped on the gas pedal and starting backing up fast with the driver's door still open. I reached out and slapped the door shut as the car moved past me. She backed around, and then turned the wheel and straightened the Malibu out, and took off, accelerating so fast that her tires squealed loudly as she left the parking lot. I watched her car stop at the end off the alleyway, turn right onto Ash and roar away down the street. I stood there for a few seconds feeling sharply disappointed and more than a little embarrassed.

I went home after my encounter with Kate LeRue feeling restless and frustrated. I changed out of my uniform to jeans and a T-shirt, and spent an hour pacing from room to room. Then I changed from jeans to running shorts, and went for an early evening run to try to dispel the unsettled feeling that had a strong hold on me.

It was a warm summer's night, the breeze balmy as it swept in off the water that was ebbing back to sea. As I ran the sun began to drop, and I knew the fiery sunset was promising to be spectacular, but tonight, I didn't care enough to watch. I even found the odor of the breeze, which was strong with the scent of the seashells and seaweed that littered the beach after the tide went out, disagreeable for the very first time. At nine o'clock, I was back home, but still couldn't shake the uneasiness, and so changed back into jeans, jumped in my truck, and drove over to the campground.

I drove through the tenting area, and then cruised slowly past Roberts's site. He was standing in front of his campfire, sifting the red, hot embers with a long switch he had cut from a tree so that sparks flew up from the flames into the air. He had most of his body turned toward the fire and he didn't look up, yet, I had a sense from his rigid posture that he knew it was me, and despite the heat, I felt an evil chill as I drove past him.

I drove home and went to bed, but was still far too edgy to fall asleep. I got back up, walked to the window, and looked out. The sky was filled with stars, but in the far distance I could see heat lightning flash in the clouds in the distance, and could hear the faint low rumble of thunder follow a few seconds later. As I watched the lightning flicker in the distant sky, I thought some more about Roberts, and about Kate LeRue and her daughter, Madeleine, and decided that until I knew what Roberts was really doing here, I would keep a very tight rein on him.

CHAPTER 22

The next morning when the first soft rose of dawn appeared in the eastern sky, I was already awake, showered, dressed and ready to head out. Just before seven o'clock, I drove to Dunkin' Donuts, bought two large coffees to go, drove to the department, went into my office, and drank mine while I waited for Caleb to join me when he came on shift at seven-thirty.

"Thanks," Caleb said, when he walked into the room at seven-twenty and took the cup of coffee I held out to him.

I nodded.

"You don't look too good," Caleb commented, after he pulled the lid back and took a small sip.

"Didn't sleep much."

"Oh," he said, and eyed me carefully as he walked over to the window. He swallowed some more of his coffee and immediately made a face.

"When did you come in?" he said.

"Around seven."

He nodded, and being the gracious man that he was, simply smiled a little bit and said. "Be right back."

I picked up a sheet of paper from my in-basket and began reading it.

"Did you drive over to the campground last night?" he asked, when he had returned with the freshly nuked cup of coffee, and had dropped down once again in the chair in front of my desk.

"Yes," I said, without lifting my eyes from the paper.

"I knew it."

I shrugged my shoulders.

"Did Sheriff Casey call back with anything on Roberts?"

I shook my head no.

"So what now?" Caleb said, after he had taken a gulp of the hot coffee.

I signed my name to the bottom of the report I was reading and tossed it into my out-basket, and then looked straight at him.

"We keep our eye on Mr. Roberts," I said, and held out the slip of paper Roger gave me.

Caleb leaned ahead, read it, and then looked at me, and with his quiet, unpretentious manner waited for me to explain.

"Roger gave me that yesterday in Gertie's. Said a guy from Georgia came in and bought a bunch of camping equipment off him, and this fell out of his pocket," I explained. "From his description of the guy, it was Roberts."

Caleb sat back hard in the chair. His pale blue eyes widened and he shook his head. "We should go talk to Mrs. LeRue right now," he said. "She must know this guy."

"I already did," I said, leaning back against my chair and folding my hands over my stomach. A band of early morning sunlight slanted in through the window blind and fell across my hands.

"I spoke to her behind Gertie's when she got off work yesterday. It didn't go very well," I said, and thought of Kate and how afraid of me she was once again and I felt an unexpected despondency settle over me. I turned my head, cleared my throat and stared despairingly at the dust motes floating around in the sunlight. When I finally gained some composure, I looked up and saw Caleb watching me with a concerned look.

"You okay?"

I nodded.

"So, what did she say?"

"She said she doesn't know Roberts."

"You believe her?"

"Yes," I said. "When I told her his name, and gave her his description, it didn't seem to shake her up at all. In truth, she seemed more afraid of me. But I'm convinced she's holding something back."

Caleb was silent a minute while he thought this all through.

"If Roberts is here to harm her, why would he bother to buy expensive gear and then set up camp at the Seashore?" he said, sounding mystified. "Does that make any sense to you?"

"No, it doesn't. But I know I'm right about this guy. I just can't prove anything yet."

Caleb observed me quietly while he finished his coffee.

"There is a problem, Jake. She doesn't seem to want our help," he said, after he had tossed his empty cup in the wastepaper basket at the side of my desk.

"I know. But we can still watch Roberts," I said, and stood to my feet and walked over to the window and looked down to Ash Street. The sidewalks were full of tourists carrying shopping bags, and eating double and triple scoop ice cream cones even thought it was barely nine in the morning. "I'm not sure what he's doing here in Leigh Falls, but you and I are going to keep a very close eye on him every minute of every day that he's here. And we're going to start right now," I said, turning from the window to face him.

Caleb rose to his feet at once. "Well then, Wyatt, let's go saddle up."

"So you've heard that one too," I said as I walked around my desk.

Caleb smiled. "It beats being called '*The Professor*'.

"You know, I think you're right," I said, and we laughed quietly as we walked out of the office.

———

Caleb dropped me off at the police department later that morning, and then went back to keeping an eye on Roberts. We had watched him all that morning and all he had done was eat breakfast, take a nap in his tent, and cruise the streets in town. I had too many tourists, and too little manpower, so other than Caleb and myself, I didn't dare put anyone else on this. I was going to relieve Caleb at five o-clock, and then Caleb would go home, grab a nap, and then return at midnight to relieve me, and we'd keep this up for as long as Roberts was in town.

I finished up some paperwork shortly before five o'clock, and then headed out of my office to relieve Caleb. I was almost through the front doors of the department when Marney shouted out my name. I let go of the door handle and whipped around, surprised by the tone of her voice. I saw her standing up behind her desk, holding the telephone receiver to her ear, her face colorless, and her eyes filling up. She nodded, spoke into the phone once more, and then hung up slowly, and seemed to gather herself before she could speak to me.

"What is it, Marney? What's wrong?" I said, moving across the room to her desk.

"That was Dennis Halton," she said, her voice faltering. "He says one of his motel guests found Freddie Leach down on the beach a few minutes ago."

"Found him, what? Intoxicated?"

"No, Jake. Found his body. He's dead."

I took a step back, recoiling as sudden shock pierced through me.

"Oh no," I said softly.

Marney shook her head from side to side sorrowfully. "Poor Agnes," she said. "She's going to take this hard."

"Yes, she is," I murmured, and exhaled heavily in despair. "Who's down there?"

"Donny Bernard."

"Did he say what happened?"

"No," Marney replied, and looked as though she was fighting back tears.

"Okay," I said, turning to leave. "Call Caleb for me and tell him what's happened. Ask him to stick around the Seashore Campground until I can get over there."

Marney reached for a facial tissue from the box on her desk. "What's he doing over there?" she asked, her voice shaky.

"Just tell him what I told you, Marney. I'll explain it all to you later," I said gently and went out.

I jumped in the cruiser, hit the lights and siren, and then proceeded down Ash Street, which was clogged solid with tourists, at about the same rate of speed as a wounded porcupine. I tooted the horn, whooped the siren, and cut around the tourist's vehicles whenever I could, and still didn't make good time at all until I was almost there anyway. I turned in off the highway, drove past the motel office, bumped along the lane that led to the cottages, and pulled in beside Donny's patrol car and a town ambulance. As I climbed out I was thinking that this was the same beach where only a little more than a week ago the three young teens from town had been partying and breaking beer bottles. Now that seemed like a year ago.

I could see a small crowd of people gathered on the motel's private beach, all of them standing huddled together in small groups, or sitting on towels spread out on the sand. My deputy, Donny Bernard, two paramedics, and Dennis Halton, were all standing at the end of the beach near the seawall. The seawall consisted of a barrier of large gray boulders below a five-foot high embankment of earth, and it ran the entire length of the motel's private beach. I noticed they were all gazing silently down to the hot sand below the embankment. I hurried over as much as were humanly possible wearing regulation shoes, and trudging across heavy beach sand.

"Donny," I said, and nodded politely to the others when I came up alongside them.

"He's over there, kind of in between those big rocks," Donny said, pointing with his chin to a secluded circle of large boulders close to the edge of the embankment about twenty feet from where we stood.

The two paramedics looked at me, and I waved them off.

"We won't be needing you guys," I said.

They nodded and turned to leave.

I headed over to the circle of boulders with Donny trailing a half-step behind.

"Did you call the coroner, Donny?"

"Uh-huh," he said. "He's on his way."

"Who found Freddie?"

"A kid chasing a Frisbee," he said, his normally deep bass voice sounding like a soprano's. "That's him there. Name's Brock Manderson," he said, pointing to a tall, athletic young guy with short, curly black hair, who looked like a college student. He was wearing green Adidas bathing shorts, no shirt, and was sitting hunched over on a boulder just below the embankment, with his elbows resting on his knees and the Frisbee held loosely in his hands.

Donny wasn't much older than the college student and under different circumstances I might have smiled at his use of the word, kid. He had just turned twenty and had only been a deputy for six months. Like most redheads, he had very pale skin and lots of freckles spread across his face, and he was so baby-faced, he looked like he didn't need to shave. I glanced at him and noted that his cheeks were unusually red, his pale blue eyes were open wide, and a sheen of sweat covered his forehead.

"You okay?" I said.

"Uh-huh," he said. "It's just the heat. It's brutal out here."

I nodded. The sun was beating down on our backs, and I could feel sweat soaking my uniform shirt at the small of my back above my gun belt, but I didn't think that the heat was the complete reason for his flushed skin tone.

He saw me watching him.

"And it's my first, ah, dead guy," he said quietly.

I nodded kindly at him and then squeezed in between two huge boulders and knelt down beside the still form of Freddie Leach and gently turned him over. When I did, his brown work hat liner slipped off his head onto the sand, and both his unzipped green parka and unbuttoned plaid flannel shirt fell open to reveal a sheet-white sunken abdomen and a rack of protruding ribs. I felt for a pulse in his neck, and then felt his body. He was stone cold, had no pulse, and rigor mortis was setting in, so I knew he had been dead for at least twelve hours. My throat and chest went tight, and my throat hurt like crazy. I held him in my arms for a minute before I laid him gently back down on the sand.

I stood to my feet and cleared my throat roughly a couple of times, my eyes stinging. Donny looked at me and opened his mouth to speak, saw my expression, and then shut it again. After I had some gained some self-control I began scanning the area. From the center of this circle of large boulders, lying on the sand where he was, he couldn't be seen from the motel above, the private beach below, or from any boats that might be out on the water. I was sure if it hadn't been for that kid with the Frisbee, he would have been here for another day or two before being discovered.

I knelt back down and ran my hands under his shirt, probing his emaciated body for any injury that might signal foul play, but not really expecting to find anything. I had already spotted an empty quart bottle of cheap whiskey lying on the sand next to his body, and figured he had passed out after consuming the entire quart, and his heart or liver had finally given out. I knew he didn't drown because of the condition of his body, and because I was well aware that the incoming tidewater didn't reach this far up on the beach. If it hadn't been that, Freddie's body would have been carried out to sea when the tide retreated again, and probably would never have been found.

Donny saw what I was doing and squatted down beside me.

"What do you think he died from?" he asked quietly.

"I'm not sure, Donny. "It was probably a combination of a couple of things. I'd guess years of alcoholism and malnutrition, but I'll have to wait for the autopsy to know for certain."

"Maybe he stumbled off the embankment onto the rocks last night," Donny said in a voice still too high, and pointed to the whiskey bottle and then up to the embankment above. "He was loaded and it would have been pitch-black out here."

"I don't think so. He doesn't have any broken bones, and there's no bruising or marks on his body anywhere that I can see. I think he wandered in here, eventually fell asleep or fell unconscious, and then passed away," I said very sadly.

Donny's face looked utterly stricken.

"Are you okay?" I asked, when I saw his crimson face pale to a pasty gray, and feared he was going to be sick to his stomach.

He swallowed hard a couple of times and then shook his head.

I pointed to one of the smaller boulders just

behind him.

"Sit down there and put your head between your knees," I said gently.

"No, no. I'm okay."

"You sure?"

"I'm fine."

I nodded, and gave him another minute to compose himself.

"Feeling steadier?" I said, slowly rising to my feet.

Donny stood to his feet and nodded. His color seemed to be back.

"Good man," I said. "Why don't you secure the area while I take a look around."

"You got it," Donny said.

I stepped out of the boulders and saw that the crowd of motel guests had moved closer than I liked. Dennis Halton had his back to me and was talking quietly with the paramedics, so I reached over and touched him lightly on the arm.

"Dennis, would you ask your guests to go back inside their rooms and stay in them. A deputy will be up to speak with each one of them shortly. I'll need to talk to you too, and Pam, if she's around. And the beach will be closed for the rest of the day."

"Sure thing, Jake. We'll be in the office," Dennis said, and moved toward the group of onlookers.

I began meticulously searching the sand in the area around the boulders and found three sets of footprints. One looked to be about a size nine, and made by a steel-toed workboot. These shoeprints ended at the circle of boulders, and I knew they were Freddie's for he wore size nine, black, steel-toed, Kodiak workboots. The second set were large, a size twelve or thirteen, and were made by a bare foot, and went up to the boulders, and I knew these were the college kid's. It was the third set of shoeprints that interested me the most.

These were very large shoeprints and I'd guess they were made by the tread of a size sixteen or seventeen hiking shoe. I followed the shoeprints to an area just below the embankment. There were more here than anywhere else and they seemed to be clustered close together. They gave clear evidence that a man, and a very big man, had been standing next to the boulders below the bank for some time.

I rose to my feet and stood just behind the shoeprints, and faced where the man had been looking, and immediately a cold chill of alarm went up my spine. Whoever had been standing here had been looking at the cottages, and from where he stood, he had an unobstructed view of Kate LeRue's cottage. I could see that Kate's car was in the driveway, but all her windows were closed, and the curtains and blinds drawn. I figured today was her day off, and she must have taken Madeleine out for a walk in the stroller because the cottage seemed locked tight, and too quiet for anyone to be in there.

"Donny," I called out.

He jogged over to where I stood.

"We've got some shoeprints here that concern

me," I said, staring down at the cluster of shoeprints in the sand.

Donny looked down at the shoeprints, and then back up to the row of cottages with a deep frown on his young face.

"Looks like somebody was standing here for a long time and looking at the cottages," he said. "Peeping tom, you think?"

I shook my head. "No. I think I know who it was, and why he was standing here."

"You do?" Donny said, a look of puzzlement on his face.

I nodded grimly.

Donny frowned at the shoeprints for another couple of seconds, and then shook his head and walked away.

I walked back over to where Freddie lay again, and looked at him a moment and felt a wave of intense sorrow go through me at the thought of where he would spend eternity, and of the almost unbearable grief Agnes would now have to live with. Losing a loved one was hard enough, but losing a loved one who had never accepted Christ and was lost for eternity only compounded the pain. And any believer who had loved that one, plead unsuccessfully with that one to accept Christ, carried a large measure of needless and undeserved guilt for the rest of his or her days, no matter what anyone tried to tell them.

———————

An hour and a half later I pulled up in front of Agnes Leach's neat, blue bungalow on McAllen Avenue. It was an attractive, middle-class neighborhood, and was lined on both sides by modest bungalows that were shaded by large oaks and pines. The street was quiet, and I could see toys, tricycles, and skateboards lying deserted on the grassy lawns, and mountain bikes standing up against the garages of some of the homes.

I got out of the cruiser and stood there for a moment. It was almost six o'clock and I could smell the scent of meat cooking in the breeze as the families of these same homes in the comfortable neighborhood gathered around their supper tables. The aroma of fried chicken wafted out from Agnes's open windows, and although I normally loved fried chicken, right now my stomach was churning so much that the smell made me sick.

I walked up the brick sidewalk that led to her front door and knocked, praying God would give me words of comfort for Agnes that might ease her pain. The inner wooden door opened, and Agnes stood there on the other side of the screen door with a look of pleasant surprise on her face. She smiled and then glanced to the left, and then to the right of where I stood on her front steps, searching for Freddie at the same time as she dried her hands on a dishtowel.

How many times over my years as a police officer had I brought Freddie home to Agnes, I thought sadly, as I watched her eyes cut left and right again, a puzzled frown creasing her forehead. She smiled, reached out one hand to open the screen door, and I felt my heart sink like a stone.

Agnes was a tall, big-boned woman, who wore her thin, gray hair cut short, trimmed neatly around the ears and parted on the left side like a mans. She had hazel colored eyes like Freddie, the same thin, narrow nose and small mouth, and when she smiled it wasn't hard to tell they were siblings. But when she saw that Freddie wasn't with me, and then caught the grimness in my eye, and the expression on my face, her smile vanished and her eyes clouded over with fear and secret dread she had lived with for many years.

"Oh no, Jake, no," she whispered, her voice barely audible.

"May I come in, Agnes," I said very gently.

"No," she moaned, and began to shake her head slowly from side to side.

"Agnes," I said softly, at the same time despising this part of my job.

"It's Freddie, isn't it?" she said, almost under her breath.

"Yes. I'm afraid I have some bad news."

Her flew to her mouth, the dishtowel fell to the floor, she released the door with the other, and it too flew to her mouth. With both hands clasped over her mouth, and her hazel eyes welling up with tears, she began shaking her head no despairingly, and stepping back at the same time. I reached out and quickly caught the screen door before it shut in my face and then followed her inside the house with a considerably heavy heart.

227

CHAPTER 23

After they had eaten an early supper on Tuesday, Kate LeRue sat on the floor of the living room of her cottage at the Blue Spruce playing with her little girl. Every twenty seconds or so, Madeleine would hand her a toy of some kind, and then would squeal with laughter and immediately hold her hand out for Kate to give it right back to her. This had been going on for about ten minutes now, and it was pretty obvious to Kate that Madeleine loved this little game more than playing with any of the toys in the way the toy designer intended.

At any other time, Kate would be laughing right along with Madeleine, especially since it was her day off, and she could spend the entire day with her. But not on this day. She hadn't been laughing or smiling much since she had spoken to Jake Cole behind Gertie's yesterday.

She thought back to when he had walked into the diner late yesterday afternoon and slipped onto his usual stool, and she had taken his order. It was then that she noticed how much more at ease she was around him. She even had to admit that she was drawn to him, and although with his deep blue eyes, and finely chiseled features, he was a very unassumingly good-looking man, it was more than his looks she was attracted to. It was more that he had a gentle containment about him that she found appealing. In fact, she knew she was drawn by his entire manner, for she had noticed that they shared the same quiet, gentle natures.

But then, when her shift had ended and he had followed her out of the diner, and had started peppering her with questions, she realized that she had made a mistake for allowing herself to feel relaxed around him. And she had felt incredibly foolish for allowing herself to be attracted to him. She recalled how, when he had held that note in front of her face, all previous embarrassment had faded, and she was at once filled with a new emotion. Anger. Anger at losing her husband to a horrible disease, anger at witnessing a brutal murder, and then to add to her misery, anger at the seemingly inability of the court system to bring the murderer to trial. A hot anger at the unfairness of it all had surged through her, overcoming the cold fear she had at first experienced when Jake Cole told her that a man from Carlow was here in Leigh Falls looking for her.

Now as she sat in her cottage, the anger long dissipated, terror threatened once again to overwhelm her. She had answered Jake Cole's questions truthfully, for she didn't know anyone by the name of Wesley Roberts. But she was convinced of one thing. He had to be the same man who had sent the photo and the threatening note. A violent tremor ripped through her body at the thought of this man harming Madeleine, and her panic intensified so greatly, it was all she could do not to grab her daughter and bolt from the cottage and flee Leigh Falls.

She pressed her hand to her forehead and forced herself to calm down and think about her options. She figured she had three options. Number one was to immediately pack their things, jump in the car, and start running right now. Change their names and find another town or city to disappear in. Number two, she could simply drive over to the police department and tell Jake Cole the entire story from beginning to end. Admittedly, he was a good cop, and a good man, and no matter what else had happened she knew he only wanted to help her. But as good a cop as he was, she feared that in the end, there wasn't much he could do to help or protect them. She had no doubt that he would feel it was his duty as a police officer to send them back to Carlow and so, to protect her daughter's life, she decided she couldn't and wouldn't go to him. And that left option number three. Stay calm, pack their things, sit tight, and then leave Leigh Falls at first light.

She dropped her head into her hands, closed her eyes, and weighed that option. After a long couple of minutes she made up her mind. They would leave at daybreak. She would bath Madeleine and put her to bed early so that she would have a good night's sleep before they began another long journey. And while Madeleine slept she would quietly pack all their belongings, load them in the truck of the car, and be ready to leave first thing in the morning. And although this guy sounded like a giant compared to her five-foot four, slender frame, she knew that no one fought more desperately or fiercely than a mother protecting her young. If he came around the cottage tonight, she would fight to the death to protect Madeleine.

She rose from the floor, walked to the front and back doors and rechecked the locks. They were both locked and bolted securely. Then she did the same with all the windows in the cottage, and made sure every curtain and blind was closed. She had turned off the air conditioning unit in the living room window earlier because it was old and noisy, and she was afraid she wouldn't hear this guy if he tried to break in. She had found a small table fan in the closet by the back door, and she had set that on an end table in the living room so that it blew on Madeleine while she played. Later, she would move it into the bedroom next to the crib so she would be comfortable enough to sleep.

Surprisingly, the air in the cottage wasn't as suffocating as she had at first feared when she turned off the air conditioner, but she knew it would become uncomfortable by late tonight. She didn't know what else to do about that though, because she couldn't take a chance on this Roberts guy slipping in without her hearing him. If he tried to break into the cottage tonight she wanted to know it, and be ready for him. With that in mind, she stepped into the small kitchen, dragged a chair over to the door and jammed it under the doorknob. It fit snugly, so she dragged another chair to the back door and did the same, and then went back into the living room, and sat down on the floor next to Madeleine again.

The shriek of a siren pierced the air and startled her so much she leapt at once to her feet. She stood frozen on the spot, her heart pounding, and listened carefully. It sounded very close to the cottage. A few minutes after the first siren died away, she heard another siren, and then a third, and all cut off suddenly right outside her door.

She forced herself to move and went to the kitchen window, opened a slat of the mini-blind just a bit, and peered outside. She saw an ambulance and two police cars parked outside her door, and all three vehicles still had their lights swirling. Panic-stricken, she raced back into the living room, delicately scooped up Madeleine into her arms, hurried into the bedroom and sat her down in the crib. Madeleine's lip started quivering, so she ran back into the living room, scooped up some toys, raced back into the bedroom and gave them to her to keep her occupied for a couple of minutes, and than ran back to the kitchen window and peered out.

She saw two paramedics, deputies, and a small group of motel guests standing together talking

Karen V. Robichaud

down on the beach, and the realization that whatever was going on had nothing to do with her slowly hit home, and she let her breath out in little short puffs. But then the thought that someone might have had an accident, or worse yet, had drowned or taken a heart attack, sank in, and she was disgusted with the sense of selfish relief that had at first flowed through her. She closed her eyes and prayed a silent, heartfelt prayer for the victim and his or her family.

A few minutes later, she opened her eyes, and with two fingers moved the slat of the blind open a little wider for a better look, and caught sight of the Jake Cole standing with one of deputies on the sand below the sloped bank. She gasped involuntarily, let go of the mini-blind, and jumped back from the window when she saw that the sheriff had turned to face her cottage and seemed to be staring directly at her.

Madeleine was plaintively calling for her now, so she walked quickly back into the bedroom, lifted her up out of the crib, took her into the bathroom, and began running the water for her evening bath. As she sat on the edge of the bathtub, gently bouncing Madeleine on one knee, she could hear her heartbeat in her ears, and could see her pulse throbbing in her wrist.

CHAPTER 24

L ate Tuesday evening I stood on my deck staring at the black water that shimmered in the silvery moonlight as it flowed to shore. The balmy, evening breeze coming off the water gently rustled the branches of the trees around my house, and the waves broke softly on the beach below my lawn. Usually, I found nights like these had a soothing effect on me, but tonight I found no comfort in all this. I hadn't shaken the sorrow that filled me after holding Freddie's dead body in my arms, or the numbing shock of Harvey Newman's drowning, and the fact that the two deaths occurred only days apart wore me down heavily.

I didn't have didn't have the pathology reports back from the medical examiner's office yet, but I suspected that Freddie's body had simply given out from the years of alcohol abuse. And I strongly suspected that the large shoeprints on the beach below the embankment belonged to Wesley Roberts. I was certain that he had been standing below the bank watching Kate's cottage. I figured he either didn't care that his shoeprints were clearly evident on the sand, thinking that no one would notice them or think much of them, which no doubt would have been the case if it weren't for Freddie's body being discovered in the same area. The other possibility was that, being from the city, Roberts hadn't been aware of the tidewater line on the sand about twenty feet closer to the water from where his shoeprints were, or maybe just didn't see it on the dark beach, and didn't realize that the surf didn't reach that far up on the beach and his shoeprints wouldn't be washed away.

Thinking of Roberts sent a rush of cold fury up my spine, for I was certain that not too long after I had driven past his campsite last night, he had slipped into the woods behind the campground and hiked over to the motel. Once there, he had stood on the beach watching Kate's cottage, probably getting ready to break in. I had a solid hunch that Freddie, who had been known to frequent the motel's private beach when he was drinking, had stumbled into the area and scared Roberts away. The knowledge of what could have happened to Kate and Madeleine if Freddie hadn't surprised Roberts, caused my heart to beat erratically, and I realized that I should have anticipated much sooner than I had, that he might make his move on Kate.

I pressed the night light button on my watch and saw that it was almost midnight, so I went up the steps to the lawn, walked around the side of the house in the dark to the driveway and got in my cruiser. Ten minutes later I pulled up alongside Caleb's cruiser, which was parked in a grove of shrubs across the road from the entrance to the campground. From there he could see the gates clearly without being easily seen himself, and since the entrance was also the only exit by vehicle, if Roberts left in his Grand Am, Caleb couldn't miss him. I had Scott Moore positioned in the woods directly behind Robert's site, and Frank Peters and Owen Mitchell posted on the highway directly across from the Blue Spruce Motel staking out Kate's cottage. If Roberts tried to hike over to the motel through the twenty acres of boggy woodland that lay behind the campground I would know it. If he made any move at all, this time I would know it.

I put one hand on the roof of Caleb's car and leaned my head down in front of the open driver's side window.

"Any movement at all?"

"Not really," Caleb said, shaking his head. "He ate supper at Darcy's Restaurant and then drove straight back here. Scott just called and said Roberts is squatting down in front of his fire roasting wieners."

"The complete camper," I said caustically, and straightened up from the window and looked across the road to the lights of the campground. It was breezier tonight and the wind carried the combined odor of salt, campfire smoke, and meat grilling on someone's barbecue.

"Jake," Scott's deep voice came over the radio.

Caleb unhooked the mike and stretched the cord out through the open window to me.

I pushed the mike key in. "What do you have, Scott?"

"I heard movement in the woods directly behind Roberts's site, and I can't see him anywhere in his campsite."

"Take another look," I said.

"Will do."

Scott's voice came back over the radio thirty seconds later. "Campfire's still blazing, but I can't see him around."

"Maybe he went in the tent."

"Don't think so, Jake. He's got a bright light set up in there. I'd see his shadow on the wall of the tent if he was inside."

My heartbeat began to quicken in my chest.

"Jake, I just saw someone running through the woods in back of his tent," Scott said. "I couldn't see him clearly, but I saw the whites of his eyes, and then caught a glimpse of a tall, shadowy figure ducking down behind a tree. Looks like he's dressed all in black."

"What if it's not Roberts?" Caleb said.

"Oh, it's him, Caleb," I said tightly.

"Jake?" Scott said. "Want me to go after him?"

"Yes, but be very cautious, Scott. Stay back a safe distance," I said into the mike.

"He's heading east toward the motel. Boy, he moves fast. He's like a cat," Scott said, his breath coming fast with the adrenaline that was pumping through his body.

"Okay. Stay on him, but don't spook him. He's going after Mrs. LeRue and I want to catch him right in the act. Caleb and I will link up with Frank at the LeRue cottage. I want to be there when he comes out of the woods across from the motel. Stay on his tail and when he gets close to the motel, lay low and cover the rear until I give the signal we're going to take him down."

"Roger, out," Scott said.

Caleb had already started the engine and we were accelerating down the highway only about two seconds after I had handed him back the mike, jumped in his car, and closed the door behind me. Less than five minutes later we screeched to a stop behind Frank's cruiser. I could see Frank inside the car working the spotlight, while Owen Mitchell was standing at the shoulder of the road, his eyes following the shaft of light that was strafing the trees.

"Kill the light, Frank!" I yelled, as I opened the door and jumped out. "You and Caleb park the cruisers in the bush off the highway," I said, pointing down road to a secluded lane that led down to the beach and was thick on both sides with tall under-brush.

The light went out a second later, the engine started, and I stood beside Owen, and watched as Caleb and Frank drove down the highway about one hundred yards and then turned right onto a narrow lane. Not long after their taillights disappeared in the thick bush, they jogged back and joined Owen and me in a huddle at the edge of the highway.

"We're going to set up like a five pointed star," I said. "Frank, you take up a position on the beach behind Mrs. LeRue's cottage. Caleb, you take up a position between the LeRue cottage and the one beside it. Owen, you go north, across the road and into the woods and lay low. I'll be in that small patch of woods on the other side of the LeRue cottage. Scott's behind Roberts so we'll have all five sides covered. Let Roberts reach the cottage, and when he makes a move to break in, I'll give the signal and we'll take him down."

"Okay," Frank said, and sprinted across the road, past Kate's cottage, and down to the sandy beach.

Owen nodded and ran in the other direction, his police regulation shoes making soft thunking noises across the paved highway.

I jogged across the road behind Frank, went down the bank, leapt across the shallow ditch, and came up the other side without taking my eyes off the row of cottages. I could see that the lights were off in all the cottages, and although they were slightly shadowed by the trees around them, the moon was up and Kate had her outside porch light on, and I could see that her car was parked in the driveway and everything looked quiet.

"Scott," I said quietly, after I pulled my portable radio free from my belt as I continued running and keyed in the mike. "Where is he now?"

"About ten yards ahead of me, I think. The

woods are as black as coal, and he's incredibly fast and light-footed for such a big man," Scott said, his voice harsh and breathless with the exertion of running with a radio in his hand, and a heavy belt with gun, nightstick and handcuffs around his waist.

"How far is he from our position?"

"Seven to ten minutes if he keeps moving at this pace."

"Okay. Stay on him, but be careful," I said.

"Roger."

Caleb jogged along beside me until we reached the cottages, and then he veered right and vanished into the shadows between Kate's cottage and cottage number four. I moved as silently as possible into a stand of dense trees to the left of Kate's cottage. The branches of the evergreens scraped and scratched my bare arms, face and uniform, and made a swishing noise as they brushed against my leather gun belt. I hunkered down behind a thick oak and kept my eyes glued to the dark road above.

The sky was clear and filled with stars, and the moon was out and cast down a fair amount of light. The only sound to be heard was my fast breathing, the hum of nighttime insects buzzing and crickets chirring in the woods around me, and the unremitting surf breaking on the shore behind the cottages. Occasionally a car would pass on the road above, but otherwise, it was dead silent out here and time seemed to slow down so that the passing minutes seemed like hours.

"Jake," Scott's voice came over the radio.

"Go ahead."

"I think I spooked him," he said with despair.

I grimaced into the blackness of the woods.

"Are you sure?"

"Pretty sure," Scott said. "I stepped on a dead branch, and the sound ricocheted like a gunshot. Right after that I heard rustling in the woods behind me, and I saw a dark shape, but then it disappeared and the sound faded away to nothing."

"He's doubling back to the campground," I said, feeling sharply disappointed.

"I think so," Scott said.

"Listen, Scott. He may have heard you, and just holed up somewhere. Stay put, lay low and listen very carefully. We'll do the same here. Wait for thirty minutes, and after that, if you still don't hear anything, come out and link up with us here at the motel."

"Roger," Scott said.

"Caleb, Frank, Owen, same thing goes. Hold your positions for thirty minutes," I said into the radio.

Thirty minutes later Scott emerged from the trees across the road, and Owen stepped out from further down and joined him. They walked together across the field and came into sight on the Oceanside Road above my position. Caleb stepped out from the shadows of cottage number four, Frank moved up from the beach, and I walked out of the woods, and we all met on the shoulder of the dark road.

"Sorry, Jake. I blew it," Scott said, his voice full of disgust.

In the moonlight I could see that Scott's sandy

colored hair, face, and his uniform shirt were all soaked with perspiration.

"Don't worry about it," I told him.

"Caleb, let's go talk to Mrs. LeRue," I said. "After that we'll go visit Roberts."

Caleb nodded.

"Scott, Owen, you guys hunker down here and keep an eye on the treeline just in case he's still in there. Frank, go back down on the beach below the embankment and keep an eye on the beach and the front of the cottage."

Caleb and I walked around to the front of the LeRue cottage and went up the short steps to the deck. I knocked on the door and noticed that despite the heat of the night, all the windows were shut tight, the blinds and curtains were drawn, and the air conditioner that was set in a living room window wasn't running.

The air must be stifling in there, I thought, and then heard a noise from inside and saw the mini-blind go up on the window of the door, and Kate's ashen face peer out through the glass. I heard her opening the locks on the doors, and then she pulled the door open and faced me, looking frightened and wide-eyed.

"Good evening, Kate," I said.

"Jake," she said, her voice tremulous. "What's wrong?"

"May I come in?" I said.

"Why? What's going on?"

"Maybe I should take a look around outside," Caleb said quietly from behind me.

I nodded at him, and he backed off the step.

Kate frowned; her eyes following Caleb as he walked slowly across the lawn in front of the cottage with his flashlight trained on the windows.

"What's he doing?" she asked.

"He's just making sure all your windows and doors are secure."

"Why?"

There was a prowler in the area."

"A prowler?" she said, her voice faltering. "Where?"

"In the woods across the road."

She frowned at me.

I took a step, but she didn't move. "We think he was heading over here."

She thought about that for a moment.

"And you think it was this Roberts guy," she said, and then made a face as if to convey annoyance and disbelief, but to me she just looked scared to death.

"I do," I said softly.

She swallowed hard and fell silent.

"Kate, are you aware that a man by the name of Freddie Leach, was found dead today on the beach directly below your cottage?"

She tried to hide it, but I caught an expression of horror cross her face.

"Freddie? That homeless man that Gertie gives coffee to every morning?"

"Yes."

"What happened?"

"I think his heart just gave out from the years of

alcohol abuse."

"I am very sorry to hear that," she said softly. "But what does his death have to do with me, or with this prowler?"

"That's what I need to talk to you about. May I come in?"

"Yes, but please keep your voice down. Madeleine's sleeping," she said very quietly, and then opened the door and stepped back so that I could enter.

"Would you turn on the light, please?" I said just as quietly, when I stepped into the darkness and the almost unbearable heat in the cottage.

She reached over beside me to the wall and flicked the switch, and I instantly winced in the bright ceiling light. I saw that she was barefoot, and wearing cotton, blue summer pajamas, and she was trying to pull slippers on her feet, but her hands were shaking badly, and she was having a hard time getting them on. When she finally had that accomplished, she looked up and her eyes betrayed the fear that she was trying to keep hidden from me.

I saw a large knife on the kitchen counter with a dishtowel half covering it.

"That's a big knife, Kate," I said.

She just raised her chin a little.

"A guy that size wouldn't have any trouble taking that from you."

"Don't be so sure," she replied.

I closed my eyes for a second, took in a quiet breath, and then opened them again.

"It's suffocating in here," I said, noticing the

perspiration that covered her face ad neck. "Do you always keep all your windows closed in this kind of heat?"

"I'm a woman alone with a small child, and you just said there was a prowler around the area. How can you even ask me that?"

"I understand that, but they've been closed since five o-clock, Kate," I said, very quietly.

"It keeps the sunlight out and the cottage stays cooler," she said, lowering her voice so much it was almost inaudible.

"I don't think it's working," I said.

She glared at me, crossed her arms over her chest, raised her chin a little more, and tried to appear defiant, and her whole body trembled with the effort. Standing there in her pajamas she looked so small, so vulnerable, that I found it almost unbearable to watch, and I had to avert my gaze from her face.

"This can't be good for Madeleine," I murmured, glancing over my left shoulder to try to see into the darkened living room. "I thought all these cottages had air conditioning. Is yours broken?"

"That's none of your business."

I took in more air, and then exhaled slowly through my nose.

"Were you home all day?" I said after a while.

"Yes."

"I knocked at your door four different times today between five-thirty and seven o'clock. Why didn't you answer?"

"I was napping."

"There was a great deal of noise. Ambulance and police sirens," I said, raising my eyebrows.

"I'm a very heavy sleeper."

"Apparently," I said.

"I didn't say I slept through the sirens," she bristled. "I did hear them, and I looked out and saw the ambulance and police cars. I was afraid someone had drowned, but after I put Madeleine to bed, I felt so exhausted I laid down, and fell asleep immediately. I'm sorry, but I must have slept right through the knocking."

I nodded. "Kate, we found shoeprints on the beach in the area close to where Freddie's body was discovered. From the pattern on the sand, it looks as though someone was standing below the embankment sometime late last night watching your cottage. Freddie must have stumbled onto the beach and scared him away. I think the same guy was on his way here tonight."

She took a breath and shuddered a little.

"Kate, why is this guy after you? Tell me what's going on."

"You don't even know for certain he was after me," she said, but didn't really sound like she believed her own words.

"Think of Madeleine for goodness sakes," I said in exasperation.

"I am," she shot back hotly, color rising in her cheeks.

I looked at her.

She averted her eyes to the floor, but then looked up quickly when a murmur and then a rustling noise came from the bedroom.

"Madeleine's waking up. Please go now, Jake," she implored, quietly, despairingly.

Caleb knocked quietly on the door, opened it, and stepped inside the small kitchen. I noticed the curious expression on his face, and knew that he had overheard us talking for some time before he decided to come in. He nodded at Kate, but when he noticed she was dressed in pajamas, he seemed suddenly shy and embarrassed and dropped his eyes to the floor.

I pulled my card from my shirt pocket and held it out to her.

"Take my card, Kate. My office, cell, and home phone numbers are all on it. If you need help, call anytime, day or night."

"I won't need help," she said, and shook her head.

"Take it, please, Kate," I urged softly, and after a couple of seconds, she slowly unfolded her arms and took the card.

"Good night then," I said quietly.

"Good night," she said softly.

I turned and nodded to Caleb that we were leaving, and then stepped out through the kitchen door, and Kate closed the door so fast behind us that it whacked the heel of Caleb's left shoe as he followed me out. In the cruiser Caleb stared at the cottage while he slowly shook his head.

"I don't understand her at all. One minute she doesn't want any help, then she takes your card like she does, and then she turns right around and slams the door so fast behind me that she almost takes my shoe right off."

"She's in trouble, Caleb," I said.

He turned his head and studied me quietly for a moment.

"Is there something going on between you two?" he asked.

"No," I said.

"I didn't realize you were on a first name basis with her."

"We've talked a few times. At Gertie's mostly," I said, and heard a catch in my voice.

He considered that while he continued studying my face.

"You like her."

I didn't say anything right away. Truthfully, I could not remember ever feeling this way about a woman before. When I wasn't near her, I thought of her constantly, and then when I was in her presence, I could barely contain my emotions, for she stirred my heart in a way that no woman ever had. I realized with astonishment that I was entirely captivated by her.

I looked at him.

"Caleb, I think I'm in love with her."

He smiled a little bit.

"I can't let anything happen to her or Madeleine."

"Then why don't we pray right now and ask God's protection over them."

I smiled and nodded at him.

Five minutes later, we drove back to the Seashore Campground, sped down the dirt lane to the back, and parked across from Roberts's campsite. He was standing in front of the campfire, dressed in black sweat pants and black Nike hiking shoes, but he wasn't wearing a shirt, and his thick chest was bare and slick with sweat. He looked up from the fire, turned around and saw us, and took two steps toward us. Caleb hit him square in the eyes with his flashlight, and he stopped, frozen on the spot, squinting into the harsh light. Caleb strafed the beam of his flashlight up and down Roberts's body, lingering on his face that glistened with perspiration in the bright light. In the glare of the flashlight his eyes seemed to have a strange icy glint.

"Back from your moonlight stroll, Roberts?" I said, stepping to within inches of his face.

"I don't know what you're talking about," he said coolly, and then turned his back and faced the fire again.

"Turn around," I ordered.

When he did, he was grinning contemptuously.

"What's your problem?"

"Where were you about thirty minutes ago?"

He shrugged, and his shoulder muscles rippled in the firelight.

"I was jogging. You mean to tell me a guy can't even go for a run in this town without being hassled by the cops?"

"We tend to get a little concerned when that guy is dressed all in black, and is sneaking around in the woods at one-thirty in the morning," I said.

He raised his wrist, glanced casually at his watch in the light from the fire, and then cleared his throat loudly. "I didn't realize it was so late, but it doesn't really matter since there's no law against jogging at night. Besides, I wasn't even in the woods. I was running along the highway."

"No you weren't," I said.

"Prove it," he said, his mouth set in a sneering line.

I watched him silently for a time.

"What size shoe do you wear, Roberts?" I said, and Caleb shined his flashlight down on Roberts's hiking shoes.

"None of your business."

They were at least a sixteen or seventeen, I thought.

"Mind if I look in your tent?"

"I most certainly do," he said, and cleared his throat again.

"You wouldn't pop your trunk for me, would you?"

"I don't think so."

Roberts took a step closer to me, his lips clamped together and his solid body tensed aggressively as he clenched and unclenched his fists.

"You listen to me, sheriff," he said chillingly. "You don't have any proof that I've done anything more than go for a moonlight run. So, you either arrest me right now, or get out of here before I file a complaint against you for harassment."

I took a step closer to him, and with our faces only inches apart, I glared at him with an anger that smoldered in my eyes.

"And you listen to me, Roberts," I said, my voice

carrying a hard edge. "You are not going to harm Kate LeRue or her daughter. What is going to happen is that I am going to lock you up. Maybe not tonight, but very soon. Do you understand me?"

I tore my eyes from him and glanced at Caleb to let him know we were leaving, and saw that his slender body was rigid as he eyed Roberts. I could understand how he felt because I was so angry myself that my entire body felt like it was on fire. I knew we could try to charge him with prowling at night, but I didn't think it would stick for there was no law against standing on a beach looking at cottages, and as far tonight went, we had no real proof it was even him in the woods. I was sure that after one phone call to a lawyer, he'd be out in less than an hour.

I touched Caleb's arm lightly, and he finally, reluctantly, tore his eyes from Roberts's sneering face, dropped the beam of the flashlight to the ground and we walked out of the site.

"I am having some decidedly unchristian thoughts about what I would like to do to that guy," Caleb muttered.

"Me too, Caleb, me too," I said.

I didn't need to turn around to know that Roberts was watching us, for I could feel his icy eyes drilling our backs as we walked to the cruiser.

CHAPTER 25

The man with the glacial blue eyes slammed down the receiver with such force it bounced right back up into the air, and then ricocheted repeatedly from side to side off the glass walled phone booth. He stormed out of the booth, got back in his car, accelerated down the dirt lane to his campsite, pulled in the short driveway, shut off the engine, and then sat in the car until the lethal rage that burned in him diminished enough that he could think more clearly.

He didn't like rich people, and he particularly didn't like arrogant, rich people who spoke with undisguised contempt to those they considered of low class. And Richard Strang, with his smug insolence, his superior affection, had just proven to be one of those people.

After a few minutes, he had calmed down enough that he was able to force Strang from his mind. He got out of the car and strode quickly to his tent and went inside. Much too tall for the tent, he hunched down on his sleeping bag and thought everything over.

He could see clearly now that this job had gone sour right front the start. Right from the very second Sheriff Cole, who very surprisingly had the sharp instincts of a big city cop instead of the small-town sheriff he was, had locked eyes with him in the coffee shop. And then late last night, as he crept through the woods on his way to try once again to break into the LeRue cottage, he had heard and then seen the young deputy trailing him, and had to turn around and go back to the campsite, only to have the sheriff and his deputy show up not more than fifteen minutes later. And from the way the sheriff spoke to him, asking him what shoe size he wore, he knew the sheriff was fully aware that he had been standing on the motel's beach watching the LeRue cottage the night before. He had no doubt at all that the sheriff would be back for him, and very soon.

He understood clearly now that he had made several critical errors. Not only had he underestimated the sheriff, but when he had seen that pathetic drunk staggering toward him, calling out to him in a slurred voice, he had foolishly put off breaking into the LeRue cottage. He could see now that he should have just waited for the drunk to leave or pass out on the beach, and then he could have gone ahead and completed the job. But he had sensed that there was someone else on the beach besides the drunk, and he had panicked and gone back to his campsite. Too late, he now realized he had made a critical error. He had assumed the tide would wash away his shoeprints, but in his haste to leave the beach, he had miscalculated the tidewater line, and now the sheriff had found his shoeprints below the embankment, and knew he had been watching the LeRue cottage and why he was here in Leigh Falls. And that fact alone would make it very hard for him to complete this assignment.

Rage flamed through him once again at the uncharacteristic mistakes he had made.

But what really rankled him was that his biggest mistake of them all was to have accepted this job in the first place. He should have stuck with what he knew, and what he knew was the city, and not the hick, seaside town of Leigh Falls, Maine.

Yet, despite the fact the sheriff and his deputies were watching him constantly, and there was a serious risk he might be caught, there were two reasons why he had no other choice but to go ahead and finish this job. The first was that he always insisted on being paid half his fee up front for a job, and he had already received that payment from Strang. In fact, he had already spent some of it on the car rental, gas, and camping gear.

The second reason was that he was more than aware that Richard Strang had the power to ruin his reputation if he backed out now, and that was exactly what the pompous fool had just threatened to do when they spoke on the phone. The tall man clenched his fists and gritted his teeth at the thought of either of those things occurring, for he knew if it did, he would never work again. And he could not allow that to happen, for he deeply enjoyed his work.

CHAPTER 26

At seven o'clock on Wednesday morning I was in my office waiting impatiently for a phone call from Sheriff Ned Casey with some information on Roberts. At fifteen past seven the phone ran out.

"Sheriff Cole," I said into the receiver, after I had quickly crossed the room to my desk and snatched it up.

"What did you say to Kate?" said a very grumpy sounding voice.

"Gertie?"

"What did you say to Kate?"

I paused and rubbed my forehead with the fingers of my left hand.

"What's wrong, Gertie?"

"Kate called me from the motel office a few minutes ago. She's not coming in to work today. She sounded really upset. Did you say something to her?"

"What?" I said.

"I saw you follow her out of the diner when she got off work yesterday. What did you say to her?"

"Nothing, Gertie. Look, I really need to get off the line. I'm expecting an important phone call."

"Well, excuse me," she said.

"Gertie," I said, and couldn't keep the exasperation from my voice.

She was silent for a few seconds.

"Does this phone call have something to do with Kate?"

"Yes."

"I knew it. I've seen the way you look at her. You're worried about her, aren't you?" she said, and then added softly. "I'm worried about her too, Jake."

"I know. I know," I said more kindly. "I can't say what's going on, Gertie. But I promise you I won't let anything happen to her or Madeleine. And if it will make you feel better, I'll go over there just as soon as I can and check on them."

"Good," she said. "And Jake?"

"What?"

"Lose the grumpy voice first," she grunted, and hung up in my ear.

Not five minutes later, the phone rang again.

"Sheriff Cole," I said.

"Good morning, Jake," said a soft southern voice over the line. "This is Ned Casey."

My pulse took off. "Good morning, Ned."

"Sorry to be so long in calling you back," he said with his warm drawl. "I had a nasty double murder up here that needed my complete attention. Just got a chance to take a breather now."

"I understand."

"Well, I have some information for you in regard to your visitor from Georgia."

"Great. What do you have?"

"I wasn't getting anywhere with his photo until today when I showed it to two of my deputies who had been out for the last two weeks. One was on vacation and the other on short-term disability. They just came back on shift this morning, took one look at it, and they both identified him at once as Wesley Garth Robisen, not Wesley Gary Roberts."

"So he's using a phony driver's license and ID."

"Yes. We think he's using the identification of a man who died three years ago here in Carlow. It happens a lot with guys like Robisen. They go down to the motor vehicle department and get a driver's license with their photo, but use the dead guy's name and birth date."

"That explains why there was no sheet on Wesley Roberts."

"Yes, it does. But, this Wesley Robisen has a very long sheet. Assault and batteries, extortion, break and enters, just to name a few. These two deputies tell me that he used to work for a well-known loan shark here in Carlow, and is a strong suspect in a vicious assault that they think was linked to this loan shark. Apparently, the victim was a forty-year old married man who was rumored to be heavily in debt to this loan shark, fell behind in his payments, and somebody tossed a pail of battery acid in his face. These two deputies were working the case, and when they interviewed the victim, he named Robisen as the man who threw the acid. But before my men could pick him up, the victim changed his mind. He said he didn't get a good look at the man after all."

"And now Robisen's here in Leigh Falls," I said, closing my eyes and massaging my forehead with my free hand.

"Yes, I'm afraid so."

I opened my eyes again. "I think he was down on the beach below Mrs. LeRue's cottage Monday night watching her cottage, maybe even getting ready to break in. I found what I am certain are his shoeprints on the sand below the cottages. But someone else was on the beach, and I think Robisen saw or heard this person, panicked, and left. He tried to go back again last night, but I had a deputy tailing him in the woods, but I think Robisen heard him, got spooked and doubled back to his campsite."

"Sounds like he's been busy."

"Yes he has. Listen, Ned, did Kate LeRue's husband owe money to this loan shark?"

"No, that's not the reason why Robisen is in Leigh Falls. Although, I admit it was my first thought too. My men tell me that Robisen and this loan shark had a falling out a couple of months ago. Rumor on the street is that he is hiring out to anyone who wants his services. This is very likely his first job."

I was silent for a time.

"So who and why has someone hired him to come after Kate LeRue and her daughter?" I asked.

Ned Casey exhaled heavily before speaking.

"Mrs. LeRue is an eyewitness to a murder of a convenience store owner here in Carlow that took place eleven months ago. I have the report in my hand right now. Do you want me to read it to you?"

"Go ahead," I said quietly.

"All right. Let me see, ah, it reads that on the night of May 18th, of last year, Mrs. LeRue witnessed the grisly murder of a convenience storeowner, a man in his early sixties by the name of Harry Morganstein. Apparently she opened the door while the robbery was in progress, and had taken one step inside when the robber shot the store owner. She was only ten feet away and saw the whole thing."

I dropped down into my chair, utterly staggered by what he had said.

"Tough thing for anyone to witness, let alone this lady, because she had just lost her husband to cancer not very long before the murder. Says here his name was Kent LeRue, he was thirty-five years old, and worked for a big computer company here in Carlow."

Oh, Kate, I said to myself, my heart filled with sadness for her.

"Who was the shooter?" I asked.

"A twenty-five-year-old drug addict from Carlow by the name of Clinton Strang. He had robbed a gas station down the street only an hour before he walked into the convenience store. After the shooting, Mrs. LeRue was able to run out of the store, got in her car, and drove straight here to the department. Strang was picked up that same night, so high on drugs that he had no recollection at all of either robbery or of the shooting. He still claims he can't remember anything about that night, and that's probably true because my men tell me his brain's been fried by drugs for a long time now. Anyway, he denied it all, and they didn't find much at the scene to prove he was the shooter, but with Mrs. LeRue's eyewitness testimony, they have him for it."

"So the Strangs hired Robisen."

"We think the father, Richard Strang, hired him."

"But you said the murder happened almost a year ago. Why did she decide to run now after all that time?" I said quietly into the receiver.

"Well, that's the thing. Clinton Strang is from a local, very well to do family here in Carlow. Their roots go way back, all the way back to being one of the first families to settle in Carlow. Clinton is the only child, the only son in the family, and his father, Richard Harris Strang is a very, wealthy man. He has lots of money to throw around. And he wasted no time in throwing a truckload of it at a shady lawyer by the name of Lester Bowden. Bowden, who is of worse character than either Clinton or Richard Strang, has succeeded in having the case delayed on one legal technicality after another. It's been dragging on for almost a year now. But, here's the kicker. Lester Bowden has run out of reasons, and the trial is scheduled to begin in less than three weeks. And as you can imagine, the D.A. up here has been going crazy trying to locate Mrs. LeRue."

I didn't dare speak for my heart was so heavy with incredible sadness for Kate I knew my voice would betray my emotions. I turned my head and stared silently out the window to the glistening water of the harbor.

"My detectives tell me Robisen is an extremely cruel and violent man," Sheriff Casey continued. "When he worked for this loan-shark he had a reputation for being very careful."

"That would explain why he has taken his time to scout out the town."

"Be my guess. He probably figured he could blend in with the tourists and get to know the town without drawing any attention. Maybe in another small town it would have worked perfectly for him. One thing he didn't count on was you. Sounds like you keep a very close eye on things in Leigh Falls."

"I try to."

"Good thing you do, Jake. You noticing him so quickly must have thrown him off and he got careless. He considers himself a professional, but he's relatively new at working on his own, and he's still an amateur. It would be nice if you could lock him up for a long time so he doesn't have the opportunity to become a professional."

"I'll do my best," I said firmly. "I have two deputies watching him as we speak, one at his campground, and another watching Mrs. LeRue's cottage. If he tries anything at all, we'll get him."

"Good. There's one more thing. The district

attorney down here has requested that you pick up Mrs. LeRue at once, and hold her for him until he can make arrangements to have her escorted back to Carlow."

My heart plummeted. "All right," I said, without any enthusiasm. "And Robisen?"

"He's all yours."

There was silence over the line for a short time.

"Are you a Christian man, Jake?"

"I am."

"I sensed you might be," he said with a soft drawl. "I've known the Lord personally for over thirty years now, and I've been a cop for almost that long. I think you know what I mean when I say that at times like this I do realize how your faith can feel more like a hindrance than a help. But it has been my experience that it is only the grace and strength of Jesus Christ that has kept me, and continues to keep me, from doing something to a guy like Robisen that I would only live to regret."

"I understand," I said, with a faint smile, for I was having some vile thoughts about what I would do to Robisen when I found him.

"Will you do me a favor, Jake? The D.A.'s really breathing down my neck on this. Would you give me a call as soon as you have Mrs. LeRue in your custody?"

"I will."

"I'd better let you get to it then. I'll be praying for you."

"Thank you, Ned," I said, and hung up.

I walked across my office to the coat rack,

grabbed my gun belt and strapped it on as I went down the stairs and headed for the door.

"Marney! Where's Caleb?" I said, and at the same time saw young Riley Shaw sitting in wooden chair by her desk.

She looked up from her computer screen and blinked twice before replying. "He's at a fender bender on Craig Street. Why?"

"Get Jack over there to replace him, and tell Caleb to meet me at the Blue Spruce Motel," I said.

"I will, but hold on a minute. Riley wants to talk to you," she said, pointing with her index finger to the skinny, brown-haired youth dressed in oversize blue jeans, a black T-shirt, and a black Nike ball hat worn backwards, who sat slumped in the chair.

"Riley, I was just on my way out. Can this wait?" I said, turning my head to the right to glance at him as I strode swiftly to the door.

He shrugged carelessly, but his facial expression was screaming no at the same time.

I paused, mid-stride, and turned all the way around to look at him.

Marney caught my eye. "I think he has something important to tell you, Jake."

"Okay, come on up, Riley," I said, and started back up the stairs to my office.

He followed me into the office, sat down in the chair across from my desk and began chewing nervously on a thumbnail.

I decided not to sit behind my desk and make him more nervous, so I dragged an extra chair from the corner of the room over next to his and sat down.

"So, what did you want to tell me?" I said.

"You're not going to like it," he said, his emerald green eyes darting around the room, landing for all of two seconds on everything but me.

"Why don't you tell me anyway," I said kindly.

He looked at me for a couple of seconds, and then took in a breath before he spoke.

"Uh, on Monday night I was on the beach near the Blue Spruce Motel with Clayton," he mumbled, staring somewhere beyond my shoulder.

"What time was this?" I asked.

"We got there at eleven, and we left, at, like, one in the morning," he said.

I nodded, my pulse accelerating as I watched him. He had been close to the area where Robisen had been lurking."

"We were um, well, we were, you know.." he said, before his voice trailed off.

I knew. I nodded for him to continue.

"Are you ticked off at me?" he said.

"A little disappointed maybe, but not angry," I said mildly.

"Are you going to tell my mom?"

"We'll talk about what you were doing down there another time. And I mean that, Riley," I said firmly. "We are going to talk about it. But, right now I really need you to tell me what you saw."

"Well, Clayton lives on Shore Street, and I live on Barrett, so we didn't walk home together. You see, we weren't on the motel's private beach, we were farther down, and so it was shorter for me to cut across the motel's parking lot up to the road and walk home from there. Saves me about ten minutes."

I nodded.

"Um, anyway, it was really hot out that night, so I took off my shoes and socks and walked along the edge of the water. I was almost at the motel, like, right down below the cottages, when I, ah, I saw," he said, and then stopped.

"Go on, Riley," I prodded gently.

He gulped in a huge lung full of air and then looked me in the eye and went on with his story.

"I saw someone standing over by the seawall just below the cottages. I thought it might be Mr. Halton and he'd, you know, freak because I was on his property, so I laid flat down on the wet sand, kind of half in the water and half out. The moon was almost full, so I could see pretty good, and it wasn't Mr. Halton. It was a tall man and he was standing like, right below the embankment, and he was watching the cottages. He stood there a long time staring at the cottages, like some kind of pervert or something. Anyway, then Freddie Leach came stumbling up the beach, and he was talking to himself, you know, like he used to, laughing and everything. I watched him go over by the seawall, and he went behind some boulders and I couldn't see him anymore, but I could still hear him. He was singing real loud. I think he scared the creep watching the cottages, because as soon as Freddie was out of sight behind the boulders, he started walking down the beach really fast. I slipped into the water and stayed there until I was sure he was gone."

"Can you describe the man?"

"I couldn't see his face real good, but I could see that he had a goatee, and long dark hair, and he had his hair tied back in a pony tail, and he was dressed all in black. And he was really tall, and big," Riley said, his eyes going wide. "Bigger than some of the wrestlers on the WWF."

CHAPTER 27

Two minutes later I went out through the doors of the department to the parking lot, jumped in my cruiser and accelerated hard out of the lot and screeched onto Ash Street.

On the way over, I called Owen, who was sitting in his cruiser outside the Seashore Campground, and when he didn't reply, I tried Frank next, who was in his cruiser directly across from Kate's cottage. But he didn't answer my call either. With my blood turning to ice-water in my veins, I called Caleb next, reached him, and quickly filled him in on everything, especially the distressing news that two excellent police officers were not answering their radios.

With more than a little uneasiness, I called Marney back at the department and told her to send Donny Bernard over to the Seashore Campground right away to check on Owen. Frank and Owen, like

Caleb, Scott and myself were working double shifts and were probably exhausted, but I knew that wasn't the reason why they weren't responding to my calls. I was convinced that something very bad had happened to them. I hit the siren and lights, and with a deep sense of foreboding, sped along the Oceanside Road to the motel while I continued to try to raise Owen and Frank on the radio.

A couple of minutes later I veered off the highway into the motel's parking lot, and sped down the lane to the cottages. I spotted Frank's cruiser parked under the shade of an oak tree across from the LeRue cottage. I couldn't see Frank in the cruiser, Kate's car wasn't in her driveway, and the cottage looked quiet and deserted. An image of Robisen harming Kate and Madeleine filled my mind and my pulse suddenly took off, and my heart began catapulting wildly in my chest. I could hear my heartbeat drumming in my ears, and I had to suppress the image and breathe through my nose until my pulse evened out some. I pulled in behind Frank's cruiser, jammed on the brake and shoved the gearshift in park before the car had even rolled to a complete stop. I threw open the door, vaulted out and ran over to the cruiser.

The engine wasn't running, the driver's side window was down, and Frank was lying across the front seat. Blood was pouring out from a gash in his head, and was streaming across his face and down over the seat, and pooling on the floor of the car. I heard the roar of an engine, glanced sideways and saw Caleb's cruiser speeding down the lane toward the cottage.

I yanked open the door and leaned in over Frank.
"Frank!" I yelled into his face.

His eyelids fluttered a few times.

"Frank," I called again.

Frank opened his eyes, blinked rapidly and began to moan.

"Jake," he said weakly, and tried to sit up.

Caleb leaned in beside me.

"Give me a hand with him," I said, putting my hands around Frank's arm.

Frank was a big man, about six feet tall, and over two hundred pounds, and it took both of us to lift him out of the car and gently lay him on the ground.

"Call an ambulance, and get the first-aid kit from the trunk," I said to Caleb.

Caleb stood up and leaned back inside Frank's cruiser and called for an ambulance. I heard him talking to Marney after that, and then he got the first-aid kit from the trunk and hunched down beside me.

"Ambulance is on the way," he said. "And I just spoke to Marney. Donny found Owen unconscious in his cruiser. Looks like someone whacked him in the head pretty good too."

"Someone by the name of Wesley Robisen," I said, clenching my teeth so hard my jaw ached.

"Is Frank okay?" Caleb asked.

"I think so. He's got a lump the size of a plum, and a deep laceration, but he seems to be fairly lucid," I said, taking a thick bandage from the kit.

"Jake," Frank said hoarsely, reaching one hand up to touch his bloodied head.

"Ambulance is on the way, Frank," I assured him, and moved his hand aside gently and then held the bandage against the wound. Like all head wounds it was bleeding profusely and soaked through the bandage in no time.

"I don't need an ambulance. I'm just a bit dizzy. Let me sit up," he said.

"Hold this tight for me, Caleb," I said, eyeing Kate's empty driveway and quiet cottage. *Where is she?* I thought, my heart jackhammering in my chest. "I need to check inside the cottage."

"Jake, what's going on?" Pam Holland hooted out as she ambled down the road toward us with two curious motel guests tagging along behind her. "Oh my goodness, what happened to Frank?"

The doors to two of the other cottages opened, and more motel guests stepped out onto the lane and inched toward us.

"People, stay back," I ordered. "Pam, would you get us a couple of towels, please."

She nodded and hurried into the nearest cottage with one of the female guests.

Frank groaned and moved around on the ground. His white uniform shirt was stained bright red with his blood.

"Jake, it was Roberts," he croaked, unaware of Roberts's real identity. "He just seemed to come out of nowhere. I caught a glimpse of him in the sideview mirror sneaking up along the side of the cruiser with a length of steel pipe in his hand, but before I could react, he bashed me in the side of the head with it. He must have hidden his car down the road and sneaked up on me. He moves like a snake."

"Frank, did you see Mrs. LeRue leave?" I asked.

"Yes," he said with a nod, and then winced at the pain that brought. "That's what distracted me in the first place. She came out of the cottage with her little girl, and got in her car just a few minutes before he belted me. I was watching her back up out of the driveway and was going to follow her, when I glimpsed movement from the corner of my eye. Next thing I knew, a giant of a man was standing at my window swinging a pipe. That was it. I know she was driving away, but I think he must have gone right after her."

I felt my body sway a little with a sickening fear.

A siren's wail sounded in the distance, and before long an ambulance turned off the Oceanside Road and sped down the narrow lane toward us. Thirty seconds later two EMT's were working on Frank.

"Okay, Caleb, let's go!" I shouted and ran to my cruiser.

Caleb nodded, head down, watching the ground as he ran alongside me.

I hauled open the door of my cruiser and slid quickly behind the wheel of my cruiser. "They don't have that much of a jump on us and there's only two roads that lead out of town. I think we can still catch them. I'll take the Drummond Cliff Road and you take the Salmon Creek Road. Call Donny, fill him in on everything, and have him link up with you there, and I'll call Eric and have him link up with me."

"Okay," Caleb said, his face tight.

"Both of those roads end at the intersection of Route 11 and 14. If neither one of us finds them before we hit that intersection, we'll join up there. But, Caleb, if you and Donny spot Robisen before you reach the intersection, be very cautious when you take him down. He's dangerous and extremely violent."

"Got it," Caleb said, moved away from my window, sprinted to his cruiser and climbed in.

I quickly backed up; Caleb did the same behind me, and we both accelerated away so fast that the rear end of our cruisers fishtailed wildly on the asphalt. I turned right and headed out of town, screaming past cars and RV's that hogged the road like huge blimps. I called Eric and filled him in and told him to meet me on the Drummond Cliff Road. I gritted my teeth at the sound of his groggy voice, certain I had caught him sleeping on shift again. I didn't have time to deal with him now though, so I pushed it out of my mind.

I held the gas pedal down, raced through town, and in short time was on the Drummond Cliff Road and climbing up the steep hill. I crested the top of the cliff, and then came down the long hill to the bottom hoping and praying to see either Kate or Robisen's cars. To my dismay, other than a one ton truck, and a Ford station wagon towing a travel trailer, the road was empty.

They must be moving at an incredibly fast clip, I thought, gunned the engine, and watched the speedometer climb past ninety miles an hour as

I came down to the bottom of the hill. I maintained that speed, and in less than five minutes screeched to a stop at the two-way intersection at the end of the Drummond Cliff and Salmon Creek Roads.

I leaned over the steering wheel and craned my head to the right and then to the left. Route 11, left, led to the town of Linden and joined on to the main highway that would lead Kate back to Georgia, and Route 14, to the right, led up to the main highway that would take her to Canada. Eric was less than a minute behind me, and Caleb, who had linked up with Donny on the Salmon Creek Road, was about two minutes away from the intersection. So far, they hadn't seen either Kate or Robisen's vehicle.

I thought for a second and then called Caleb, told him I was going to head down Route 14, and when they got to the intersection, he and Donny were to take Route 11 and continue their search. I called Marney and told her to call in the night shift deputies, and have them set up roadblocks at the two entrances to town in the event that Robisen headed back there, although I didn't think it was very likely.

That done, I whipped the steering wheel to the right and stomped on the gas, the tires squealing in protest and leaving a long black mark behind me on the highway. I bore down on the gas pedal until the speedometer moved to ninety again, and the pine trees that lined both sides of the road were just a green blur rushing past the windows. I had my driver's and passenger side windows rolled down all the way, and the morning air blasting in smelled of the mingled scent of pine and salt

When the odometer clicked ten more miles, my breath suddenly caught in my throat. I could see Kate's Malibu moving up ahead with Robisen's black Grand Am following closely behind. Despite the gust of cool air whipping into the car, as I took in the scene before me, sweat broke out on my forehead and lower back. As I drew closer I could see the top of Madeleine's head slanted sideways in the car seat, and realized that she was sleeping. I saw Kate's dark hair lifting in the wind that whipped inside through the open driver's window of her car, and had to inhale deeply to steady my nerves.

I steered with one hand, unhooked the mike and pressed the key in with the other and called Caleb and Donny to tell them to turn around and head this way immediately.

"Jake, we're five or six minutes away," Caleb said, sounding worried.

"Try to make it faster," I said. "We're climbing Hope Hill now, and Stanton's Bluff is dead ahead. I think Robisen's going to try to force her car over one of them."

"Four minutes," Caleb said, and I knew he was going to hold the pedal to the floor all the way here.

Where's Eric? I thought, glancing into the rearview mirror.

With my heartbeat climbing much higher than my speedometer, I prayed a fervent, silent, prayer to God for his protection over Kate and Madeleine.

At this high rate of speed, even without a direct hit from Robisen's car, I feared Kate might lose control of her car and they would never survive the crash.

As the two cars reached the top of Hope Hill and began descending down the other side I lost sight of them for a couple of panic-filled seconds. Still praying, I pressed the gas pedal all the way to the floor and held it there. As I came over the top of the hill I saw that the distance between Robisen's vehicle and my cruiser was now less than three hundred yards and closing fast. I moved within a couple feet of Robisen's bumper, and saw him glance up into his rearview mirror at me, and then he grinned icily. He was so dangerously close to Kate's bumper my stomach felt like a fist was clenched in it, for I knew that even if she made it to the bottom of Hope Hill without him hitting her and shoving her over the edge, Stanton's Bluff was just ahead.

CHAPTER 28

Kate's mind reeled with terror, and she was afraid she was going to be violently sick to her stomach. She swallowed a couple of times, forcing the bile back down, while keeping her white-knuckled hands locked tightly on the steering wheel. She risked a quick glance into the rearview mirror and saw that the driver of the black car had moved to within inches of her rear bumper, and she feared he was going to smash into them any second now.

After another moment, she risked looking into the mirror to see into the back where Madeleine slept in her car seat, and could have wept as she glanced at her precious daughter. If only she could have gotten away sooner. Even after Jake Cole and his deputy had left the cottage last night, her plan, which was to be on the road before first light, and cross the border at Calais, Maine into St. Stephen,

New Brunswick sometime around noon, hadn't changed.

She had been all ready to leave, had been since five o'clock when she had bathed Madeleine, put her to bed early, and then quietly packed and loaded the suitcases in the trunk of the car which was parked in the back of the cottage, and was out of sight of Jake Cole and his deputies, who were down on the beach.

And she hadn't been lying when she told Jake that she had been asleep when he had knocked at the door to the cottage shortly after five-thirty. She had been so emotionally and physically exhausted, that after loading the suitcases in the trunk, taking out a map and planning their route, she had gone into the bedroom, changed into her pajama's, laid on the bed on top of the blankets, and had instantly fallen into a very deep sleep.

But her plan had fallen apart when, after Jake and his young deputy had left the cottage around one-thirty in morning, and she had looked out the window, and to her shock, saw a town police cruiser pull up and park right outside her back door. And it stayed there the rest of the night. At dawn she had watched out the window, hoping and praying the deputy sitting behind the wheel would leave, and finally he did, but only to be replaced by another deputy.

At six-thirty, Madeleine was up, fed and dressed, and as Kate watched her, she decided it was time to leave, deputy or no deputy. Carrying Madeleine in her arms, she stepped out of the cottage, walked right past the police cruiser, and walked up to the motel office to use the phone to call Gertie to tell her she wouldn't be in to work today.

That done, she walked back down the lane to the cottage, and before she went inside, waved at the big deputy in the cruiser, who smiled and waved back. Then, with her heart thumping fiercely, she came back out of the cottage not two minutes later carrying Madeleine and one small overnight bag in her arms, had walked to her car, strapped Madeleine in her car seat, climbed in, and tossed the bag on the passenger seat, and while the deputy watched with a curious expression on his face, started the engine and backed up out of the driveway.

But before driving away, she had glanced over her shoulder to the police cruiser, and to her horror, had seen a very tall man creeping up on the unsuspecting police officer sitting in the cruiser. *It's him*, her panic-stricken voice had screamed over and over in her head. She honked her horn three times to warn the deputy, and then, with her heart thumping madly in her chest, she had floored it and sped away.

But before she had even reached the top of Drummond Cliff, she had noticed a black car, driven by the same huge man, following her. When he had moved his car to within inches of her bumper, she glanced in the rearview, their eyes locked, and he gave her such a chilling, depraved smile, her heart had fluttered strangely, and terror shot through her with such potency she shuddered and almost lost control of the car right there.

A harsh thud suddenly yanked her from her thoughts, and with alarm, she discovered, too late, that she had let her mind wander and the man had smashed his car into hers. She pressed the gas pedal down harder and accelerated up the markedly steep hill, and was almost at the top, when another resounding thud rocked her car so violently that her head snapped back with such force that she bit her tongue and could taste blood. Only seconds later, the man rammed them again, and then all at once, the wheel jerked out of hand just long enough that she lost control, and the car began careening from one side of the road to the other.

She grabbed the wheel and hung on, fighting for control, as her car swerved into the oncoming lane and then back again. Each time her car veered across the yellow line and into the left lane, she was in danger of hitting an oncoming car head-on, or of going off the road and smashing into the sheer wall of rock that bordered the left-hand side of the road. And each time her car veered sharply to the right, she headed straight for the edge of the cliff, and would glimpse the churning, blue-green water crashing into the large gray boulders that lay at the base of the cliff. She cried out to God for help as blood filled her mouth, and bile rapidly rose in her throat, threatening once again.

"Mommy!" Madeleine cried out from the back seat, jolted awake a moment earlier when their car was brutally rammed.

Kate had to swallow a mouthful of blood before

she could speak.

"It's okay, Madeleine, Mommy's here," she said, flicking her eyes from the road to the rearview. To her immense relief, she saw that other than being frightened, Madeleine looked unharmed.

"Mommy," Madeleine said, and her mouth puckered, trembled and Kate knew she was going to cry.

Kate didn't dare speak to her again. The car was still veering wildly from one side of the road to the other and they were in great danger of going right over the side of the cliff. One minute the car's tires were sliding on the asphalt and the next they were digging into the grass that grew along the guardrail that ran along the edge of the bluff. She wanted so badly to hit the brakes, but didn't dare for fear she would send the car spinning completely out of control. Her entire body was tensed so tightly; her wrists and forearms were shaking and ached painfully as she fought to keep the car from reeling right over the edge and into the deep water of the Atlantic Ocean.

CHAPTER 29

I had just spoken to Caleb, who told me they were just two minutes away, when Robisen drive his car into Kate's. My stomach seized into a knot as I watched him ram her two more times, shattering her taillights, and propelling her car right off the asphalt and onto the grassy shoulder of the road. Her car began veering crazily from one side of the highway to the other, at times grazing the low metal guardrail that ran the length of the edge of Stanton's Bluff.

"Oh Kate," I moaned softly when her car skewed off the road onto the shoulder, its back tires kicking up dirt and grass as it headed straight for the edge of the bluff. At the last second, it slewed wildly to the left, and was heading away from the edge and back to the roadway, but was now moving in the wrong lane and heading for oncoming traffic. As we climbed the steep hill, two vehicles coming toward Kate, both minivans driven by young couples with children, narrowly missed hitting her head-on, their horns blasting warnings as they went by her.

"Lord, please help them," I prayed aloud, my voice drowned out by the shrieking of my siren. I shoved the gas pedal all the way to the floor, pulled out into the left lane, and bore down on Robisen's car. My sheriff's cruiser was outfitted with a steel push bar on the front fender, so with the engine whining in protest, I held the gas down, and came up alongside the Grand Am, and then whipped the wheel to the right and drove the push bar into his car. The impact jarred his car hard enough that two wheels went off the asphalt and onto the grassy shoulder, and I could see him fighting the wheel to get the car back onto the road.

I eased over to the right until my cruiser was right up against his, and held his car over there, preventing him from getting his wheels back onto the asphalt. We were side by side, metal screeching against metal, and when I glanced at him, he turned his head, flashed me a deranged smile, and then pointed first to Kate's car, and then to the edge of the cliff.

Anger locked in my throat and I jerked the wheel to the right, jammed the gas pedal down, and rammed him again. I caught the front corner of his car and the fender crumpled and the headlight shattered, he lost control, and all four wheels slid off the road and onto the grass. The passenger side of the Grand Am was screeching against the guardrail, and he was now in peril of going over the edge himself.

I gunned the engine, maneuvered my cruiser past his and caught up to Kate. I glanced in the rearview mirror and saw that Robisen had steered his car back on the highway and was now rapidly closing in on my rear bumper. I kept my eyes glued to Kate's car and stayed with her as she slewed back and forth across the yellow line. I could see Madeleine's small head showing just above the back seat and Kate's shoulders tensed as she tightly gripped the wheel of the wildly careening Malibu, and the sight just about killed me.

I gunned the motor when I saw Robisen in my sideview mirror pulling out into the left lane and accelerating in an attempt to overtake me. I stayed ahead of him, and he gave up and slipped back in behind me, and then began repeatedly ramming his car into the rear of my cruiser. In my sideview mirror I saw his car slip out once again into the oncoming lane and try to come up alongside me. I eased my foot off the gas and let him catch me, and when we were almost even, I stomped on the gas, hauled the wheel all the way to the left, and drove my cruiser into the side of the Grand Am. The front passenger door of his car took the full brunt of the hit and buckled in, and then his car's rear end began fishtailing savagely back and forth across the yellow line. When it served at a right angle in front of me, I hit the gas hard, and smashed the heavy steel push bar into the front of his car again. I saw his bumper come loose and hang down, so that it was scraping along the asphalt and sending sparks high into the air as his car began whipping around in wide circles in the center of the road. I pressed the gas harder, and with the engine screaming, shot past him and went after Kate.

"Great," I muttered under my breath, when I spotted a huge motor home crest the top of the bluff and begin its heavy lumbering descent down the hill.

The forty-foot RV rumbled closer and I could see that the driver, an elderly white-haired man, appeared frozen in open-mouthed shock as he spotted Kate's car careening back and forth across the yellow line, and my sheriff's cruiser, with it's siren wailing and lights flashing chasing her.

I hit the button to the siren and whooped it quickly a couple of times to snap him out of his stupor, and then held my breath as his RV moved closer to Kate's Malibu. Somehow, the driver managed to steer the RV to the right at the same time as Kate's car angled to the right in her own lane, and the RV wallowed heavily past with mere inches to spare. I flicked my eyes from Kate's car to the rearview and saw the RV roll on, seemingly picking up speed as it coasted down the steep hill. I saw that it was now heading straight for Robisen's Grand Am which had come to a dead stop in the middle of the blacktop.

Eric, I said and groaned inwardly when I saw a police cruiser screech to a stop alongside the Grand Am in the oncoming lane and directly in the path of the RV. The driver's door flew open, and I saw Eric jump out and run over to the Grand Am with his gun drawn. He was so intent on capturing Robisen, he never even heard or noticed the RV bearing down on his cruiser. I saw the RV's brake lights flash on, and stay on, before it suddenly swerved to the left to avoid the police cruiser and then broadsided Robisen's Grand Am with a terrible force. The collision, seemed surreal, like it was happening in slow motion, for Robisen's car appeared to lift gently from the road, and then float in slow motion over the guard rail before disappearing over the edge of the bluff. I couldn't see it anymore, but I knew it was now plunging over two hundred feet to the wave-tossed water below.

I flicked my eyes from the rearview, back to Kate's car, and then back to the rearview mirror again in time to see the RV shudder horribly from the impact, and then its rear end skewed sideward and skidded to a stop only about three feet from the guard rail. Eric's cruiser still sat untouched on the road, and I caught a quick glimpse of him pulling himself to his feet not far from the RV, and knew he had barely escaped with his life.

I didn't stop, but shoved the gas pedal down heavily until I caught up with Kate, who had by this time miraculously gained some control over her car, and had it straight in her lane, and was now gently and carefully applying her brakes. I watched her brakes flash on and off every couple of seconds and then her car slowed to less than thirty miles an hour. At the very apex of Stanton's Bluff, Kate eased the Malibu to the shoulder of the road and braked to a stop. My heart flooded with incredible relief and joy. I shut off my lights and siren, and pulled in behind her, silently, but profusely thanking God for His answered prayer.

And then all at once, the Malibu's brake lights went off, the car screeched back onto the asphalt and Kate accelerated away.

"What are you doing, Kate?" I murmured under my breath as I pulled back out onto the highway and followed her.

The Malibu continued moving down the hill, so I pressed the gas pedal down until I caught up to her near the bottom of the hill. I saw her glance into the rearview mirror at me, and I gestured to her to pull over, but she just shoved her mirror up so that she couldn't see me any longer. I looked at the speedometer as I followed behind her. She had slowed to forty-five miles an hour. She wasn't speeding, but she wasn't stopping either.

Two vehicles were coming toward us in the other lane, so I waited until they passed and then turned on my lights and siren again, pulled out, and drove up alongside the Malibu. Kate was staring straight out through the windshield, her face pale and grim, her hair flying in the wind, and her hands gripping the wheel tightly. Madeleine was in her car seat looking out the side window at the flashing lights on the roof of my cruiser. She saw me and waved her funny little wave, and a lump formed in my throat.

Kate wouldn't look over at me so I whooped the siren a couple of times until she did, and then motioned with my hand for her to stop. She glared at me, shook her head once, emphatically, and then lifted one hand from the wheel and waved me away.

I blew out my breath and shook my head and then gunned the engine and accelerated past her, and then pulled back into the lane, and stayed right in front of her. I took my foot off the gas and coasted along the blacktop, tapping my brakes cautiously every few seconds, trying to slow her down and bring her car to a stop behind me. She pulled out and tried to pass me once, but I sped up and blocked her. After another minute, I had the cruiser and her Malibu both slowed to ten miles an hour, and she gave up, pulled her car over to the grassy shoulder of the road and came to a stop.

CHAPTER 30

I pulled over in front of Kate and slammed on the brakes at the same time as I radioed Caleb and told him to work the RV accident scene. Then I threw open the door, vaulted out, and ran back to the Malibu.

Kate was staring straight ahead through the windshield, her knuckles white as she clutched the steering wheel, her face pale and tight with fear. I leaned in the open window and turned the key in the ignition and shut off the engine. Madeleine began crying so I straightened up again, and went to the back door, opened it and leaned inside. Tears were streaming down her cheeks, and she had two fingers jammed in her mouth, but when I examined her I found to my vast relief that she was uninjured.

"You're okay, precious. Everything's okay now," I said soothingly and patted her arm to comfort her. I wanted to pick her up out of the child seat, but I thought it might upset her more than she already was, so I decided to let Kate do it. I moved back out, left the back door open, stepped to the front door and looked in again and saw that Kate still wasn't moving. I carefully studied her face for any sign of injury. Other than looking whiter than any human I had ever seen, she too, appeared to be okay too.

"Kate," I called gently.

She stared straight ahead through the windshield with a distant look in her eyes.

"Mommy!" Madeleine cried loudly.

That seemed to snap out of her daze, and she looked over her shoulder to the back seat, her eyes frantically searching for Madeleine. She kept her hands, which were shaking badly, clasped on the wheel, and her eyes on her daughter while she spoke softly to her, but Madeleine continued wailing at the top of her lungs. She wanted out of her seat and into Kate's arms.

"Kate," I tried again.

"Is she okay?" she said, her eyes frantic as she studied her daughter.

"She's fine," I said. "But she needs you to hold her. Please, come out of the car."

"Are you sure she's okay?" Kate said, unable or refusing to let go of the wheel.

"Yes, I'm sure."

"Where is the man that was after us?"

I paused for a second. "His car went over the bluff. He's dead."

She swallowed, and then looked at me, her blue-green eyes pleading.

"Then let us go, Jake."

"What?"

"Please, Jake, let us go."

I took in a breath. "Kate, you know I can't do that," I said very gently.

"You can't do that," she shot back fiercely. "Then you look me right in the eye now, Jake Cole, and tell me that if you send us back to Carlow we'll be safe. You tell me that the Richard Strang won't just hire someone else to kill us."

I didn't say anything because I had been a cop long enough to know better.

"I thought so," she said so low that I almost didn't hear her.

I felt like I was being torn asunder. Kate was a witness to a brutal murder, and it was my sworn duty as a police officer to send her back to Carlow so she could testify. But as a man, who loved her with a love so deep and unexpectedly intense, it was my heart's desire to take her and Madeleine away from here and hide and protect them forever.

"Mommy, want out," Madeleine pleaded.

Kate turned slightly in her seat and leaned back over the seat until she could reach Madeleine's leg, and caressed her knee gently.

"Mommy's right here," she spoke quietly to her.

Her words and touch seemed to have a calming effect on her daughter for Madeleine stopped crying, sniffed two times, and then reached for a toy that was clipped to her car seat and hugged it to her chest.

Kate turned to me again, pleading. "Jake, please. Let us go."

"Kate, even if I could do that, what good what it do?" I said, my heart full of sorrow. "You said yourself that Richard Strang would hire someone else just like Robisen to come after you. How long do you think it would take before he tracked you down?"

"I'll go to Canada," she said.

"Canada," I repeated, and shut my eyes for a second.

"Yes, Canada. For Madeleine," she said passionately. "I have to try."

"Mommy," Madeleine tried again when she heard her name spoken.

"Madeleine, please," Kate said. "Mommy can't hold you right now."

"Kate, please listen to me," I said. "I have spoken with Sheriff Casey in Carlow and he is a good man, a Christian man, and a very good cop. I know he'll make certain you and Madeleine are both protected and,"

"Oh, save it, Jake," she said, cutting me off. "We both know better than that."

"Then think of Madeleine," I said. "If you don't go back and face this you will always be on the run. Is that the kind of life you want for her? To live in onc strange city or town after the next. With no home she can call her own?"

"I don't see how that's any of your business. You're not her father, Jake," she said in a furious whisper.

I took a deep breath. "I know that, Kate," I said softly. "But I care what happens to her. I care very deeply what happens to you both."

That seemed to catch her by surprise and she looked straight at me, opened her mouth, and then closed it again, and looked away. Finally, she dropped her hands from the wheel and slumped back against the seat in resignation.

"Mommy," Madeleine called, her voice trembling a little.

"Kate," I said gently. "Come out of the car."

"Would you get Madeleine for me please? I need a minute and I know she will go to you," she said quietly.

I nodded and went to the back of the car and leaned inside.

"Hi there, precious," I said softly.

Madeleine beamed and held her arms out to me. I smiled back, unfastened the straps, and lifted her gently up into my arms. She wrapped her arms around my neck and hung on, and my heart almost melted to nothing.

Madeleine chattered away to me about the 'frees'. She pointed to the tall spruce and pine trees that lined the other side of the highway, and despite everything that was happening, I couldn't help but smile at her. When I looked back at Kate I saw she had her seatbelt off, and was moving to get out of the car, so I opened the door with my free hand, put my free hand lightly around her arm and helped her from the car. Once out, she leaned back against the front fender, her face more gray than white now, but still terribly drawn. She took in a breath, and then reached for Madeleine, who by now was squirming impatiently in my arms to get over to Kate.

I handed Madeleine to her, and then moved to the back of the car and leaned in to remove the car seat. Once I had it out, I walked back over to my cruiser and fastened it in the back seat. When I had finished securing it, I stood by the open door, with one arm resting on the doorframe and waited, watching Kate.

She took a deep breath and then, holding Madeleine tightly in her arms, she walked over.

"You don't know what you're doing, Jake."

"Trust me, Kate," I said.

"I can't."

"Then trust God with this," I said kindly.

Kindly said or not, that earned me a very nasty look.

"That's easy for you to say," she snapped angrily.

"No," I said solemnly. "It's not."

She just looked at me for a moment before leaning into the back seat with Madeleine. When she was finished strapping Madeleine in her car seat, I opened the front passenger door for her, and when she was in, I walked back over to her car and locked the doors, and then climbed behind the wheel of my cruiser.

"I'll have your car towed to town," I said.

She was looking straight ahead, her face drawn and pale, and didn't say anything to that.

"It will be okay, Kate," I said softly.

She remained stone still and silent.

Feeling like a monster, I started the engine, made a U-turn in the road and headed back to town.

CHAPTER 31

Shortly after arriving at the department I took Kate and Madeleine into my office, and then asked Marney to sit in there with them while I placed a phone call to Sheriff Casey. He wasn't in his office, so I left a message with the dispatcher for him to call me as soon as he got back.

A couple of minutes later I went back into the office with a cup of coffee for Kate, and a juice box for Madeleine, and Kate took the juice but refused the coffee. After that she just sat in a chair at the wooden table, cuddling Madeleine in her lap, and giving her sips of the apple juice, and continuing to ignore both Marney and me. She hadn't spoken one word to anyone since I had brought her in; other than to murmur words I couldn't hear to Madeleine.

"Is there someone I can call for you, Kate?" I asked, for the third time.

Without looking at me she shook her head no, but her posture said it all. *Get Lost.*

I looked at Marney and she just shrugged as if to say, 'well, at least that was some kind of a response'.

I didn't blame Kate one bit though. She had every reason to be angry at me, and afraid of what lay ahead in Carlow for her and Madeleine. I had promised her that I would do everything in my power to see that Sheriff Casey arranged flawless protection for them, and before I let them out of my custody, I swore to myself that I would keep that promise.

There was a knock at the door, and Caleb poked his head in.

"Call for you, Jake."

I stepped out of the office and went down the stairs and used Caleb's phone. I punched a number and spoke into the receiver.

"This is Sheriff Cole speaking."

"Good day, Jake. How are you?" drawled a smooth southern voice over the line.

"I'm fine, Ned. How are you?"

"I'm very well, thank you. And I'm happy to hear you were looking for me. I just got back in now and I was about to phone you myself. I have news for you, and I'm assuming you have some for me too."

"I do," I said.

"Well, since I'm a southern gentleman, I'll let you go first."

I smiled. "Okay. First thing is that we found Kate LeRue and her daughter. They're both safe and sound in my office right now."

"Good man. I am so very happy to hear that. What about Robisen? Anything there?"

"Wesley Robisen is dead."

"What? You're kidding. What happened?"

"He went after Mrs. LeRue in broad daylight. She got away in her car and he followed her. He tried to run her off the road and over a two hundred foot cliff called Stanton's Bluff. I caught up with them and rammed Robisen's vehicle with my cruiser and he lost control of his car and spun out in the middle of the road. Stopped dead in the center of the yellow line with a forty-foot RV barreling down on him. The RV hit him broadside and shoved his car right over the bluff," I explained quietly, not wanting to embarrass Eric, who was sitting red-faced at his desk only five feet away, listening to my conversation as he typed up his report of the accident. I knew he had shown great courage in going after Robisen alone, and I was thinking there might be hope for him yet.

"Did you recover the body?"

"Not yet. Diver's are still out there searching."

"Sure he's dead?"

"No doubt at all. The RV driver and one of my deputies both saw Robisen, belted in and slumped unconscious behind the wheel, just before the car slipped over the edge and dropped down into the water. It's a sheer drop of two hundred feet straight down into the ocean."

"Is that so? Well, forgive me for saying this, but that's no great loss to the world."

I smiled faintly.

"Speaking of no great losses, I have some news that will be of considerable interest to Mrs. LeRue."

"What is it?"

"Not more than an hour ago I received a phone call from the district attorney. It seems that Clinton Strang's father suffered a massive heart attack while playing golf early this morning. He dropped dead right on the green."

I shook my head slowly, feeling dazed by the news.

"You still there?"

"Yes," I said quietly. "It's just a bit of a shock."

"I know what you mean. Anyway, the district attorney is pretty sure that Mrs. LeRue is no longer in any danger. We are positive it was Richard Strang who hired Robisen, and certain that Mrs. Strang, the mother, didn't have any knowledge of it. The D.A. told me that he knows her, and she's a very nice lady. She threw Clinton out of the house last month, and he's flat broke and has been living on the street. He doesn't have either the money or the brains to hire someone to come after Mrs. LeRue. And with what you have told me about Robisen, it does seem certain that Mrs. LeRue can safely return to Carlow to testify."

"Yes," I said, and rubbed my cheek with the fingers of one hand while I thought.

"Well, good then. My men will probably arrive sometime tomorrow afternoon to escort Mrs. LeRue and her daughter back here to Carlow."

"There's one other thing," I said.

"I know what you're going to say, Jake," he interrupted with a kind tone. "I know that you care for this woman. I can hear it in your voice whenever you speak of her. I promise you I will protect this woman and her child as if they were my own. Nothing will happen to them."

I smiled, feeling greatly relieved.

"I'll give her the news. I think she may feel better about going back now."

"No doubt. And you may tell her what I said. She will be fully protected."

"Thanks again."

"No problem."

"Listen, before you hang up, Ned. I'd like to thank you for all your help."

"Don't know if I was that much help, but it was nice working with you too, Jake. If you ever need our assistance down here again, please don't hesitate to give me a call."

"And vice versa. Call me anytime."

"Thank you, I'll remember that. You have a real nice day now."

"You too," I said, smiling when I hung up.

CHAPTER 32

On the Sunday following the July 4th holiday I awoke to a bright sunny, summer's day. The sky was a clear, sapphire blue, and the breeze coming off the water was stimulating, and sharp with the scent of brine. I felt lighthearted as I drove over to Jeb's, picked him up, and then headed across town to the church.

Jeb squirmed on the seat and talked hyper-fast, and without ceasing, during the drive across town to the church. His mom had finally relented and tomorrow at the crack of dawn, he and I were going to drive over to the Downey's Kennels in Linden, where he would chose a puppy. He had his heart set on a Golden Retriever, and he was driving me right up the wall talking about it. Monday morning couldn't get here fast enough for the both of us.

I was glad that Sandy had given in to his request for a dog. I was sure her decision was due in part to the fact that she was now seeing Pastor Rayner and his wife regularly for counseling. I knew she had a long way to go before she climbed completely out of the pit of despair that had held her prisoner for these past five years, but she was making progress and that was all that mattered.

As I pulled in to the church parking lot I spotted Kate LeRue's black Malibu parked in the lot. I felt my heartbeat instantly quicken and chided myself for that reaction, for we hadn't spoken since the day I stopped her on Stanton's Bluff. She and Madeleine had returned to Carlow, and Kate had testified against Clinton Strang. The trial lasted three days, and the jury came back after only one hour with a guilty verdict, and he was sentenced to life in prison without parole.

Kate was now back working at Gertie's, but each time I ate my meals there, she avoided serving me, and if our gaze did meet she would drop her eyes and look away. I had been so afraid that Kate would choose to remain in Carlow, and I would never see her or Madeleine again, that I didn't really mind the cold shoulder so much. I never could have imagined that I would ever love someone so deeply, and I comforted myself with the knowledge that I was a very fortunate man, for many people lived their entire lives never experiencing a love that intense. And just knowing she had chosen to return here brought me such happiness that even if she never spoke to me again, I was prepared to live with simply seeing her around town. Anything was better than if she had left Leigh Falls.

"Uncle Jake, why are you wearing a suit?" Jeb said, yanking me from my thoughts of Kate.

"Felt like a change," I said, and as we walked to the front entrance of the church I straightened my dark blue tie over my white shirt, and adjusted the jacket of my light blue summer suit.

Jeb watched me with a frown.

"But you never wear a suit."

"Like the saying goes, I guess there's a first time for everything," I said, wishing he would just drop it. The suit was hot and itchy against my neck, and that was irritating enough without his questions.

"You always say it's too hot in the summer to wear a suit," he said.

"It's not that hot."

He snorted in disbelief.

We walked side by side in silence for half a minute.

"Well, I sure wouldn't wear a suit just for some girl," he said, shaking his head and looking clearly disappointed in me.

Before I could think up a reply to that I noticed Leighton Marshall to my right, standing in front of his navy blue Buick Roadmaster. He raised his hand and gestured to me to join him under the shade of the trees that lined the lot behind his car.

"Oh, brother. It's the mayor again, Jake," Jeb groaned loudly and made a face.

"Jeb."

"Well, why can't he go to your office to talk to you like other people do?" he said.

"He's afraid of Marney," I whispered.

Jeb snorted and then giggled, and then giggled harder and louder, clutching his side.

"Jeb."

He couldn't stop.

"Go on in. I'll just be a second."

For once, Jeb, who couldn't wait to tell his friends he was getting a dog, only nodded and ran to the front doors, his small body still shaking with giggles. I wasn't completely sure his mirth was entirely caused by me telling him about Leighton's fear of Marney. I suspected my suit had something to do with it too.

I took in a deep breath and then walked over to Leighton. He was as flawlessly dressed as ever in a gray-pin striped suit, a crisp white shirt, red silk tie, and a matching red silk handkerchief in his suit pocket.

"Beautiful morning, Jake" he said.

I smiled. "Yes, it is. Looks like it's going to be a fine day."

"That's a nice suit. Don't think I've ever seen you wear a suit before."

I shrugged and tried to look more at ease in it than I felt.

Leighton ran his fingers across his bangs and combed them over. He looked over at the church and then looked me directly in the eyes.

"I believe I owe you an apology, Jake."

"Oh?"

"I was wrong in trying to tell you how to do your job. I hate to think what would have happened to

Mrs. LeRue and her child if you hadn't been so prudent."

"Don't worry about it," I said.

He blew out his breath quietly. "No, no. I said some things to you I need to apologize for. I know it's a poor excuse, but I love this town and I love the people. I feel a great deal of responsibility for the town's economy and to the people here who elected me. At times I let my emotions over-ride any good sense I might have," he said, and shook his head.

"Water under the bridge, Leighton."

"That's very gracious of you."

We fell silent and I could hear the voices of the congregation singing the words to the chorus *'Shine, Jesus, Shine'* coming out from the open windows. I thought I could hear Jeb's voice, singing off-key, too fast and much louder than anyone else. I was sure I wasn't the only one who would be glad when he finally got his dog.

"I think it's time we talked about something else too, don't you?" Leighton said.

I took a sharp breath, but didn't speak.

"Jake?"

"We're going to be late."

Leighton gave me a sad smile. "I don't think they're going to miss watching us scowl at each other, do you?"

I looked away, and slipped a finger under my shirt collar to scratch my neck and didn't speak.

"It was an accident, Jake," Leighton said softly.

I faced him.

"An unnecessary accident, Leighton," I said angrily.

"You know I had his driver's license pulled right after the accident. He hasn't driven a car since that day."

"Yeah, well, maybe you should have done that five years ago," I said coldly.

"I made a mistake, Jake."

"A mistake?" I said hotly. "You called some government officials and had your half-blind, deaf, and mentally incapacitated, eighty-year old brother's license reinstated after he caused a horrific accident in Florida that took the lives of two teenage girls."

"Half-brother."

"I don't care what he is, Leighton," I flared. "The man was driving in the wrong lane down a four-lane highway, and never even noticed he caused an accident. He just kept right on going. You knew that, and you went ahead and made those phone calls regardless."

Leighton dropped his head and stared at the ground.

"I'm so sorry, Jake," he said despairingly.

"I will never understand how you could have even considered doing that."

Leighton looked at me. "Jake, please try to understand. After his first accident in Florida he called me and he was really upset. He said the media down there was vilifying him, and he wanted to get away for awhile. We were half-brothers, but he was a lot older than me. By the time I grew up he had already moved out of the house, so I thought it'd be nice to help him out, and at the same time we could get to know one another. I never thought the man would cause another accident the very second he arrived in Leigh Falls, and certainly not one that would cause Craig's death," he said, shaking his head sadly.

"Well, he did, and now Craig's dead. And when you made those calls, you became as much responsible for Craig's death as your brother. In my mind, even more so, since your brother suffers from senile dementia, and you don't."

"Jake," he said solemnly. "Believe me, I have never regretted any decision I have made as much as I have that one. I thought the world of Craig, and I've had a hard time living with it."

Not as hard as Sandy and Jeb, I wanted to yell back, but didn't because when I looked at Leighton's face, he seemed genuinely broken and filled with deep remorse.

"When you told me the other day that it was getting harder and harder to tell that I was a Christian, those words cut through me like a knife," he went on after drawing a shaky breath. "But the more I thought about it, the more I realized they only hurt so much because they were true. I can see now that my growth as a Christian has suffered terribly since that day. But, Jake, what about you? We have both been sitting in this church Sunday after Sunday with this festering between us like an open wound. You haven't been able to forgive me, and you can't tell me that that hasn't hurt your Christian walk in some way too."

I stared silently, angrily, at the ground.

"Jake, I am so sorry, and I'm asking you to forgive me."

"I don't know if I can, Leighton," I said quietly.

"I think you need to as much as I need you to," Leighton said.

I breathed out through my nose, and kept my eyes on the ground. I knew Leighton was right. I had been harboring bitterness in my heart ever since the day I learned that Jack Allaby, the man who caused Craig's accident, was Leighton's half-brother. And that bitterness had progressed to deep anger when I discovered that Allaby had been involved in a fatal car accident not more than three months before he drove to Leigh Falls, had lost his license after the accident and Leighton had fought successfully to have it reinstated. And what further fueled my anger, was that after Allaby had caused the accident on Drummond Cliff that took Craig's life, Leighton has paid his brother's fines, swiftly hustled him on a plane, and sent him back to Florida before anyone in town found out that Jack Allaby was his brother. To this day, other than the coroner and myself, no one else in town knew the truth.

I turned a little and looked across the road to the line of evergreens, and it was at that very moment that Jesus seemed to be saying to me,

'Jake, I have forgiven you for so much, can you not forgive him for so little?'

My Savior's words hit me hard and I shuddered at the depths of my own failure as a Christian. I understood clearly that I had been disregarding His still small voice when He spoke softly to me of my need to forgive Leighton. Despite the nagging sense of disquiet I had felt in the very center of my being, I had refused to obey Him.

As I stood there looking at this broken man in front of me, the awareness of my own failure as a Christian increased, and my heart softened toward him. As a man who had been forgiven, as a man who claimed to have been forgiven by Jesus Christ, and who proclaimed Jesus Christ to be his Savior and Lord, I had utterly failed. I felt broken myself, and knew what my Lord was asking of me, what he been so lovingly demanding of me for so long now. I could do no less than to forgive Leighton. I turned away from Leighton slightly again and looked to the treeline, and prayed a long, silent, prayer of confession, asking for His forgiveness, and then prayed that He would fill me with the strength and grace I needed to forgive this man standing before me.

"Well, I guess I'll head inside now," Leighton said, after some time had passed. "But Jake, I'll say it one more time. Whether you believe me or not, and even if you can't find it in your heart to forgive me, I am truly sorry."

I turned slowly around to face him.

"Hold on a minute, Leighton."

He paused and looked straight at me, waiting.

"I believe you," I said. "And I was wrong. I should have forgiven you years ago."

He looked startled and then hopeful.

"Leighton, I forgive you," I said, and was glad to find I truly meant it.

"Thank you, Jake," he said, sounding considerably relieved.

I held my hand out.

He smiled and shook it, and I smiled back, and we walked into church together. And the profound peace and joy that I knew flooded both our hearts was almost beyond description.

After Sunday School, I stopped in the foyer to talk with Caleb, Ashlyn and their two children, Gabe and Haley.

"Nice suit," Caleb said, after Ashlyn took the children into the sanctuary. "Didn't know you even owned one."

"Well, now you know."

"Uh-huh," he said with a grin.

I nodded greetings to people who said hello as they passed us in the foyer. I pretended not to notice their grins when they saw my suit.

"You and Leighton seem to be more at ease with each other this morning," Caleb said.

I nodded and smiled at him.

He studied me thoughtfully for a moment.

"You've forgiven him," he said quietly.

I looked at him in astonishment.

He shrugged. "I always thought the trouble between you two had something to do with your brother's accident and that he was involved somehow.

The elderly driver; he was related to Leighton, wasn't he?"

"He was his half-brother. But, how did you figure that out?"

He grinned and shrugged again. "Super cop."

We laughed together quietly and walked into the sanctuary. I slid into a pew near the back, and he continued on down the aisle to where Ashlyn and his children sat in a pew near the front. I didn't realize until I was already seated, that I was sitting directly behind Kate LeRue. I spent the next forty minutes trying not to notice how pretty she looked in her mauve, two-piece suit, or how I liked the way she had pulled her dark, glossy hair back behind her slender neck. However, my eyes seemed to drift to her of their own accord, for I admired everything about her, and was drawn to her in a way that never ceased to stagger me.

Suddenly I was snapped out of my reverie by the shuffling of feet. The service had ended, apparently with me so lost in thought I hadn't even noticed, and people were now readying to leave. I rose to my feet at once, and then stood at the end of the pew waiting for a break in the crowd so I could step out into the aisle. From the corner of my eye I could see that Kate was standing at the end of her pew and was also waiting to step out. I risked a glance at her, and saw that she was looking straight at me.

"Hi, Kate," I said quietly.

"Hi, Jake," she said, held my eyes for a moment, and then stepped out into the aisle.

Well, at least that's progress," I thought, for it was the first time she had said anything at all to me since the day I brought her to my office.

That fact elated me so much my heart began pounding hard in my chest, and as she walked past me I didn't dare say anything and just stared stupidly at her. I stepped out into the aisle behind her and followed her into the foyer, where she turned right and went downstairs to the nursery and I got in line to shake hands with the pastor and his wife.

Five minutes later, I stood beside my cruiser waiting for Jeb, and saw Kate and Madeleine emerge from the front doors of the church. Kate was holding Madeleine's hand and walking slowly to match her daughter's short toddler steps. Jeb ran over just then, yanked open the passenger side door to the cruiser, and was half way inside when he spotted Kate and Madeleine going by and he froze.

Oh-oh. Unsuspecting victims for his dog story, I was thinking, and leaned into the open driver's side window to speak to him, but was too late. He had already hopped back outside.

"Mrs. LeRue!" he screamed.

She looked over, surprise on her face.

"Guess what! I'm getting a dog!" he yelled happily.

I closed my eyes. When I opened them again, I saw that Kate and Madeleine were walking toward us and my pulse instantly quickened.

"Jeb, don't talk her ear off about the dog," I warned him.

He nodded resolutely before he shut the door and flew around the car to where I stood.

"Hi Mrs. LeRue. Hi Madeleine," Jeb whooped out as they neared us, his voice way too loud.

"Jeb," I said. "Settle down a little."

"Hello, Jeb," Kate smiled at him.

Madeleine smiled at him too, and then looked up and reached her arms up to me.

"Hi there, precious," I said, smiling at her.

"Want up," Madeleine said, smiling back at me.

"She seems to have taken to you. Do you mind?" Kate said.

"Not at all," I said, beaming with delight, and then bent over and gently scooped her up into my arms.

"So, Jeb. You're getting a dog tomorrow?"

Grinning, Jeb nodded his head vigorously.

"What kind of dog do you want?"

"A golden retriever. Uncle Jake's taking me to Linden tomorrow morning to pick one out."

"That sounds great, Jeb," Kate said, sounding genuinely happy for him.

"I'd better go now, Mrs. LeRue," he said, flicking his eyes to me. "I'm not supposed to talk your ear off about it."

Kate looked at me and laughed softly.

"Bye-bye, Madeleine," Jeb said, giving her a wave before running across the parking lot to join a group of boys his age who were chasing each other on the side lawn of the church.

"Bye-bye," Madeleine said to his back, squeezing one hand open and shut in her now familiar wave.

Kate followed Jeb with her eyes, and then looked back at me and was silent.

"He's pretty excited."

Kate smiled. "I see that."

I smiled. "So, I hear you're going to stay in Leigh Falls," I said.

"Yes. It's a nice town and the people are wonderful. I think it will be a good community for Madeleine to grow up in."

I nodded, feigning a semblance of composure I didn't at all feel, for her words had sent my heart leaping with joy.

"I won't be working at Gertie's after August though. I heard that there was an opening for a fourth grade teacher at Leigh Falls Elementary School. I applied for it and the principal called me Friday and offered me the position."

"I didn't know you were a teacher."

She smiled a small smile. "I taught for seven years before I married Kent."

"In that case, congratulations on your new job. I think," I added quietly after a couple of seconds.

She tilted her head slightly and looked at me with a puzzled expression.

"I only say that because Jeb's entering the fourth grade in the fall. It's a small school and he's bound to be one of your students."

We both chuckled at that.

"Gertie will miss you terribly," I said, after we had stopped.

Kate nodded. "I'll miss working for her too. But I suspect that this town gets pretty quiet after the tourist season ends and she won't need my help anymore."

"That's true. In the winter you would never know it was the same town. Not a tourist to be seen."

"I don't think I'll mind," she said.

"I certainly don't."

"Well, yes, I have heard something about that," she said, a smile playing at the corner of her mouth.

I smiled too, and then we lapsed into silence again.

The sun was high in the blue, blue sky, and the breeze had picked up some and was stirring the leaves in the trees above our heads, and the birds, which were flitting from one branch to the other, sang happily. Madeleine's eyes grew wide as first one sparrow, and then another, trilling loudly, set down on a branch right over our heads. She grinned and pointed at the sparrow.

"Bird," she said, and looked me dead in the eye with her big, blue-green eyes.

"Yes, it is," I said, and smiled at her.

Two seconds after that something on the ground caught her attention and she wanted down. Kate gestured to me that it would be all right, so I shifted her in my arms and let her down gently. She squatted down by my feet and started picking up rocks and seemed content to stay there, so I looked at Kate.

"Who will watch Madeleine for you?"

"Miranda Renard's mother. Madeleine loves her, and Gertie and Pam have both recommended her quite highly."

"Yes, Jackie's very good with kids," I said.

A silence fell between us again, and we watched the cars pulling out of the parking lot. Only eight cars left now; two of which were my cruiser and Kate's Malibu.

"Kate," I began quietly. "I need to explain something to you."

Kate kept her eyes on Madeleine, but she nodded and seemed to be waiting for me to go on.

"I did want to let you go that day on Stanton's Bluff. But I couldn't do it. And not only because I'm a cop, but because I felt that God was asking me to give Him complete control of the situation. And believe me Kate, trusting Him that day with both your lives wasn't easy. In fact, it was indescribably terrifying," I said sincerely.

She raised her eyes from Madeleine to study me quietly.

"But I am glad I did trust Him now. He answered my prayers in a way that I couldn't have anticipated or imagined," I said.

"I understand, Jake," she said quietly, seriously. "From the very moment we left Carlow, I could sense His leading us here to Leigh Falls. And then one night in the cottage I was reading my Bible, and I was sure that God was speaking to me through Ezekiel 34:28.

'And they shall no more be a prey to the heathen, neither shall the beast of the land devour them; but they shall dwell safely, and none shall make them afraid.'

After she had quoted the verse to me, she

tucked a loose strand of dark brown hair behind her ears, and then looked at me; her blue-green eyes earnest.

"It was as if He was telling me through that verse to stay in Leigh Falls. Like He was telling me he would take care of us and we would be safe here. I just had to trust Him. But then, when you told me that a man from Carlow was in town, and had been around the cottage, I completely panicked. And I ran. And I wanted to keep running."

She looked at me and I nodded sympathetically, and she inhaled and then exhaled very quietly before she continued.

"I admit I was hurt and angry with you at first when you wouldn't let us go. But later, when we were driving back to town in your cruiser, I came to the end of trying to handle it all myself and I turned everything over to Him. I gave Him complete control of Madeleine's life, my life, the trial, everything. I decided that no matter what happened, even if a good opportunity to run came up again, I wouldn't go. I would trust Him to see us safely through the situation."

She stopped speaking for a moment and gazed lovingly down at Madeleine, and then looked back at me.

"It probably sounds strange, Jake, but trusting God with her life was so much harder than trusting Him with Kent's life when he was diagnosed with cancer. I can honestly say it was the hardest trial I've ever gone through in my Christian walk."

"It doesn't sound strange at all, Kate," I said softly. "It's perfectly understandable. It's much more difficult when it your child's life that is in danger."

She nodded slowly and looked down at Madeleine once again.

"I am so glad I did chose to trust God, for I have learned so much about trusting Him. And just as He promised, He has taken care of us, and we are safe here and no longer afraid."

I smiled back at her and nodded in empathy, for I too, had learned a great deal about trust and forgiveness in the past two weeks.

We were silent again and I was aware of the voices in the parking lot fading as the congregation slowly drifted to their cars and left. I glanced around and saw that there were only four cars left in the lot now. I caught Jeb poking his head around the last group of people huddled outside the front doors, and knew he was telling them about his dog again and gestured to him with one hand to come over.

"I guess I should get going," I said. "I think Jeb's worn out his welcome here."

Kate glanced over at Jeb and laughed.

"Yes, I should too," she said, and then bent down to lift Madeleine up from where she sat on the ground playing with rocks.

"Good-bye, Jake," Kate said.

"Good-bye, Kate."

"I'm glad we talked."

"Me too," I said.

She looked at me with a warm smile.

"And thank you for everything."

"You're welcome," I said, and smiled easily back.

Kate took a couple of steps toward her car.

"Kate," I called out.

"Yes," she said, and turned around, blinking in the sun.

My pulse had picked up considerably, and my hands had started shaking, so I opened my suit coat and shoved them in my pants pocket.

"Jeb and I are going to grab some lunch at Salty's Take-out, and then head out to the Blue River for a picnic at the falls. Would you and Madeleine like to join us?"

Our eyes met and held.

"That sounds nice," she said with a smile.

"Great," I said, smiling back.

"I'd like to run to the cottage first though, so Madeleine and I can change into more comfortable clothes."

"Sure, we always change first too. Why don't we meet at the take-out in half an hour," I said calmly enough, considering that my heart was beating way too fast to be healthy.

"Okay," Kate said, and smiled warmly again..

Two minutes later I had rounded up Jeb and we were leaving the parking lot headed for home.

"Where're we going?" Jeb asked, watching me.

"Home to change, and then to Salty's to meet Mrs. LeRue and Madeleine. I invited them to have a picnic lunch with us at the falls."

"And she said yes?" he said in astonishment.

"She did."

"Even after you arrested her?"

"I didn't arrest her, Jeb."

He stared at me, his forehead crinkling with lines while he thought that over.

"Are you okay with this?" I asked him.

"Uh-huh," he said.

We drove in silence for a couple of seconds.

"Uncle Jake?"

"Yes?"

"I guess the suit worked," he said with a grin.

I laughed quietly.

"Uncle Jake?"

"Yes, you can hit the lights and siren."

Printed in the United States
1171100001B/13-42

9 781591 605232